CW00403874

THE LAST DAYS OF US

CAROLINE FINNERTY

Boldwood

First published in Great Britain in 2021 by Boldwood Books Ltd.

Copyright © Caroline Finnerty, 2021

Cover Design by Head Design

Cover photography: Shutterstock

The moral right of Caroline Finnerty to be identified as the author of this work has been asserted in accordance with the Copyright, Designs and Patents Act 1988.

All rights reserved. No part of this book may be reproduced in any form or by any electronic or mechanical means, including information storage and retrieval systems, without written permission from the author, except for the use of brief quotations in a book review.

This book is a work of fiction and, except in the case of historical fact, any resemblance to actual persons, living or dead, is purely coincidental.

Every effort has been made to obtain the necessary permissions with reference to copyright material, both illustrative and quoted. We apologise for any omissions in this respect and will be pleased to make the appropriate acknowledgements in any future edition.

A CIP catalogue record for this book is available from the British Library.

Paperback ISBN 978-1-80162-527-2

Large Print ISBN 978-1-80162-523-4

Hardback ISBN 978-1-80162-522-7

Ebook ISBN 978-1-80162-520-3

Kindle ISBN 978-1-80162-521-0

Audio CD ISBN 978-1-80162-528-9

MP3 CD ISBN 978-1-80162-525-8

Digital audio download ISBN 978-1-80162-519-7

Boldwood Books Ltd
23 Bowerdean Street
London SW6 3TN
www.boldwoodbooks.com

For Mary, for always making me feel so welcome in her family and for being a truly lovely grandmother too.

This is the story of us: my family – JP, Harry, Robyn and me – my whole world. We were once just like any other family; life was a mundane tangle of school runs, after-school activities, a never-ending laundry pile and bedtime stories. But it was my ordinary life, and I treasured every minute of it. You know those beautiful moments, the ones where you step outside yourself for a split second to appreciate what you have and just soak it all up? Where you recognise that this snapshot in time is utterly perfect. Where your heart swells and you know that this – this is the very place you have been waiting to reach your whole life. This is where you are meant to be, and this is what it's all about. But then, there are sometimes defining moments where things can change instantly, splitting your life into 'before' and 'after' and you know nothing will ever be the same again.

I'm glad that I didn't know then that my world was set to fall apart...

1

Cinnamon and nutmeg floated on the sugar-scented air, entwined with the smell of cloves and star anise. It was Christmas Eve and the children and I were in the kitchen making gingerbread men to leave out for Santa Claus. Mince pies were baking in the oven and mulled wine was brewing on the hob for JP and me to drink later on, after the kids were tucked up in bed.

I had been looking forward to this day for weeks. To me, Christmas Eve was the best day of the whole year. I loved the anticipation, the piney smell of the real (never fake) noble fir tree, the aromas wafting from the kitchen, the excitement written on the kids' faces. Christmas Eve was like a beautifully wrapped present, as you waited to reveal the gift of Christmas Day.

I had an image in my head of the perfect Christmas, almost like an image from a catalogue. I knew I was a hopeless dreamer, but I couldn't help but get swept up in the merriment of it all.

I helped Robyn, my four-year-old daughter, to press her cutter down into the dough as Judy Garland's caramel-smooth voice was singing 'Have Yourself a Merry Little Christmas' on the radio:

Have yourself a merry little Christmas,
Make the yuletide gay,
Next year all our troubles will be miles away...

I sang along but didn't quite reach the high notes like Judy.

'Do you think Santa likes gingerbread?' Harry asked from underneath a cloud of icing sugar.

'Well, he's eaten it every year that we've made it for him, and we've never had any customer complaints,' I joked.

He laughed, showing large, gappy teeth. His adult teeth were starting to fill in the spaces where the baby teeth had been pushed out. They still looked too large in his small mouth; it was as though his face was playing catch-up. A trace of freckles that had appeared in the summertime still dotted the bridge of his nose. At nine years old, my boy was growing up fast. *Too fast*, I thought with a sigh.

'Can I make a gingerbread lady?' Robyn asked.

'Of course not,' Harry retorted, 'they're called gingerbread *men*!'

'We can have gingerbread men *and women*,' I said in a bid to keep the peace. 'We're all about equal opportunities in this family!'

'Oh, can they have a little boy and a little girl like our family, Mammy?' Robyn asked with wide-eyed excitement.

'Sure, sweetheart.'

She used a chubby hand, with its knuckles softened by baby fat, to push her soft golden curls out of her eyes and grinned up at me. I watched her whole face screw up in concentration, as her small fingers attempted to cut out the gingerbread family. Her fingers were still so young, she was just learning to grip and fold as she tried to ply the dough to make mini gingerbread children.

I stopped to look at the scene before me, like an observer in my own life. It was at moments like these that Harry and Robyn still made me catch my breath. My son and daughter stood before me, working together to make treats for Santa. How had I got so lucky? Ten years ago, I would never have believed this scene could be mine. That children could be in my future. I still had to pinch myself that this was real – that these children were ours: JP's and mine.

We had longed for our babies so much. We had waited and tried so hard to have them. My sister Fiona always joked that I had wanted a baby since I was eight years old. I was the girl on our street who would ask the neighbours if I could push their baby around the estate in the pram. So, I knew as soon as JP and I had married, I wanted to begin trying for a family of our own. While friends of mine wanted to wait a few years to have some fun times with their new husband first, I had insisted that we start trying on our honeymoon. But despite our initial leap out of the starting blocks, we endured years of gruesome disappointment after gruesome disappointment as we tried to conceive.

In the end, JP and I had undergone six rounds of IVF to have Harry. Unless you have experienced that gut-wrenching pain that infertility wreaks upon your life, then you have no idea of the hollowed-out feeling you experience as, once more, cramps forewarn you that you have failed yet again. That *you* have let your husband down. That *you* are the reason he isn't yet a dad, while the rest of his friends are rejoicing in fatherhood.

There were endless injections, drug regimes, blood tests, internal examinations and procedures – we had been tested to our limits – but I could honestly say that all the heartache had been worth it the very moment Harry, a mewling, pink-faced bundle, was placed into my arms. So, JP & I could hardly dare to believe our luck when I had fallen pregnant naturally with

Robyn. Harry and Robyn were our precious babies – each a miracle in their own way.

I reached over and pulled the two of them into a bear hug.

'Hey, Mam, what are you doing?' Harry said, laughing and wriggling away from me. He was reaching that age where he was starting to get embarrassed by physical affection.

'Where's Daddy?' Robyn asked.

I glanced at the clock on the fridge door, the door that was covered in the kids' artwork, appointment reminders, school permission slips that needed to be signed and all the other things that came with children. It was growing dark out. *Where was he?* He had said he needed to go into the office for a few hours to wrap up a couple of things before the Christmas break.

JP was the finance director for a US tech company headquartered in Dublin. I was used to him working long hours to meet deadlines and occasionally needing to go into the office on weekends or public holidays. I hadn't returned to work after maternity leave with Harry; after waiting so long to have him, I couldn't bear to leave him to head back to the rat race. Then Robyn had come along too and I loved being there with my children for every milestone in their life. I wanted to be there for every tummy ache and scratched knee. I felt very fortunate that JP's salary meant we could afford that choice.

JP had said he wouldn't be long, but that had been four hours ago... Surely, he should be home by now? Then it hit me, he was probably rushing around Dublin city centre trying to buy me a Christmas gift. He was always leaving it until the last minute. I could imagine him now in a sweat, racing through Brown Thomas on Grafton Street or maybe even Weir's, frantically choosing whatever was left at this time on Christmas Eve, while some predatory sales assistant took full advantage of his desperation. I couldn't help but laugh at the image in my head.

'What's so funny?' the kids asked in unison, looking up at me.

'Oh, nothing,' I said, with a wave of my hand. 'I think Daddy is probably doing some last-minute Christmas shopping.'

* * *

When we were finished, we loaded the tray of gingerbread men (and women) into the oven and I sent the children upstairs to get changed into their new Christmas pyjamas. I briefly wondered how many more years I had left where they would let me dress them in matching nightclothes, but I pushed the thought out quickly again. *Just enjoy the moment, Sarah*, I told myself.

I looked outside, where, beyond the window, darkness had fallen. I put a candle in the window, as was the tradition on Christmas Eve, then I moved around lighting my collection of Christmas-themed candleholders. Every year, JP would groan when I took them out of storage on 1 December and set about decorating every shelf, windowsill and mantlepiece in the house. I adored how the yellow candlelight shone through the miniature windows of the pretty, little snow-capped houses, or how the nose on my snowman-shaped holder glowed orange when the candle inside it was lit.

Outside, I had light-up reindeer grazing in our front garden and multicoloured lights strewn along the trees. JP thought they were kitsch – and they probably were – he preferred the more sophisticated style of our neighbours' white lights and fresh holly wreaths, but I couldn't help going overboard on the Christmas decor because I loved the smile it brought to the kids' faces.

I glanced at the clock again. Wouldn't the shops all be closed by now? They always closed a little earlier on Christmas Eve. Where was JP? It would be time for the children to go to bed soon and he always helped them leave out the treats for Santa and the reindeer, before we tucked them up together and read ''Twas the Night Before Christmas'. A bad feeling washed over me. It wasn't like him to miss this. I really hoped nothing had happened to him.

I lifted my phone from the countertop and called him. I waited as it rang for what felt like an age, but he still didn't answer. I prayed he was okay. A sickly feeling of dread snaked its way down my body, and I felt goosebumps prickle all along my arms. Where the hell was he?

2

I woke with a start. My heart was racing and I felt panicked. Somebody was calling my name. My arm was being pulled. Something terrible had happened, I could sense it like a black veil sitting upon the cool morning air. I opened my eyes and let them adjust to the half-light of the room.

'Mammy! Wake up, Mammy, it's Christmas!' Harry and Robyn shouted in unison. 'Can we go down and see if Santa has come yet?'

Their words jolted me awake. My bedside clock told me it was 5.54 a.m. I turned to wake JP, but the other side of the bed was startlingly cool. It was then that what had happened the night before came crashing down upon me.

I had wrapped all the presents for the children, then waited up for JP to come home until I could hardly keep my eyes open any more. I had lost count of how many times I had dialled his number, but his phone had rung out unanswered. I had called his friends, but nobody had seen him. In desperation, I had even phoned all the Dublin hospitals, but they had confirmed that they hadn't admitted any patients matching his name.

'Where's Dad?' Harry asked, looking around the room as if expecting his father to jump out and surprise him.

'I'm not sure, sweetheart,' I said. I heard the concern lacing my own voice. I could remember still being awake at 3 a.m. and he hadn't come home, and I must have fallen asleep after that.

'Come on, Mammy, get up.' Robyn tugged my arm again. 'We need to see what Santa branged us!'

'*Brought* us,' I corrected on autopilot. 'Okay, I'm coming now.' I climbed out of bed and wrapped my ancient, ragged cardigan around me to shield myself from the cold morning air. The wool was bobbly and fuzzy. There were old holes in the sleeves where I was now sticking my thumbs through and yet I couldn't bear to throw it out. I had been wearing this cardigan for as long as I could remember. It had kept me warm while I studied for my college finals, I had worn it through my pregnancies and had breastfed my babies in it. Each hole in the wool seemed to represent a different chapter in my life.

The three of us descended the stairs together and the smell of stale alcohol hit me from the hallway before we even reached the living room. Disappointment began swirling through my veins like warm liquid, curdling somewhere near my heart. I hesitated at the door, apprehensive of what was waiting on the other side for us.

'Come on, Mam!' Harry said impatiently, noting my hesitation. 'We need to see if Santa came!'

'No, wait, don't go i—' I raised my hand to stop them, but before I could, the kids had pushed the door open and went running into the room. They froze when they saw their dad passed out on the sofa. He was snoring heavily and the smell of stale air, a combination of rich food and alcohol, was pungent in the air. In the corner, underneath our Christmas tree, lay the toys they had listed in scrawled handwriting in their letters to Santa, all wrapped up, waiting to be opened. But instead of rushing over to open their presents, they both turned back to me with a mixture of worry and fear filling their eyes.

'Why is Dad sleeping here?' Harry asked, looking up at me for answers.

I noticed that JP was still dressed in the same trousers and sweater that he had left the house in the day before. His shoes lay kicked off in the middle of the floor. A short glass with a residue of amber-coloured liquid sat on the rug beside them.

'Should we wake him up, Mammy? He's going to miss opening the presents,' Robyn said.

The same refrain kept shooting through my mind: this wasn't how it was meant to be. It was Christmas morning – it wasn't supposed to be like this. In the run-up to Christmas, I had imagined this moment a thousand times in my head and it had never been like this.

I stepped over his coat, also thrown on the rug, and shook his shoulder. He grunted and turned over. I shook him again.

'JP,' I called. 'Wake up.'

There was no sign of life.

'JP,' I tried again, sterner this time.

He woke with a start. 'What is it? What's wrong?' He shook himself and began rubbing his eyes.

'Santa came, Dad!' Robyn announced, looking at me in confusion.

'Santa!' He sat up theatrically and looked over to the tree. 'Well then, we need to see what he brought for us, don't we?'

My heart broke to see relief wash over their innocent little faces. Their eyes darted to me for reassurance and I quickly arranged my face into a smile.

JP jumped up and scooped a giggling Robyn off the floor before hurrying over to the tree with her. Harry ran behind. I followed after them, marvelling at his ease. How he could just turn it on. How could he just switch into 'Fun Dad' mode, while my heart was reeling, and my mind was racing with so many questions? Where had he been? What was going on?

As the children began unwrapping presents, I felt an overwhelming sense of sadness. I knew my expectations were too high – I blamed the beautifully orchestrated marketing campaigns. In the adverts and films I watched on TV, happy families hugged each other tightly after exchanging their perfectly wrapped gifts. Of course, I knew that life wasn't like a Hallmark movie.

'Look, Dad, Santa brought this one for you,' Harry said, thrusting the gift towards him. I watched as JP ripped off the paper decorated in holly leaves that I had wrapped the night before. I had carefully chosen bows to complement the colour of the paper, while he had been god only knew where. He untied the ruby-red grosgrain ribbon before tearing open the paper. He pulled back the box that was inside to reveal a watch.

'Wow... thanks, Santa.' He looked over at me.

'Happy Christmas,' I said. We locked eyes briefly before his darted quickly to the floor. Why couldn't he look at me? He closed the lid of the box and placed the watch back down on the floor.

The children continued ripping open their presents until the room was a sea of paper and they were squealing and shouting with glee as Santa ticked off everything on their lists.

Soon all the presents were open, but suddenly Robyn's face grew serious.

'What's wrong, darling?' I asked.

'Where's your present, Mammy?' Although she was only four, Robyn was my sensitive child; she was always in tune with how everyone else was feeling.

'Oh, don't worry, I have loads of things,' I said, quickly brushing her off.

Harry put his remote-controlled car down on the floor. 'Santa forgot Mam?' He looked crestfallen.

I looked over at JP; he was pretending to be engrossed in the instruction leaflet that came with one of Robyn's dolls.

'Come on, who's hungry?' I said, forcing myself to sound bright. I didn't want anything else to ruin Christmas morning. I climbed back up from the floor.

'Me, me, me!' the kids chorused, their concern over my lack of presents already forgotten.

'Mam?' Harry came up beside me as I took sausages and rashers out of the fridge a few moments later.

'Yeah?' I said, shutting the fridge door.

'How did Santa come down the chimney if Dad was in the room?'

Here were the questions. I knew they would come.

'Well… em… he must have come before Dad came home.'

'But then why didn't Dad wake us up when he saw Santa had come?'

'Well… maybe he came when Daddy was asleep?' I tried.

'But why didn't Daddy sleep in your bed with you?'

'Look, why don't I see if have any batteries for that remote-controlled car?' I said, trying to change the subject.

I walked past him into the utility room where JP was standing reading something on his phone. He quickly slipped it into his back pocket when he saw me.

'Where were you last night?' I asked. 'You said you were going into work for a few hours and then you never came home!'

He turned away from me. 'I was out.'

'I was worried about you.' I was whispering so the kids wouldn't hear. 'Couldn't you have called me and let me know you were okay? I've had to field a load of questions from them—'

'Will you stop nagging me – it's Christmas morning, for God's sake!'

I felt hot tears filling my eyes, stinging and burning with their ferocity. I didn't understand what was happening. I was worried about his behaviour. I guess if I was honest with myself, he had been acting strangely for a while now. He had been short-tempered and disinterested in everything I said.

'Mammy, what are you and Daddy talking about?' Harry came into the utility room and was looking at both of us for an answer. I could see the worry pooling in his eyes.

'Nothing, sweetheart,' I said, quickly brushing my tears away, leaving my cheeks damp.

* * *

After we had eaten breakfast, I went upstairs to shower and change before our guests arrived. We were having JP's parents Joan and Richard for Christmas dinner and my sister Fiona and her partner Seán were going to join us too. As our mother and father were both dead, we always spent Christmas together. I knew JP's parents would be calling straight after mass, so I needed to hurry.

I was just putting on a little make-up to disguise my tired eyes when I heard the doorbell go downstairs. A few seconds later, I could hear Harry screaming, 'Granny and Grandad are here!'

'Mum, Dad! Happy Christmas!' I could hear JP sing from the hallway as he welcomed them into our family home.

I took a deep breath inwards to calm myself before heading downstairs to greet them. 'Happy Christmas,' I said, forcing myself to smile.

My father-in-law, Richard, was carrying gifts and we attempted an awkward hug around his full arms. My mother-in-law, Joan, handed me a poinsettia in one hand and her coat in the other without even a greeting.

'Can I get you both a drink?' I asked, following them all into the living room.

'Well, it is Christmas morning,' Richard said, in a jubilant tone. 'Sure, we might as well!'

'You're looking a little tired, John-Paul,' Joan remarked. 'Were the children up very early?' She only ever called him by his full name, never the abbreviated version.

'Just before six,' he yawned.

'I remember those days,' Joan laughed.

I disappeared into the kitchen, glad at the opportunity to have a moment alone to compose myself. I had to get it together. It was Christmas Day; I couldn't let what had happened earlier ruin the whole day for everyone.

I plastered a smile on my face and returned to the living room a few minutes later with a bottle of champagne and the flutes I kept for special occasions. I noticed they had already started exchanging gifts without me.

'Look, Mammy, look what Ganny got me,' Robyn cried, holding up a *Frozen* board game.

'Oh wow, that's amazing. Say thank you to Granny.'

'Thank you, Ganny,' she repeated.

JP took the bottle from me and began uncorking it. The kids squealed as the cork popped and golden champagne frothed over the rim of the bottle. He began to fill everyone's glasses.

'To family,' he toasted. And for a moment we almost looked happy.

3

We had just seen off our guests and I was in the kitchen with the lights dimmed low. JP was tucking the kids up in bed; they were exhausted from the day. Robyn had fallen asleep on the sofa, clutching her new Baby Annabell doll in one hand and her beloved Mr Bunny in the other, and Harry's eyes had been drooping closed as he tried his best to stay awake.

I was standing at the sink, my sleeves pushed up, scrubbing the roasting tins with Brillo pads. My shoulders burned with knots and I was drained from the day, not helped by the lack of sleep the night before. Sinéad O'Connor was softly crooning her version of 'Silent Night' on the radio in the background and the hairs on my arms stood to attention as her voice soared to catch the high notes.

JP came back down the stairs and I swung around from the sink.

'That went well then,' I said sardonically as he entered the kitchen. I was referring to our Christmas dinner when I had noticed my mother-in-law using her knife and fork to lift up her meat. She had flipped it over on the plate, examined it and then done the same again on the other side.

'Maybe it's my eyesight...' Joan had said, raising her glasses to her eyes. 'I'm not great if the light is a bit dark, but mine's looking a bit pink. Here, have a look, John-Paul,' she'd said, sliding the plate towards him. 'What do you think?'

'Yeah, I see what you mean, Mam,' he had said, peering down at the plate.

'Really?' I'd said, trying to keep my cool. JP rarely cooked so he wasn't the best person to judge. I had spent hours preparing this meal for our family with very little help and I was tired. 'I don't think I undercooked it...' In fact, the opposite was true, I had overcooked it; it had been a bit on the dry side, if I was being completely honest with myself.

I had leaned across the table to look at her meat, which to my eye was perfectly cooked. It was milk white.

'I think it's okay,' Richard had said, taking another bite.

'It's delicious, Sarah,' Fiona, my ever-loyal sister, had added.

'It is,' Seán had agreed.

'I won't risk it,' Joan had said, shaking her head and pushing the plate away. 'An undercooked turkey is very dangerous, you know.'

'Well, I can see if I have another slice...' I had offered, pushing my chair back and standing up to leave the table.

'No, you're okay.' She had sat back and folded her arms across her lap. 'I'm not very hungry now...'

'I'll eat the meat, Mammy,' Robyn had said, sensing the tension in the room.

'Why didn't you stick up for me earlier?' I demanded now from JP. 'You could see that that turkey was perfectly cooked!' I looked at him, willing him to say something to acknowledge what had happened during dinner earlier, but, infuriatingly, he just shrugged his shoulders at me. I felt anger warm my veins.

'That's it?' I asked in disbelief. 'That's all you're going to say? I put so much effort into this day; making sure everyone had the presents they wanted, cooking for us all. You should have backed me up, you knew the meat was perfectly fine!'

'Stop playing the martyr, Sarah. Can you just leave it out for once?' He sighed heavily, walked over to the fridge and took out a beer bottle.

I felt as though my heart had stopped. Something had changed between us and I hadn't noticed when. The way he was looking at me right now, it was almost as if he hated me, but I couldn't recall doing or saying anything that might have offended him.

He raised the beer to his lips and took a long, slow gulp.

I peeled off my rubber gloves and tossed them onto the draining board. I turned around to give him my full attention.

'What's going on with us, JP?' My voice trembled. 'I don't understand why you're acting like this.'

He opened his mouth to speak, but the words seemed to stick on his lips, and he swallowed them back down again.

'What is it? What's happening here?' I pushed again, taking a seat at the table. I needed to sit down; my body seemed so heavy. 'Is there something on your mind? If you tell me what is wrong, then maybe I can help?' My tone was softer now.

He rubbed his hands down his face before shaking his head.

'JP, what's wrong? You're scaring me, this isn't like you. I'm so worried about you. I can't keep living like this... it's horrible.' I felt as though I was a passenger in an out-of-control car and didn't know the destination.

'Me neither,' he said, shaking his head.

There was something in his tone warning me. I was crossing a line and I wasn't sure if I was ready for what awaited me on the other side, but I had no choice but to continue.

'Wh-what do you mean?'

'I'm not in love with you any more, Sarah,' he mumbled so low that I wondered if I had misheard him.

'Sorry?' I said, thinking I couldn't be hearing him right. It was like his words had come out all jumbled up. All wrong. I needed to hear them again so I could put them the right way around.

'I haven't been in love with you in a very long time.' He was looking down at the floor, pawing at the tiles with the toe of his shoe.

The words hit me with the sudden shock of a wasp sting as I realised what he was saying to me.

'But why? Why are you saying this?' I was reeling. His words were rubber ping-pong balls and they were bouncing off my brain because my head couldn't process them.

'I don't want this any more, I think it's best for everyone if I move out – give us both some space to figure out what we really want,' he continued.

'But you can't! We're your family, JP! Me, Harry and Robyn – we're your *family*! You can't walk out on us!' The whole thing seemed preposterous. What was going on inside his head? It didn't make sense.

'I'm so sorry, Sarah – I really tried. For a long time, I've tried to make it work, but I can't do it any more…'

'You can't do what?'

'I'm sorry, Sarah, I didn't want to do this on Christmas Day, but I can't keep on living a lie – I think it's best for everyone if I move out for a while.'

I felt panicked, as if I was slipping further down under currents of oily water and I couldn't break through the surface as I thought of the implications not just for me but for the kids too.

They were my world. Why wasn't he being rational? If something broke, you fixed it; you didn't just cast it out, especially when you had spent fifteen years of married life with that person. 'Please, JP, please, I don't understand? Just tell me what I've done – we can work it out! Whatever is wrong, we can try to fix it!' I begged.

He shook his head. 'I've made up my mind—'

'But what about the kids? What are we meant to tell them? How are we going to explain it to them?'

'I'm not sure,' he admitted, 'but kids are tougher than we think. Yes, it will be hard on them at the start, but they'll be okay. We'll sit them down in the morning and explain it to them.'

I couldn't understand why he was being so heartless, so cruel. This wasn't like him. This wasn't the JP that I knew and loved. Was this some kind of midlife crisis?

'But where will you go?'

'I'm not sure yet...'

'You can't do this – they need you – *we* need you. We can try counselling... loads of couples need counselling... why can't we try that?' I pleaded in a small voice that didn't even sound like my own. Although we hadn't been getting on for some time now, I just hadn't seen this coming. I felt totally blindsided. The room was spinning around me. A juggernaut had jackknifed through my life, my world, my family, my heart, and I couldn't stop it. 'Please, JP, don't do this,' I wailed.

'I'm sorry, Sarah – I can't—'

Then it suddenly hit me; his unexplained absence the night before, the way he was always checking his phone. The way he wouldn't look me in the eye lately. 'Is there someone else? Is that what this is about?'

'I'll sleep on the sofa.' And then he turned and walked out of the room.

4

I woke to find my head pressed against the table. It took me a second to work out why I was asleep in the kitchen, and then the crushing realisation of what had happened the night before hit me like a punch. I had sat at our kitchen table crying until everything was raw: my skin was raw from salty tears; my throat was raw from heaving sobs; my heart was raw from the slash of JP's words. The washing was still piled up in the sink from when it had been abandoned the evening before. JP had taken up residence on the sofa and, as I heard snores coming from the living room, I'd wondered how on earth he was able to sleep?

I'd stayed sitting at the table until the light outside changed from the black dark of night to the pinky-orange shades of dawn. How I wished I could stop time from marching forward. I longed to be able to hold back the day because I knew what was awaiting our children when they woke.

Our children who were our world – or, at least, I had thought they were.

We weren't just husband and wife, we were parents. I always believed we had had an implicit, unspoken pact that we would never do anything to hurt them. Whenever we heard stories about marriages disintegrating or people walking out on their families, I thought we were both in agreement that we would never do something like that, *we* could never do such a thing to our children. We were better than that. So, where had it changed for JP? Was our unspoken agreement just in my head? Maybe it had been one-sided; had it been only *my* pact all along? They say that infertility is one of the biggest stresses that a marriage can face, but not for us it wasn't. We rode that storm out together, so as I sat at my kitchen table, I was wracking my brain to figure out where it had all gone so wrong for us. How had we fought our biggest battle and won, but defeat was yet to come?

The dawn sky was now alive with the chorus of morning song, the birds welcoming the arrival of a new day. A new day that I wished my kids didn't have to face. This was to be a turning point in their lives, a watershed moment that would define everything from here on in. This would be the day that they would learn that their mother and father were not the rock that they had once thought. The core was about to be ripped out of their world.

* * *

Just after seven, I heard footsteps on the stairs and Harry came into the kitchen, his sandy hair sticking up chaotically from sleep.

'Mam, you're up before me?' He was usually the first person up. He would normally stick on the TV or play on his tablet for a little while, sometimes helping himself to biscuits, while JP and I slept on a bit longer.

'You know I love you so much, don't you?' I said, hearing the emotion thread my voice.

'Of course,' he wrinkled his nose in that way he had that was so like his father as he tried to figure out what was going on.

Robyn came down the stairs next. She burst through the door and when she saw me sitting at the table, ran straight into my arms and climbed up on my knee.

'Did you sleep well, Robby-roo?' I asked, brushing her hair back off her forehead.

She nodded sleepily in my arms. She was wrapped in her big, fluffy dressing gown and was clasping Mr Bunny tightly to her chest. I had placed that teddy comforter into her cot on the day she had been born and she had slept with it every night since. I snuggled my face into her warm neck. She was divine.

I looked beyond the patio door to see a robin pecking at the ground.

'Look, Robyn,' I said, pointing at the small bird.

'My birdy!' she cried, leaping up and rushing to get some bread out of the press to feed him. 'Me want the story, Mammy.'

I took a deep breath. 'Did you know that we called you Robyn,' I began as tears welled in my eyes at the memory, 'because on the day that you were born, a robin fluttered down and landed on my windowsill in the hospital and he looked at me with his dark eyes.' I choked, trying desperately to keep my emotions in check. 'And I knew then that he was telling me that we had to call you Robyn.'

She smiled at the familiar story; she never tired of hearing it.

JP came into the kitchen then. I still hoped that maybe it had been the alcohol clouding his judgement; he had drunk several glasses of wine with dinner and then had poured himself a large tumbler of whiskey after our guests had gone home. Perhaps he hadn't been thinking straight.

He didn't look at me as he walked over to the fridge and filled a glass of water for himself. As the cool water rushed into the glass, I wondered if having the time to think during the night had helped him. Helped him to see sense. Maybe he had changed his mind. Had realised that what he had said was madness – complete madness.

'Hi, Dad,' Harry sang as if it was just a normal day.

JP turned around from the fridge. 'Harry, Robyn, can you sit down for a second...'

My heart fell down to my feet. This was it. He wasn't even going to wait until they had eaten breakfast or dressed. The kids looked at me to see what was going on.

'Your mammy and I need to talk to you about something,' he continued.

No, I screamed in my head, *it's you – you need to talk to them. I don't need to talk to them about anything. I don't need to destroy their lives – you do.*

'Are we going to Disneyland?' Harry asked, taking a seat at the table. His eyes were full of excited hope and a big grin spread across his face.

I felt an enormous pang in the pit of my stomach.

JP looked at me in bewilderment, wondering what was going on. I groaned internally. The ads were on TV again, squashed in between episodes of *Pokémon* and *Peppa Pig*, the ones where serious-faced parents sat their children down and then announced grandly that they were actually taking them to Disneyland, resulting in much cheering and whooping from the kids. My heart felt as though it was being squeezed in a vice grip; Harry's voice was so small, so innocent, and I wanted to scoop him up off the chair, run out of this room and keep him in a world where your parents sitting you down to talk was because they had an exciting surprise for you, not because your dad was leaving the family home. I wanted to lock both children away somewhere where I could stop their universe from being shattered.

'What the hell is he talking about?' JP muttered. Harry had clearly put him off course.

'I think he means the ads on TV where the parents sit the kids down and tell them they're going to Disneyland...' I mumbled.

'No, Harry,' JP said, shaking his head and looking mildly irritated. 'We're not going to Disneyland.'

'Oh,' Harry replied, sinking down again with disappointment. 'Then what is it?'

'I need to go away for a while,' JP said.

'With work?' Harry asked, wondering what the big deal was. They were used to their dad travelling with his job.

'Not exactly,' JP replied. 'I need to go and live in another house. Now, you'll still see me all the time, but I just won't be living in this house any more.'

'But why do we need two houses?' Robyn asked.

'Sometimes grown-ups need their own space,' JP said.

A fat tear rolled down my cheek. I tried to catch it with my fingertip, but it landed instead on my Christmas jumper that I was still wearing from the day before. The smiley reindeer face with its red light-up nose beaming up at me suddenly felt mocking.

'Mam? Why are you crying? What's going on?' Harry turned to me and demanded an explanation.

'We love you,' I said, and then I couldn't hold it together any more. Tears coursed down my face. 'We both love you so, so much.'

'You'll still see me,' JP said, glaring at me, his face angry and full of warning for me to keep it together.

'I don't want Daddy to go away,' Robyn stated. 'Kiss and make up,' she ordered.

That's what I always said to her and Harry whenever they fought about something.

'I'm sorry, sweetheart.' I wiped my cheeks with the back of my hand.

JP shoved his chair back with a screech and got up from the table. I heard his footsteps climbing the stairs.

'What's going on, Mam?' Harry asked as he began to cry.

'Your dad loves you so much, he just needs a little bit of space,' I soothed as I cuddled my two sobbing babies in close to my chest.

* * *

JP came back down the stairs a short while later with a large suitcase in his hands. It was part of a set that we had got as a wedding present. We had taken them on honeymoon with us, and every family holiday since.

'I think I have enough to keep me going for a while here,' he said sheepishly.

'But where are you going to stay, JP?' I asked.

'I'm not sure yet...'

'Don't go, Dad,' Harry said, running over and grabbing on to his father. 'The Liverpool match is on today – we can watch it together.'

My heart tore into shreds. Harry was putting his best case forward to get his dad to stay, but he was too young to understand that, if we weren't enough, a Liverpool match wasn't going to cut it.

JP made for the door, but Harry gripped him tighter.

'No, Dad,' he said, clinging to JP's leg. 'I don't want you to go. Neither does Mammy or Robyn. Isn't that right, Mam?'

Tears choked in my throat and I couldn't answer him. How could JP be so heartless?

'Tell him, Mam!' Harry begged, 'Tell him you don't want him to go!' His eyes were beseeching me to stop all of this craziness.

'It's okay, Harry,' JP said. 'I'll see you both really soon.'

'Please, JP, just think about it. Think about what you are doing! Think about the kids – if you can't stay for my sake, stay for theirs at least!' I stepped forward and placed my hand on his arm in a last-ditch appeal.

'Don't make this any harder than it needs to be, Sarah.' He brushed off my hand and headed out the door to his car. We all followed after him, watching as he opened the boot using his key fob. He rejigged his golf clubs to make room for the case. Then he slammed the boot shut and climbed into the car. He didn't look at the three of us as he reversed out of the driveway and out of our lives.

HARRY

I don't know what is happening. Dad has gone away and I don't know how long he's going to be away for. He said it's just for a while, but he even took the suitcases that we always take on our holidays. I asked Mam if he was gone on holidays too, but she shook her head and started crying and said she didn't know, so I think it's really bad. If Mam doesn't even know what's happening, then how am I supposed to know what is going on? Robyn thinks he's just gone to work, but that's because she's only four, so she doesn't really understand things like I do.

Mam was crying again today. She's always crying, and she thinks I can't see her when she hides in the kitchen or she pretends she is getting something out of the fridge, and her voice goes all funny when I ask her a question, but I'm not stupid. I'm way better at hiding when I cry than she is, she never sees me crying in my room.

It's all Dad's fault that everyone is crying. The house is all weird now and I don't like it. I just want him to come home and then everything can be the same again.

5

When I woke the next morning, it hit me fresh again. It was surreal, like I was an actor in a film. This wasn't my life. This wasn't JP – this wasn't *my* JP.

St Stephen's Day had gone past in a blur. I don't know how long I had stood on our cobblelock driveway for after he left, but it was long enough to see our next-door neighbour's blind twitching as she wondered what was going on. We lived in Seaway Close, a small housing estate in Malahide, a suburb on the north side of Dublin, where neat, detached, red-bricked houses fronted onto a small green. Our neighbours were mainly older couples whose children had flown the nest. I would invite them all around for barbeques every summer, but other than exchanging polite greetings when I met them on the street, I didn't know them well. I had brought the children back into the house and we had all sat shell-shocked on the sofa. Usually, we spent the day with just the four of us taking it easy after the pressure of hosting our families on Christmas Day. We would eat the turkey and ham leftovers, then the kids would chill out with their selection boxes by the fire and watch a movie, while JP and I shared a bottle of red wine and ate cheese, but instead the three of us had stayed in our pyjamas all day, curled up together on the sofa.

The children had so many questions for me; questions that I wasn't able to answer. Where had Daddy gone? When would he be home? Why did he take our suitcases? Had he just gone on a holiday? I had my own questions. Did he just need space away from his marriage for a while? Or had he fallen out of love with me? Perhaps it was stress. I knew he was under a lot of pressure in work, the company hadn't met their targets for the financial year and as the person responsible for reporting directly to the US, it was weighing heavily on him. Had it all got on top of him and this was his way of coping? I was wracking my brain for a reason for all of this. More worryingly, a voice in my head kept asking if there might be someone else involved, but no... I really didn't want to let my head go there...

When the children had eventually stopped crying that evening, they had fallen asleep on the sofa, their small faces sticky with tears, and I had carried them up to my bed to sleep because I couldn't bear to be alone.

JP was the only man I had ever loved. We had met when I was seventeen years old and I was a shy first-year student in Trinity college. We had both studied economics – I still thought it was funny to have worked so hard for that degree and now all those macro and micro theories that I had sweated so much over were so irrelevant in my daily life as a stay-at-home mum. I had known JP to see from lectures; you couldn't miss him, he was very good-looking and my two friends, Linda and Mel, and I had nicknamed him 'Johnny-Popular', because he always surrounded by a crowd.

JP and I had been paired together for a project and one day, while we were working on the assignment together, I got a call from Fiona to say Dad had taken ill suddenly at work and had been rushed to St Vincent's Hospital. JP had listened as I had taken the call and, after I hung up reeling from the shock that had been foisted upon me, the words 'Dad' and 'hospital' tumbled from my mouth. He took control while my head was spinning; he ushered me out to the car park and drove me to St Vincent's. I don't think I even said goodbye to him as I hurried out of his car and ran through the sliding doors of the hospital, but Dad was already dead by the time I got there – the result of a massive heart attack. He was just fifty-three years of age.

At the funeral, I was shocked to see JP in the long line of mourners who queued to shake our hands. He called me the next day to see how I was and then the day after that and every day until I returned to college. When I went back to Trinity, still stunned by my new reality, still grappling with the shock of how fast my world had changed, he would sit with me and put a mug of hot, sugary tea between my hands when I was too full with grief to eat. It was as if my dad had passed JP the baton as he had been leaving this world and sent him to take care of me.

So, you see, I had always felt connected to JP on this level. We were more than just boyfriend and girlfriend; we were soulmates. My dad had brought us together. That's why this was all so shocking. It was as if I didn't recognise him any more. The whole thing was ludicrous. I still harboured hope that he might have had a change of heart overnight. A night away might have given him enough space to realise all that he was leaving behind, but when I checked my phone to see if he had called or even texted, there was nothing there.

I suddenly felt a wave of anger warm my body. He owed me – no, not just me, the kids, *us* – he owed us an explanation. You can't just get up and walk out on your family without telling them why. How could he do this? How could he walk out on them – the most beautiful, precious little people on the planet? I had always believed that our kids were our world, so when did *his* world change?

What was I supposed to do now? What was I supposed to say to them? I felt I had no words to explain it. I couldn't even fathom it myself. It wasn't as though I had had time to prepare myself. As a mother, whenever there were things I was unsure of, I would turn to Google or online support forums. When Harry had had silent reflux as a baby, or when Robyn wouldn't sleep and when toilet-training threw up problems, I would go online and seek out the best advice. But this was the biggest parenting challenge ever to come my way and I was thrown in at the deep end. I had no idea how I was supposed to handle it when I wasn't even sure myself what was going on. Was this just a temporary thing for JP? Did he just need some space for a few days and then he would be back again with his tail between his legs? Was it a midlife crisis that, in a few weeks, we would both sweep under the carpet, never to be referred to again? I didn't want to think of the alternative… God, if he would just come home, I could sort it all out. I knew I could fix us.

As I lay in bed that morning, I could hear the sound of laughter, from some cartoon the kids were watching, squealing up from the living room. I needed to see them, I needed to feel the reassuring weight of their arms around my neck or the touch of their silky skin against my own. I pulled myself out of bed and headed downstairs.

I stuck my head around the door to find them eating from cereal bowls sitting in front of the TV. Their routine was reassuring.

I went into the living room and wrapped my arms around them, burying my face into the smooth skin of their necks and breathing them in. They wriggled out to get a view of the TV again. I was relieved to see that it was almost like they had forgotten yesterday's events. They knew JP as well as I did, and it was as if they knew this whole thing was just temporary and their dad would be back soon. The dawn of a new day had fortified me – this was utter madness. JP would be back, he wouldn't leave his children – whatever he felt about me, I knew he loved the bones of those children. He would come back.

I left them alone to watch their TV programme and went into the kitchen and began clearing up yesterday's dishes that I hadn't been able to face the day before and stacked them in the dishwasher. As I worked, my eyes landed on the collage of family photos that hung on the wall in the dining area. There was one taken the night JP and I had got engaged. We had gone on holiday to Thailand and had been both bedraggled and jet-lagged when we finally landed in Bangkok. As soon as we reached our hotel room, I had just flopped down onto the bed, feeling tired down to my bones as the rickety air-conditioning unit lost the battle against the dead heat of the city, but I had felt a presence at the side of the bed, and when I opened my eyes, JP was on his knees, looking terrified. In his hand he had a small black box, where a diamond solitaire was perched on a cushion inside, and I think I had agreed to marry him before the words even left his lips. He had laughed then and explained how he had had grand plans of proposing at Maya Bay because I had been obsessed with the book *The Beach* and the movie adaptation had been filmed there, but he had been too excited to keep it a secret any more. I could see in his eyes just how much it meant to him to get it right. It was the sweetest proposal and I told him it was a million times better than any perfectly executed, well-rehearsed proposal on a white-sanded paradise could have been.

Suddenly, I came undone at the memory; my heart felt as though someone had ripped it from my chest and trampled all over it afresh. The breath snagged in my lungs and I fell to my feet beside the open dishwasher. How had I gone from being that girlfriend he desired so much that he couldn't wait to spill a proposal from his lips, to the wife that he no longer loved or needed?

Just then, Harry and Robyn came into the kitchen and dumped their cereal bowls in the sink.

'What's wrong, Mammy?' Harry asked, his brow furrowing downwards.

Tears streamed down my face, and I couldn't stop them. They were pouring out of me, and I could see that the children didn't know what to say to me. I hated the look of fear and helplessness on their young faces, but I just couldn't stop the tears from falling.

'Nothing,' I said, sticking my head inside the dishwasher.

'Daddy will be back real soon, Mammy,' Robyn said. 'He's just gone to work.' She explained it in a voice like she was the mother and I was her child.

'Are you mad with us?' Harry asked.

I wiped my tears away and turned around, but they kept on coming. 'Of course I'm not,' I said, trying to wipe the damn things away again.

'How long is Dad going away for?' Harry continued.

'I'm not sure, pet.'

'But when is he going to come home to our house?' Robyn asked.

The question blindsided me. I knew Robyn meant it as an innocent enquiry, but it was her innocence that made it all the worse. She thought this whole arrangement was temporary and that he would be back home with us all again soon.

'Well... eh... sometimes grown-ups fall out of love with each other and they just want to be friends and when that happens, they have to live in different houses.'

'But Dad loves us, doesn't he?' Harry asked. 'He hasn't fallen out of love with us, has he?'

'Of course not!'

'Well, if he loves us then, why doesn't he want to live with us?' Harry said.

I was stumped by the line of questioning. I could see the natural logic of a child who had yet to experience unquantifiable things like feelings and attraction.

I fumbled for the right words. 'I know this is hard for you both to understand right now. I think when you're grown-ups you might. But I need you both to know that your dad and I love you so, so much, more than you will ever know.' I wrapped my arms around them, burying my hot tears into the smooth skin of their necks. And at that moment, I almost hated JP. I hated what he was doing to me, but I hated what he was doing to our family even more.

Just then, my phone rang, and my heart somersaulted. I scrambled to answer it, but, with a sinking feeling, I saw that it wasn't JP. Instead, it was my sister Fiona.

'Sarah, is everything okay?' she asked before I even had time to say hello. Her voice sounded thin, like stretched elastic, like she was holding something back.

I took a deep breath. I wasn't ready to admit yet that JP had left, even to Fiona. Somehow, I thought he might still come back and we would keep what had happened between ourselves, only ever referring to it in some secret code such as 'JP's moment of madness'. In my fantasy, I even imagined us laughing about it over a glass of wine together. I wouldn't ever need to tell anyone, and we could go back to being JP and Sarah again, the way everyone knew us.

'Yeah, of course. Why?' I forced myself to sound normal.

'Well, it's just that I was in town earlier... Seán and I were going to go for breakfast in O'Hanlon's and well... eh... well, I saw JP. He... uhm...' She paused to choose her words. 'He wasn't alone, Sarah...'

I felt as though the wasp had returned and was now stinging my whole body all over. I couldn't speak. Blood rushed into my ears and they began ringing loudly.

'Sarah, are you still there? Sarah?'

'I'm here,' I said in a small voice that didn't sound like my own. 'Who was he with?' I knew that whatever Fiona said next would change the course of my life.

'A woman – well, "woman" is stretching it. She was no more than a girl really. About twenty-six or seven maybe? A wispy blonde thing... plastered in make-up and tan – you know the sort...' She paused and lowered her voice before adding the killer punch. 'It didn't look platonic.'

The wasps were swarming all around me now, chasing me down in a blur of black and yellow.

'Did you go over to them?' I asked.

'No! I think I was too shocked. Even though we had just walked into the café, we turned and left straight away. I didn't want him to see us – I don't know why... Should I have said something? I was just caught off guard. What's going on, Sarah?'

'JP left us yesterday.'

'What are you talking about?'

'He left us, well, *me* really...' The words seemed to be spilling out of my mouth as if it was somebody else saying them. 'He said that he wasn't in love with me any more. That he hasn't been for a long time now.'

Fiona took a sharp intake of breath; I could hear it whistle between her teeth. 'I'm coming over there right this minute.'

6

A little while later, I heard the doorbell going downstairs and I knew it was Fiona. I could hear the children answering it and telling her I was upstairs. After her phone-call, I had gone up to my room so that the kids wouldn't see me crying. Sure enough, her footsteps came treading up the stairs and, moments later, there was a soft knock on my bedroom door.

'I'm so sorry,' Fiona said, coming into the room in a flurry of colourful scarves and sitting on the side of the bed, throwing her arms around me.

Fiona worked as a freelance graphic designer. She had been given all the creative genes, whereas I couldn't even draw a straight line. She had taken a circuitous route through life: she had attended art college, then dropped out and gone travelling; whereas I was the diligent, straight-laced, studious sister who had gone straight from school to study economics at university, where I had met JP, we had married, finally had our babies and I had decided to stay at home with them. While Fiona was spontaneous, I was a people-pleaser who played by life's rules. That's why it was so hard to accept JP leaving because it wasn't in my plan. JP had broken *our* rules.

'Why didn't you tell me? I feel awful now for telling you over the phone like that. I had hoped you would say that it was a work meeting or something and you knew all about their lunch date.'

'Nope,' I said, shaking my head as tears streamed down my face. 'It was a bolt from the blue.'

'The worst kind. Who is she? Is she someone that he works with?'

I wiped my running nose with the back of my hand. 'Hand on heart, I have no idea. I'm guessing a work colleague, but who knows... He joined a gym recently, so maybe he met her there? Oh, God!' I said as it suddenly dawned on me. 'This is such a cliché!'

'The reason clichés exist is because they're true. Did you have any idea, any idea at all, that he might have been seeing someone else?'

I shook my head. 'I feel like such an eejit,' I sobbed, 'but honestly, Fiona, I didn't see this coming. I know we had been arguing more than usual lately, but don't all couples have their ups and downs?'

'What about counselling, did you suggest that?'

I shook my head. 'I tried but he had already made up his mind – I don't get a say, apparently.'

'You wouldn't throw out a washing machine that had broken down,' she said angrily. 'You would call out a repair person and try to get it working again. Not that I am comparing you to a washing machine – sorry, Sarah,' she added clumsily, 'or not that you've broken down... there's nothing wrong with you... Oh, God, I'm just making this worse... you know what I'm trying to say... But if something still has good qualities and it just needs to be worked on, then you get help!'

'So why is he throwing me out then? Maybe I have no good qualities left?'

'Oh, I'm sorry,' she sighed, 'I'm not helping, am I? I just don't know what to say.' She shook her head. 'I don't know why he has done this, Sarah, but karma is a bitch. Now come on, get up out of that bed,' she said. 'Harry is surrounded by empty biscuit packets and Robyn is mainlining Skittles down there.'

'I can't—'

'Yes, you can. I'll help you.' She sat down onto the side of the bed.

'Can't I just stay here? I don't want the kids to see me like this.'

'Come on, Sarah. I know what's happened to you is terrible – it's awful, I won't pretend it isn't – but you have to stop feeling sorry for yourself. There are two children downstairs who are depending on you.'

'My husband left me for another woman – I think I'm allowed to feel sorry for myself!'

'Yes, if it was just you that was involved here, I'd cut you some slack, but you have two children to think of, Sarah, two children that are also suffering. They need you now more than ever. They've lost their dad! You have to pull yourself together for their sake. You're the one who has to keep the show on the road now their father has let them down. That's what mothers do – they're the glue that holds everything together. Now come on, get up outta that bed!'

Her words, although hard to hear, hit home and, grudgingly, I found myself pulling back the duvet and planting my two feet on the floor.

'When did you last wash yourself?' Fiona continued, tutting.

'Christmas morning.'

'Jesus wept! Right, into the shower, straight away,' she ordered.

I didn't even protest as she steered me by the shoulders into the bathroom.

'I promise, you'll feel so much better afterwards.'

'A shower isn't going to bring my husband back,' I grumbled.

I just stood under the showerhead letting the water cascade around me. I didn't have the energy to lather soap around my body.

When I was finished, I saw Fiona had left two fluffy towels and my robe to heat up

on the radiator and, as I wrapped them around me, their warmth was like a hug. I wiped away a patch of steam on the mirror and saw my face – red, blotchy and angry – looking back at me.

'Do you feel better?' Fiona asked when I emerged from the bathroom.

'Not really,' I admitted.

'I have lunch waiting for you in the kitchen.'

'I'm not hungry.'

'Well then, you can just have a cup of tea.'

I followed her downstairs and looked into the living room, where the kids were lying on the floor, chins resting on their hands as they watched TV. They were engrossed in the cartoon so I sat down at my kitchen table in front of a plate of bacon and avocado on toast. I was touched that she had made my favourite lunch for me, but I couldn't stomach food and pushed the plate away.

Fiona boiled the kettle and made a pot of tea before placing it down on the table and pouring two mugs.

I reached forward and clasped the mug between my palms, embracing its warmth.

'What kills me is how powerless I feel. That I don't get a say in any of this. What about me? What about what I want? Isn't marriage meant to be an equal partnership, so how can one person just decide that it's over when the other person doesn't want it to be over?' I blurted.

'I've no answer for that except that life is unfair, but you're strong, Sarah. You're much stronger than you give yourself credit for. You've just had one of the biggest shocks of your life, it'll take time, but you will heal. I know you will.'

I knew she was trying to help, but I honestly couldn't ever see myself getting over this.

'Don't give him any more power over you,' she continued. 'Those beautiful children need you.'

I looked at them through the glass panes in the door leading into the living room. 'They are so beautiful,' I echoed. 'How could he leave them?' A sob choked in my throat.

Fiona shook her head. 'I have no answer for that, but from this second on, you're going to keep your chin up and get on with your life. Screw him.' She placed her hand over mine on the table and gave it a squeeze. 'I will help you through this, okay?'

Suddenly my phone began to ring and, when I checked who it was, I saw that it was JP.

7

Three days later, I watched from the window as JP's blue BMW coupe turned into the driveway. He was coming over to collect the kids. It was the first time they had seen him since St Stephen's Day, the day he had left. When I had confronted him on the phone about the girl Fiona had said she had seen him with, he had let out a breathy sigh and said, 'Her name is Megan. I'm sorry, Sarah, I never meant to hurt you—'

'Why didn't you just come clean and tell me?' I had asked. My voice wasn't angry, just sad. Sad for the lies and deceit. That was almost the worst part of it all. He wasn't just my husband, but my best friend too, and the betrayal was so hard to bear. How could I ever trust anyone ever again if JP – the love of my life – could do that to me?

'Look, I know I should have told you, but I didn't want to rub salt in the wound at the time… I guess you would have found out sooner or later anyway.'

'How did you meet?' I don't know why I was asking these questions, was I trying to torture myself? But I felt I needed to make sense of it all. He seemed to have detached himself from me so easily, like you would unhitch a trailer from a car, without a guilty second thought.

'We work together.'

'Is that where you are now? Are you staying with her?'

'Yeah,' he'd admitted. 'We're renting a flat in town.'

After I had hung up, I'd felt stupid. Mortification warmed my body, leaving me feeling sticky and wishing that I could crawl out of my own skin. How did I not realise that there was a reason he was leaving me? Of course there was. Men didn't just walk out on a relatively happy family life for no reason. There was always a reason.

I could imagine them holed up in their love den, laughing at my innocence. You know when you hear those stories on the radio chat shows, I always used to think – they *must* have seen it coming, there *must* have been signs. And, of course, when I look back, there were signs, but I still hadn't spotted them.

I was now tormented, wondering how long had he felt this way for? For how long had our marriage been a sham? I was thinking back over every little detail and analysing it like a forensic crash investigator would scour the roadside for clues after a bad traffic accident. I couldn't help but think back to my last birthday when JP had surprised me by taking me out for dinner. He had arranged for Fiona to babysit. We had laughed and talked, and we had had a lovely night... or at least I had thought we had, but maybe he had been unhappy then and I just hadn't seen it? Had Megan been on the scene at that stage? Had he sat through the dinner, wishing he was with her instead?

We had gone on holidays with the kids at their Halloween midterm break and JP had acted like a caged bear all week. At the time, I couldn't understand why he was being so moody and tetchy and just assumed he was stressed out by work, but now his behaviour clicked into place for me.

The loneliness and the feeling of being lost was the worst part; it was not just my husband who had gone, my whole identity had been stripped away. I had been with JP for almost twenty-five years – over half my life. It was like we had fused together. I didn't even know who I was any more.

'Come on, get your coats and hats on, your dad is here,' I called.

Harry didn't need to be told twice and he ran out to the cloakroom under the stairs.

'I'm tired, Mammy,' Robyn said, making no effort to move from the window. 'I'll stay with you.'

I guessed she was a bit anxious. She wasn't the only one, I thought wryly.

'Aw, pet, don't you want to see your daddy? It'll only be for a little while. You'll have fun.'

'I don't want to go.' She shook her head.

'You don't have to stay for my sake, Robyn. I'll be just fine, it's okay for you to go with your dad, I don't mind.'

'But my head is owee,' she protested.

I placed my palm on her forehead and it didn't feel hot. 'You don't have a temperature...' Was she feigning illness? This was what I didn't want. My super-sensitive four-year-old was already feeling torn. JP had only been gone for a matter of days and already the impact on the children was devastating.

'I said I don't want to go!' she shouted. Robyn's legendary stubborn streak was rarely revealed, but when it was, she could be mulish, and I knew no amount of coaxing would get her to change her mind if she didn't want to do something.

Harry opened the door and ran straight out to his dad, but Robyn stayed where she was.

'Come here, Robby-Roo,' I said, taking her hand in mine as we followed Harry out to the driveway.

Low winter sunlight bounced off the metallic paintwork of his car. It was pristine as usual. It had obviously just been through the car wash. I couldn't even wash my hair, but not even walking out on his family had stopped JP from taking care of his car, I thought bitterly. His car was his pride and joy and I had once joked that he loved the car more than me. Now I realised with searing irony how close to the bone I had been.

'Hey, kids,' he sang as he stepped out of the car, almost as if he was just returning home from a day at work. I noticed that he was wearing a leather bomber jacket that looked as though it belonged on somebody twenty years younger than him. I was so used to seeing him in his work suits during the week, or in chinos with a polo shirt when he was being more casual at the weekends. Although he was still an attractive man, his black hair had started to grey ever so slightly around the temples, so the jacket looked bizarre on him.

'Hi, Dad!' Harry ran forward and jumped on him.

'Hi, Robyn,' JP called, but she just buried her face into my hip. 'Robyn, aren't you happy to see me?' he asked. He came over towards us and reached out his arms to take her from me, but she just clung tighter to my hand.

'I don't want to go,' she said, shaking her head.

'Come on now, Robyn,' he coaxed. 'I thought we'd grab a pizza at Paccini's, how about that?' Paccini's was a long-established family-friendly restaurant. The kids loved it because the waiters gave them mini chef's hats and aprons and they let them roll their own dough and add their own toppings.

'No, I'm too tired.' She shook her head.

'Go on, Robby-Roo, it'll be fun,' I tried. I couldn't believe she was passing on the opportunity to go to Paccini's. The thing was, despite everything that had happened, I really wanted Harry and Robyn to see their dad; I didn't want them thinking that any of this was their fault. I wanted some kind of 'normality' for them in this horrible situation.

'I said no!' she shouted, causing me to step back in shock. It was so uncharacteristic for her to behave like this. I guessed she was angry, and this was her way of expressing it.

'She has been saying she isn't feeling well. I hope she's not coming down with something...' I said, defending her. Robyn was dogged when she made her mind up. It was a trait I usually admired, except when I was on the receiving end.

JP crouched down in front of her, but she pushed him away. He stood up again and irritation flashed in his eyes.

'Right, come on, Harry, let's go,' he said, getting back into the car.

* * *

When JP dropped Harry home after eight, he rang the bell and wordlessly handed our son to me before walking back to his car. Fifteen years of marriage, twenty-five years together, two kids, and this was what we were reduced to, I thought as he reversed out of the driveway.

'Did you have a nice time, Harry?' I forced myself to sound bright. I knew this was my biggest test as a mother – a test I had never thought I would have to face until it landed on my doorstep. I needed to paint this situation in as positive a light as I could manage so that my children wouldn't become casualties in this mess.

He shrugged his shoulders. 'It was all right. Where's Robyn? I brought her home some pizza,' he said, handing me a takeout box.

'You're so thoughtful. She's already in bed though.'

Robyn had asked to go to bed soon after Harry left, which was strange because she never willingly went to bed. When I had asked which story she wanted me to read, she had said that she just wanted to go straight to sleep. She was definitely coming down with something, I had thought as I tucked her up with Mr Bunny. She had fallen asleep before I had even left the room.

'So, did you have a good time?' I pressed.

'Yeah...'

'What's wrong, Harry?' He wasn't meeting my eyes and I got the sense there was something he wanted to tell me but wasn't sure if he should. 'Is there something worrying you?'

'Dad has a new girlfriend,' he said as tears pooled in his eyes.

I felt myself freeze. Damn it anyway! I hadn't told the children about her yet. I wasn't sure when I should do it; they were only just getting their heads around the fact that JP had left. I wanted to let them adjust to that blow first before heaping more hurt onto them, but apparently JP didn't feel the same way. Could he not have waited until Harry had got over the shock of him leaving? He should have discussed it with me first. This was too much for a nine-year-old to process.

'Oh, Harry, love,' I said, throwing my arms around him. 'Did he tell you about her?' I asked, dreading the answer that I knew he was going to give me.

'She came too, Mam. Her name is Megan.'

Anger warmed my veins. How could JP do that to him? Surely, he wasn't that stupid to bring her along so soon?

'Oh, sweetheart,' I said. 'I'm sorry.' I cuddled him in close to my breast and felt his warm tears soak through my cotton T-shirt. I guessed Harry had believed JP's departure to be a temporary thing. He had always seen his parents as a unit and now he was facing the crushing realisation that our unit was shattered.

'Will you tell Dad that I don't want to go next time? It's too weird. Dad is meant to be with you.'

My heart felt as though it was being splintered into tiny smithereens at his innocence. Harry thought I could fix this, that I had some say in what was happening to us. He didn't understand that I was just as powerless as he was.

HARRY

I can't tell anybody because I'm trying to be brave, but I miss Dad soooooooooo much. We always watch the Liverpool matches together or go out for a kick-about on the green and it's not the same without him.

Dad still hasn't come home yet and he's being really mean because he's making everyone sad. Dad left us because he wanted a different wife instead of Mam, but that's not fair on Mam because she didn't get a different husband.

She's called Megan, but they didn't get married yet because he is still married to Mam. She's really young – even younger than my teacher. She looks a bit funny and she's really orange, not like when you go on holidays and you get a suntan, she's actually orange like the fruit. Her nails are really long and pointy, and she always wear loads of make-up and she keeps having to fix it whenever she sees a mirror. Dad was acting all funny when she was around, and she kept calling him 'babes', but he's forty-three so he's not a baby, and they hold hands (eugggh), even though Mam and Dad never do that. Dad likes her better than us, that's why he wants to live with her. Robyn is clever, she faked being sick so she didn't have to go to Paccini's. I wish I had thought of that and then I wouldn't have had to meet stinky Megan.

I asked Dad to come back home because everything went wrong when he left, but he said that he can't, and I said, 'why?' and he said, 'because sometimes mams and dads need to live in different houses'.

I want to make Mam happy again and I asked her if I got her a new husband would she stop crying and then she started crying even more, so I don't think she wants one, which is good because I don't know where you get husbands from, so now I'm working on a plan to break up Dad and Megan, it's called 'Harry's Secret Plan to Bring Dad Home'. Step One is that I'm going to pretend I'm sick the next time he comes to pick me up like Robyn did so I don't have to go with him. Then Step Two is I'm going to annoy Megan, so she will break up with Dad. I just want everything to go back to the way it used to be. I know Mam gets really sad whenever I say that to her, but it's all because of stupid Megan. I hate her! She made everything go bad.

Tomorrow is New Year's Eve and normally Mam and Dad let us stay up really late to watch the fireworks on TV and we all make a wish, but the only thing I want for the new year is for my dad to come home.

8

January came in raging and roaring. Cold and wet and bleak. Although it hadn't yet snowed, dark clouds, heavy and threatening, hung in the sky. The kids had gone back to school and I was alone in an empty house for the best part of the day, with only my thoughts and wounded heart for company.

It had been three weeks since JP left and over the last few days it had slowly dawned on me that his departure wasn't a 'moment of madness', but, instead, it seemed to be a new way of life for us. I missed him so much, I was still crying myself to sleep every night. I would wake up in the morning to find my pillow damp from tears and a dehydration headache pounding. I would open the wardrobe and see his clothes still hanging beside my own. Sometimes I would lift out a T-shirt just to breathe in his manly smell and rub the soft cotton along my skin. His photos still hung on the walls, his crime thrillers still sat on our bookshelves, his toiletries still stood on the bathroom shelf – everywhere I went there were reminders of him and the life we used to share together.

The children had amazed me with their resilience. I had

contacted their teachers to tell them that JP and I were having marital difficulties so they could be on alert if there were any issues with Harry and Robyn, but thankfully both of them seemed to be coping well with the altered landscape of their lives. They were slowly accepting their changing circumstances with the adaptability that young kids are remarkable at. I was so proud of them.

Word had slowly filtered out to our wider families and friends and what bothered me the most was the silence. Nobody from JP's family had made any contact with me since that fateful Christmas Day. I was sure they must have heard the news though, if not from him, from somebody else, but they hadn't picked up the phone. I knew by the way other mums avoided my eye at the school gate that they had heard what had happened too. I even saw friends of ours, other couples that we had gone for dinner or drinks with, turn down a different aisle just to dodge me in the supermarket. I guessed people didn't know what to say to me, they would rather avoid me than stand and have an excruciatingly awkward conversation. I still hadn't been able to find the words to tell my friends Linda and Mel what had happened yet because I felt like such a failure.

I had recently logged into our bank account and was relieved to see JP had lodged money to cover the mortgage and our living costs for a few months, but I couldn't rely on him doing this forever. I knew he might ask for a divorce down the line, after we had been separated for two years, as was the requirement under Irish law. There might even come a time when we would have to sell the family home, I had seen it happen when a couple's assets got divvied up in the divorce settlement. I loved being a stay-at-home mum, there was no more important job in my eyes, but I might have no choice but to go back to work. It was daunting to think about dusting off my CV after spending so long out of the workforce.

One morning, I was in the bathroom undressing to get into the shower when, in some sort of perverse self-flagellation, I made myself stand and face my reflection head-on in the mirror. Usually, I averted my eyes to avoid looking at my body, but that day, I forced myself to look at the image staring back at me. I hated the way the loose skin from my mum-tum hung over my underwear and how the silvery grooves of my stretch marks made my stomach look like elephant skin. I placed my hands on either side of my abdomen and stretched out the loose skin to try to remember what it had looked like before. Then there were the dimples of cellulite on my thighs and the way my breasts had gone south after feeding two kids – to me, my body was revolting. I had let myself go. I should have tried harder to stay in shape. I had joined a gym when Robyn had begun playschool and I finally had a few hours to myself again every morning, but I hadn't gone back to it after the first week. Was it any wonder JP had left me?

Suddenly, I heard Robyn crying and calling out for me. I quickly threw on my dressing gown and followed her small voice down the landing.

'What's wrong, pet?' I asked, hurrying into her bedroom.

'I'm sorry, Mammy, I got sick.' She was standing looking at her soiled carpet in dismay.

'Hey, don't worry, sweetheart. Are you okay?'

She nodded.

It was the second time in as many weeks that I had woken to find she had vomited. I guessed there were a lot of bugs doing the rounds at this time of year and children Robyn's age seemed to pick up everything. I knew half of her playschool class had been out sick with various illnesses recently, but she had been complaining of not feeling well a lot lately and I was starting to think her illness was psychosomatic. It worried me that she could be doing this at just four years of age.

She had made excuses not to go the last two times that JP had called to collect them, and then Harry had tried it too and I knew JP thought it was my fault. I had mentioned it to Fiona, and she had suggested that the kids might need counselling. That had been a shock to me, I had always thought I would be able to protect them from whatever life threw at them, but my daughter had clearly been affected by our break-up.

I got her cleaned up and as I set to work scrubbing the carpet, she asked me if she could have Cheerios for breakfast. I was baffled at how she still had an appetite.

We went downstairs and, after she had finished her cereal, she raised the bowl up to her lips to drink the leftover milk, leaving a big milky moustache behind on her face.

'Can I wear my princess dress to playschool?' she asked.

'You want to go to playschool?' I was dumbfounded, but that was the thing with kids, they just bounced back. They were so resilient.

'I feel better now,' she sang as she ran off towards the playroom to find the dress.

Even though she did seem to be fine again, the playschool's sickness policy meant I would need to keep her at home. Although I was probably being overcautious, I decided to make an appointment with our doctor just to put my mind at ease.

* * *

I had tucked Robyn up underneath her duvet on the sofa; she was sucking her thumb and snuggling Mr Bunny as she watched *Paw Patrol*. I was relieved to see that she had managed to keep her breakfast down and had been in great form since she had been sick that morning. I guessed it was some sort of bug she had picked up in playschool.

I had called Fiona and asked her if she could take Harry to school for me so I didn't have to disturb Robyn. Thankfully, as a freelancer, she had a lot of flexibility with her hours. I had just seen them off and was standing in the utility room, loading Robyn's soiled bed sheets into the washing machine, when I heard the doorbell ring and, when I answered it, I saw that it was my mother-in-law, Joan. I hadn't seen her since Christmas Day, and I had wondered when I was going to hear from her.

'Sarah,' she said curtly, casting a critical eye over my greying fleecy dressing gown.

'Come in, Joan,' I said, feeling mortified that she had caught me still in my pyjamas. She was wearing a rose-coloured tweed two-piece suit with matching court shoes and her white hair was carefully styled. She was always dolled up as if she had somewhere important to go to. A former air hostess during the glory days of airline travel, she had never lost any of her glamour.

She made her way into the living room. I watched her eyes as they landed on the toys scattered around the room and Harry's pyjamas that he had left in a pile on the floor when he got dressed for school earlier. I hadn't had a chance to pick them up.

'Oh, hello, Robyn,' she said in surprise.

'Ganny!' Robyn tossed the duvet aside, jumped up and ran to hug her grandmother.

'Oh, I've missed you, darling girl,' Joan said, lifting her up and kissing her cheek.

I realised that JP leaving us had repercussions for them too. They hadn't seen the children since Christmas when usually they would have seen each other every week.

'Why isn't she in playschool?' Joan asked me.

'She was sick earlier this morning,' I said.

'Well, she seems fine now.' She looked at Robyn, who was grinning in her arms.

'You know what kids are like,' I said, shrugging my shoulders. 'Anyway, the playschool has a forty-eight-hour exclusion policy when a child has vomited,' I added, because I knew she felt I was being overcautious. *I should cancel my appointment with Dr Peters*, I thought. I didn't want to waste his time... 'Can I get you a tea or coffee?' I offered.

'A tea would be lovely, thanks.'

She followed me into the kitchen and took a seat at the table as I began to boil the kettle.

'I just wanted to see how you've been,' she began as I placed the mug down in front of her and took a seat opposite her.

I was touched by her concern because JP was the apple of her eye and, for her, could do no wrong. JP had lost his younger sister, Ellen, when she was ten years old, after being knocked off her bike in a road traffic accident on her way home from school. JP had become an only child overnight and, understandably, his mother had been very protective of him ever since. I had been wondering how she had taken the news of his departure. As a devout Catholic and a regular mass-goer, I knew it would have been a huge blow to Joan to learn that her son had walked out on his wife. Even though JP and I had both been raised as Catholic, we weren't very religious. Although we had got married in a church and had chosen to baptise our children, we rarely went to mass, and Joan called us *à la carte* Catholics.

'I miss them, you know,' she added, and I could see water gather at the corners of her eyes. 'Richard too – both of us – we're not used to going without seeing them for so long.' Her voice quivered.

'Joan, I know this is hard on everyone.' I placed my hand over hers on the table and gave it a squeeze. 'But you can see them whenever you want, you know that.'

'It's not meant to be this way,' she continued, shaking her head.

'This isn't my doing, Joan – JP walked out on us – he left me for a younger woman.' I wondered exactly what version of events JP had told his parents.

'But all marriages have their ups and downs, Sarah, you just have to try a bit harder. Men have been having affairs since the year dot and women just quietly turned a blind eye to it for the sake of keeping the peace. Once the men were discreet, their wives ignored it and just went about their business as normal, but it's only now, since all these bra-burning feminists have come on the scene, that everyone has to make a big song and dance about it. You aren't the first woman to be wronged by an errant husband, Sarah, and you won't be the last.'

'JP left me on St Stephen's morning! He didn't give me the option to "turn a blind eye to it". Do you think I want this? I'm devastated! I begged him to stay, but clearly his feelings for her – this Megan woman – trump his family. Did he tell you that they're living together?' My voice snagged as emotion caught up with my anger. 'I still love him, Joan, but I don't have a say in it,' I explained sadly.

'Well, if I were you, I'd be asking myself some deep questions.'

I was stunned by the vitriol in her words. 'What's that supposed to mean?'

'I mean why did he stray in the first place? As a wife, there are certain things you can be doing... Keep yourself looking well, for a start.'

I automatically fingered my hair, which I knew was wild and wispy around my face, but I would have tidied myself up a bit if I had known she was calling. My mother-in-law had never approved of my casual dress sense. Over the years, I had lost count of the times she had passed comment when she would call round and I would be wearing a tracksuit. Or if I didn't turn up to a family occasion with a fresh blow-dry and a full face of make-up, I would see disapproval in her eyes. For Christmas every year I was gifted make-up palettes in lurid colours, with names like 'Scarlet Siren', presumably in the hope that I'd start to up my game in terms of my appearance. I would donate them to the charity shop the following week. JP and I used to laugh about it. I was able to let it roll off me. I was comfortable enough in my own skin for it not to bother me, but now, when I was at my lowest ebb, her criticism stung.

I stood up, indicating that this conversation was over. 'I don't think that's very fair, Joan.'

She stood up too, holding onto her handbag and heading down the hallway towards the door before stopping and turning back to face me. 'I'm sorry, Sarah, I've said my piece, so I'll go now, but please just try to work things out with John-Paul – you have to try and save your marriage – for all our sakes.' She nodded towards the living room. 'Tell Robyn I said goodbye. I hope she feels better soon.'

9

I sat stunned at my kitchen table for a long time after Joan had left. It was clear that she was pinning the blame for the disintegration of my marriage squarely on my shoulders, but surely she knew, I loved JP. If there was anything – anything at all – that I could have done to save my marriage, I would have done it, but I was powerless. Her words had been like salt in the wound; Joan seemed to think JP had left because I had let myself go and, now, I was questioning myself yet again. Was it really all my own fault that JP had walked out? Could I have done more to stop him leaving? If I had dressed better or lost some weight maybe? And it had been months since we had had sex – why had I said I was tired whenever JP tried to make love to me? Why hadn't I ever been the one to instigate it, instead of always leaving it up to him? Now I wished more than anything that I had tried harder.

I hadn't told anyone, but I had looked up Megan's Instagram page a few days ago. Her account was set to public, so it was easy to find her. I had tortured myself by flicking through photo after photo of her posing and pouting with her friends with strings of hashtags underneath that I didn't understand. Long blonde hair cascaded down her back and she looked as though she had bathed in fake tan. I had stared at this woman – well, she didn't look much older than a girl really – with her perfect teeth smiling back at me; this woman, who had stolen my husband and taken my children's father away from their home. This woman who had broken down the foundations of my life. I wondered what she saw in a man that was almost twenty years older than her. Was it all a game to her? Did she comprehend the gravity of what she had done to my family? I had swiped through her photos, feeling so frumpy and out of touch. So old. I couldn't help but think it was no wonder he left me – how could I even possibly compete? I would have left me too if someone like Megan came along.

As much as it pained me to admit it, Joan was right, I didn't make much of an effort with my appearance. When I had worked in the bank, I used to treat myself to a blow-dry every week and sometimes my nails too, but doing all of that seemed pointless now when I was mostly in the house with the kids. Back then, I used to nip into the shops on Grafton Street on my lunch break. Now I couldn't remember the last time I had bought new clothes for myself instead of the kids, but my priorities had changed since I had become a mother.

I stood up and walked over to the mirror that hung above the dining table. Although I usually avoided looking directly at myself, I forced myself to look at the reflection staring back at me. My lines were deep, like valleys, my face starting to sink as it lost a battle with the forces of age, and shadows had appeared where I never had them before. I caught hold of the skin on either side of my face and pulled it back, making my face instantly more youthful. When had I got so old? I had never been obsessive about my appearance; I hadn't really worried about lines and wrinkles the way some women did, but maybe I should have. If I had, my husband might not have left me for a younger woman.

'Why is your face weird, Mammy?' Robyn asked from behind me as she came into the room.

'Oh, I was just making silly faces in the mirror, sweetie.' I lifted her up and we stuck out our tongues and pulled at our eyes to make funny faces. We were laughing so much as we contorted our faces and I was so glad to see Robyn was back to her usual happy self again. As we giggled at our reflections, I couldn't help thinking, what the hell did a few wrinkles matter when I had the most perfect children?

* * *

After we had collected Harry from school, the three of us set off for Dr Peters' surgery. Robyn had been in great form for the rest of the day and I had been about to cancel my appointment, but I knew the surgery would charge me a no-show fee if I cancelled so late in the day.

'Maaaaam,' Harry called. 'Tell Robyn to stop!'

I glanced in the rear-view mirror where Robyn was poking Harry.

'Robyn, stop annoying your brother,' I warned.

She sat back in her seat with a mischievous twinkle in her eyes as she began swinging Mr Bunny around by his ears. That poor, tortured rabbit. I smiled, but I was glad she was back to her sparky self.

We took a seat in the waiting room where there were ghost-like children sitting on their parents' knees, patients too sick to keep their eyes open. Meanwhile, Robyn continued trying to wind Harry up. I cringed, feeling silly for being there. She was definitely not a sick child.

We were eventually called in by Dr Peters and we followed him into his surgery and took a seat while Harry ran over to play with the Lego that he kept in the corner of the room for children to play with.

'How are you today, Mrs McIntyre?' he asked.

I replied with my standard line: 'I'm good, thank you.'

'What can I do for you?'

Dr Peters was an older doctor, nearing retirement age. Wispy tufts of white hair sat on either side of a kindly, round face. He had been our family doctor since Harry was born and I trusted him with my life. Robyn too had been going to him since she was just a few weeks old and, as I sat in front of him listing off her symptoms, he didn't seem too worried. I felt like a fraud as she chatted away to him, telling him about her friends in school and how she and Lily both wanted to be Elsa when they were playing together yesterday, but Lily wasn't wearing the right dress so how could she could be Elsa?

Dr Peters chuckled as she chatted. 'Look, it's probably just something viral that she picked up. If you saw the number of children that I get coming through the doors here with all sorts of crazy things.'

I sent Robyn over to Harry to play with the Lego. 'Well, it's just... a few things have happened lately...' I said once she was engrossed in playing. 'I was wondering, well... do you think kids can, you know... experience... imaginary symptoms if they're worried about something?' I was trying to ask as tentatively as possible. I wasn't ready yet to tell Dr Peters about JP, I didn't trust myself not to get upset if he showed me any sympathy.

'How do you mean?' He peered at me over the top of his wire-rimmed glasses.

'Well, it's just it's the second time it's happened, and she's been a bit lethargic recently... and sometimes she complains of headaches... but, well, I don't know... maybe she's just looking for attention?'

'Well, if you want, we could get some blood tests done, just to give you some peace of mind?'

I shook my head. I felt embarrassed for wasting his time when he had a waiting room packed full of really sick people outside the door. Even just saying it out loud made me realise how ridiculous I sounded. I was starting to feel like a hypochondriac. Like I was imagining everything – wishing my children sick as a cry for help. Wasn't there a name for that – Munchausen syndrome by proxy or something?

I picked up my bag ready to leave, but then I felt a little wobble in my resolve. There was something niggling at me in the back of my brain. 'Yeah, maybe... I think so.' I placed my bag back down on the floor.

'Okay, we can't do paediatric blood tests here, so I'll write you a referral for the Dublin children's hospital,' he said as he clacked away on his keyboard, and I knew by his tone that he thought I was another overcautious parent clogging up the health system. And I probably was, but I just wanted to be sure. After everything that had happened over the last few weeks, the ground underneath my feet had been shaken and I just wanted some certainty in my life. I needed to know that Robyn was okay.

10

One Sunday evening a few weeks later, Fiona and I were sitting in the living room as rain ran down the windowpane in rivulets. I was keeping an eye on the driveway for JP's car. He had taken the children over to see his parents for the evening. I knew Joan and Richard found it difficult not seeing them as much as they usually would. It had taken a lot of persuasion, but I had eventually managed to convince Robyn to go along with them too. Although they had only been gone for a few hours, it still felt too long. I missed the children when they weren't there, the house was too quiet. It was hard to imagine that in a previous life whenever the kids were being noisy and spreading mess like a tornado, I had sometimes fantasised about living alone in a quiet, orderly house. Now I hated being by myself. Sometimes I would meet Linda or Mel for coffee; I had finally plucked up the courage to tell them and they were being a great support. I had been worried they would look upon me with pity, but they had rallied around me and bolstered my shattered self-worth and reminded me of the good things about myself. Other times, Fiona would call over to keep me company; she knew I found it lonely without the children's laughter echoing around the walls.

I couldn't believe that JP had been gone for almost two months. February had pushed out January and in some ways it felt like it was only yesterday since he had left, but in many more, the last few weeks had been the longest of my entire life. He was still living with Megan and thinking about them together hurt as much as it did the first time I had found out about them. Valentine's Day had stung, going into shops decorated with paper hearts and red balloons and seeing ads full of loved-up couples on the TV. It wasn't helped by a florist knocking on my door asking if I could take in a delivery of a dozen red roses for my neighbour because she wasn't at home. The kids had tried cheering me up by making a card and picking snowdrops and daffodils from the garden, so I had plastered a smile on my face for their sake. Even though JP and I had never made a fuss about Valentine's, he would always arrive home with flowers to mark the day and it was a reminder of all the little things I missed about my husband.

JP was a person I didn't recognise now; he dressed differently, acted differently, like he had erased our whole life together. I was getting through each day as it came to me. I couldn't think too far ahead because if I did that, I would feel an overwhelming sense of suffocation and fear about what the future held for me. For all of us. So, I took one day at a time and, somehow, I got through. I had had a roller-coaster few weeks, but I was slowly starting to see the light. Fiona had helped me to update my CV and I was keeping an eye out for part-time work. I was emerging from the awful darkness and was able to see a future for me up ahead in the hazy distance that didn't involve JP. The pain still felt raw and some days were worse than others, but I was learning to accept my new life. Life didn't seem as bleak as it had back in January, and I thought, with time, one day I might even be able to smile again.

Eventually, just after eight, I saw the lights of his car in the driveway and I hurried out to meet them. JP and I exchanged the usual awkward greetings that were our new normal. We were able to remain civil to one another and I was very grateful for that.

'Did you have a good time?' I asked the children as they climbed out of the car.

I was glad to see Harry had a big smile plastered across his face, but Robyn was more subdued, and I could tell she was tired.

I had just turned around to head back into the house when JP called me back.

'Can I talk to you for a sec?' he asked. Nothing good ever followed when JP asked to talk to me.

'Go on into the house before you get soaked,' I called to Harry and Robyn. 'I'll be in in a sec.' I turned back to JP.

'Everything okay?' I asked as the rain landed in cool droplets on my skin.

'I think we might need to take Robyn to get her eyes checked... she seems to be squinting,' he continued.

'She's just tired,' I said, folding my arms across my chest. 'It's way past her bedtime.' I glanced pointedly at my watch.

'Yeah, you're probably right,' he agreed.

We stood in awkward silence for a moment, each of us stuck for words and eventually he got back into his car and I went into the house. Although I didn't like to admit it to JP, I had noticed Robyn squinting too and it wasn't just when she was tired, sometimes she would be sitting eating her cereal in the morning and her eye would start to close on one side. Then there had been the strange vomiting episodes when she woke in the mornings but would be fine again moments later. I had been putting it down to tiredness or the viral bugs that tended to swarm around preschools at this time of year, but maybe it was all connected? There had been so many little things niggling at me lately. Alarm bells were starting to fire in my head, and I was beginning to think I was going crazy.

Two weeks previously, I had taken Robyn to the Dublin children's hospital to have her blood tests as Dr Peters had suggested. She had screamed the place down as the phlebotomist had tried to locate the vein. Although I did my best to distract her, it was futile. We had passed really sick children in the corridors on the way in; a bald girl not much older than Robyn had been walking along beside her mother with drip attached to her arm and, in that moment, I was so grateful that hospitals and needles weren't part of our daily life. When Dr Peters had called to tell me the results, I had hardly dared to breathe.

'Sarah, I was just calling to let you know that the hospital has forwarded the results of Robyn's blood tests and I'm sure you'll be glad to know that everything looks good.'

I had exhaled heavily, feeling my shoulders climb down from my ears. It was a relief to know that I had been worrying about nothing.

'How's she been since?' he had continued.

'Good, she's been great,' I'd lied. For some reason I didn't tell him that she had got sick again the previous morning. If her blood tests were good, then she was good, I had thought. They would have shown if there was something wrong. That day I had breathed a huge sigh of relief as I had hung up the phone, but now there it was again, that nagging voice was back, telling me that something wasn't right.

'How're my most favourite people in the world?' I said, swinging my arms around both children as I went back inside the house. 'Did you have a good time?'

Robyn smiled up at me, but her face didn't look right. I rubbed my eyes, thinking that perhaps my vision was blurry, but when I looked again, Robyn's face was definitely drooping slightly on one side, causing her eyelid to sag down above her eye. I could see why JP thought she was squinting. I felt a prickle of goosebumps breaking out across my body. This wasn't right.

'Fiona,' I said. 'Is her face okay?' I mouthed.

'What?'

I pointed at my own face and then at Robyn's.

Fiona dipped her head to get a closer look. She stood back and cocked her head to inspect her further. 'Now that you say it, it does look a bit funny, doesn't it?' she said.

'What looks funny?' Robyn asked.

'This...' Fiona said, sticking out her tongue so that Robyn began to giggle. As I looked at Robyn's beautiful face lit up with laughter, I still felt unsettled.

'Maybe she needs glasses?' Fiona suggested later while the kids were in the bath. 'Remember I had a lazy eye when I was around her age and had to wear a patch for months – you used to call me Pirate Girl.' She laughed at the memory.

'Yeah, you're right,' I said, forcing myself to laugh along too.

'She's grand, Sarah, stop stressing,' Fiona assured me.

'I know,' I replied, trying to shake off my unease. 'She's fine.'

HARRY

Mam has stopped crying every day now, she smiles more, and she got her hair cut too and she looks really pretty again. She's like the way she used to be before Dad went away, but I don't want her to look too pretty though in case she gets a new husband before I get Dad home. On Valentine's Day I made Mammy a card and Robyn picked flowers for her in the garden because we didn't want her to be sad again if she didn't get any cards or flowers and she said we were the best kids in the whole wide world.

We went to Granny and Grandad's house today and Robyn actually came with us. She never wants to go with Dad when he picks us up, she always pretends she is sick. I tried doing it a few times too, but they wouldn't believe me. She's a reeeeally good faker. She even made her eye go all funny when we were over there!

I'm still working on the next step in my plan to get Dad home, but today Step Two kinda just happened. When he was dropping us home, Megan rang him on the speakerphone in the car. Dad was meant to pick her up, but he was late dropping us home so then Dad and her had a big fight. Then Dad said the F-word and then Megan said the F-word twice! His face went all red and he told Megan to 'calm the fuck down and stop making a scene with the kids in the car' and she screamed back 'how dare you tell me to calm the fuck down and maybe you should calm the fuck down'. Robyn and I were trying so hard not to laugh, and we have a new nickname for her now we're calling her Crazy Megan. I think my plan to break them up is working...

11

The following morning, I walked down the footpath outside the playschool, feeling the winter sunshine warm my cheeks. I stood chatting with some of the other mums while we waited for the door to open. It was a glorious day. Wispy clouds stretched like pulled cotton wool hung suspended in the sky. We were on the cusp of spring and over the last few days the strengthening sun had started to push out the colder winter days.

'Are you sure you're okay?' I asked, crouching down in front of Robyn as I went inside the playschool. Her eyelid was still drooping, and I hadn't slept all night worrying about it. I couldn't ignore the bleeping in my brain. It was getting louder. I had made an appointment with the optician in town for that afternoon and I really hoped she would be able to tell me what was going on with my daughter. I just wanted some kind of explanation, something that could be fixed with a pair of glasses or even an eyepatch like Fiona had had, if that's what it took. Whatever was wrong, I just wanted to get it sorted before I lost my mind completely.

'Yes, Mammy,' she said. 'Look, there's Lily, I want to go now.' She wriggled away from me and ran off to play with her friend.

I waited until the other parents had left and her teacher Louise had all the children settled so I could have a word with her.

'I just wanted to check that Robyn has been getting on okay lately?'

'She's fine – she's full of beans, always first to share her news with the class too! Why? Are you concerned about something, Sarah?'

I looked over to where Robyn and Lily were playing with Lego blocks. From this distance, her face looked the same as it always did. I couldn't see the lopsidedness. Perhaps it had all been in my head? Maybe I was looking for things that didn't exist, but then JP and Fiona had noticed it too…

I hesitated for a moment, then shook my head. 'No, sorry, it's nothing…' I gathered up my bag to leave.

'Wait, Mammy!' Robyn cried, running after me and throwing her arms around me. 'You forgot my kiss.'

'Oh, silly me!' I bent down and felt the press of her soft, wet lips against my own. I was relieved to see she was her usual spritely self once more. 'I love you, baby girl, have a great day.'

She turned and ran back to her chair, but she didn't make it and instead collapsed beside it. Louise and I both hurried over, assuming she had tripped on something, but we soon realised that there was no hazard in her way. I reached out to help her up, but it was as though she couldn't get her legs to work. I felt my own legs get weak with shock and I held on to the table to steady myself. I knew by the way Louise stepped in and lifted her onto a chair, that she was just as concerned as I was. Something was wrong with my daughter and it wasn't just in my imagination.

'I need to call her doctor,' I said. On the periphery, I could see a sea of small, round, curious expressions staring at me, wondering what was going on, but it was only Robyn's drooping face I could focus on.

'Go and use the staffroom,' Louise said, as she pointed me towards a door at the back of the room. 'I'll sit here with Robyn.'

I didn't move, it was as though my feet were concreted to the floor. I could see the fear in Robyn's eyes, and I didn't want to leave her alone. 'Go on,' Louise encouraged. 'I'll be right here with her, Sarah.'

Reluctantly I left her with Louise and went into the staffroom.

I was beginning to think I was going round the twist. Her bloods had been okay – if something was wrong, they would have shown up something, wouldn't they? With trembling hands, I immediately called the surgery. I didn't care if Dr Peters thought I was mad, I just needed reassurance. The bleep in my brain had now grown into a screeching siren. I explained to the receptionist what had happened, and I was so grateful when she put me straight through to his office and I heard Dr Peters' calm voice on the other end.

'Is that you, Sarah? Is everything okay?'

'Well, it's Robyn, I'm very worried about her...' I heard the crack in my voice as it threatened to give way to tears. I explained to him what had happened and about how one of her eyes was drooping, and I knew by his questions that he was concerned. He told me to take her to A & E to be checked out, but he reassured me that it was probably nothing to worry about. He reminded me once again that her bloods had all come back fine. I took a deep breath to slow my heart rate down and listened to this man full of wisdom, with a vast medical knowledge. He was right, I needed to calm down.

I helped Robyn out to the car. Although she could now walk again, her gait was wrong, and it was like she was leaning to one side. Once she was belted up, I drove to the Dublin children's hospital.

She was unnaturally quiet on the journey there – normally she chatted non-stop in the car – and I knew she was scared by what was happening to her body. I thought about calling JP to let him know, but I didn't want to worry him unnecessarily. Dr Peters had said it was probably nothing serious. I decided I would call him when we were on the way home afterwards.

When we arrived at the hospital, we went inside and were seen straight away by a middle-aged, rotund triage nurse with a kindly smile who didn't seem too perturbed as I listed Robyn's symptoms. We took a seat in the waiting room, decorated with colourful cartoon characters like Peppa Pig and Fireman Sam. I was glad it wasn't too busy; there was a baby with roaring red cheeks, clearly under the weather, and a boy around Harry's age came in with a suspected broken arm after falling in the school-yard. I smiled in solidarity at the other parents, each of us wrapped up in our own worries, wishing we were anywhere else but there.

While we sat in the waiting room, Robyn was really subdued. She didn't play with any of the toys in the play area and just sat quietly beside me instead. I took out my phone and began typing her symptoms into Google, but the search results that came back ranged from minor childhood ailments to illnesses that didn't bear thinking about, so I put my phone back in my bag again. There was no point worrying myself silly. We would find out what was going on soon enough.

After an hour waiting, we were seen by the paediatrician. He read through the notes on Robyn's chart given to him by the triage nurse.

'Just to be on the safe side given some of the symptoms you

described, I think we should do a brain scan. I'm sure it's nothing, but I would like to rule out anything sinister.'

'Sinister?' My head stuck on the word.

'Let's just get the scan done and then we can see,' he said.

'We had her bloods done recently and they were fine,' I added. I was begging him to tell me this was all okay.

He nodded. 'I'm sure all is good, Mrs McIntyre, try not to worry, but I wouldn't be doing my job properly if I sent you home without further thorough investigation. The scan will tell us more.' He left us alone as he went on his way.

Just hours ago we had been sitting around the table eating breakfast and now Robyn was going to have a scan on her brain! I couldn't even begin to get my head around it.

I left Robyn alone in the cubicle we were waiting in and stepped outside the door into the corridor. I took my phone out of my bag and, with trembling hands, tried to ring JP. It took me three attempts before I finally managed to press the right buttons.

'Sarah?' he said when he picked up. 'Is everything okay?'

'You need to come to the children's hospital...'

'Woah, there – slow down – what are you doing in the hospital? I'm just on my way into a meeting—'

'Robyn collapsed at playschool, so I rang Dr Peters and he told me to come here.' My voice sounded calm and in control as if it wasn't coming from me at all. 'The doctors want to do a brain scan.'

'I don't like the sound of that.'

I felt the same but didn't want to let him know that. If I showed JP my very worst fears, I was worried he would confirm them. That this could be serious. 'Look, it'll be fine,' I said as breezily as I could.

'Right, I'm on my way.'

'Call me when you get here, and I'll come and meet you.'

I called Fiona next and told her what was going on and asked if she could collect Harry from school and take him home. She reassured me that Robyn would be fine and made me promise to call her as soon as we had any update.

A short while later, JP came rushing through the hospital doors. Wordlessly, I led the way back to the cubicle where sunlight streamed in through a small window, making the room feel so hot. Robyn was busy colouring a picture, her face was screwed up in concentration as she worked hard to keep the crayon inside the lines. She looked fine, surely whatever it was that was wrong with her couldn't be too serious?

'Hey there, princess,' JP greeted her.

'Hi, Daddy.' She smiled at him.

He turned to me. 'What do you think it is?'

'Look, you know what doctors are like, they have to cover themselves – they have to err on the side of caution. Let's not jump to conclusions and worry ourselves stupid when it's prob-ably nothing,' I said. 'Look at her, she's fine.' We needed to stay calm here. This was all going to be okay, because it had to be okay. The alternative was unthinkable.

'You're right,' he agreed. But despite his best reassurances, I could see the fear inside me was mirrored in his eyes.

A short while later, we were told they were ready for her MRI. Robyn screamed while they inserted the IV cannula required for the general anaesthetic that she needed to help her lie still due to her young age and I felt a maternal pull to take her in my arms, run out of the hospital and stop all of this. As they wheeled her trolley away and it was swallowed by the flap of a set of double doors, I found myself making the sign of the cross.

'She's going to be fine,' JP said, noticing me. His arm reached out and we had an awkward moment as it looked as though he was about to hug me. We both watched his arm as it hovered midair and then he thought better of it and it fell back limply by his side.

'Yeah,' I said, trying to sound bright.

Despite all that we had been through in recent months, I was glad he was by my side right then. It was comforting to have another person who knew Robyn just like I did; who loved her from the moment she came into this world.

We sat back on the chairs beside Robyn's empty bed and waited. My mind raced trying to think of something to say to JP. It made me sad to realise we had spent twenty-five years together and yet I couldn't think of single thing to talk to him about. The one topic we had in common was our reason for being in the hospital, but we were both deliberately not going down that road. Suddenly, his phone rang, jolting me out of my thoughts.

I listened to the one-sided conversation for a moment and quickly picked up that it was Megan.

'I'm not sure,' he said, standing up and starting to pace around the small room, which made it feel even more claustrophobic. 'I don't know how long these things take... Well, why don't you get a taxi then?'

He was becoming increasingly irate with every sentence he spoke.

'It's not every day your daughter has an MRI on her brain!' he said, hanging up abruptly. He tossed the phone down onto the bed. 'Sorry about that,' he mumbled.

'Megan?' I enquired.

He nodded, clearly too incensed to talk.

'If you have somewhere else you need to be, I'm going to be here anyway...' I said.

'No, this is the only place I need to be...'

I nodded and we each fell silent.

It was less than an hour later when Robyn was wheeled back

in and I was relieved to see she was already coming out of the anaesthetic. I reached over and stroked her smooth, plump cheek. A small patch of drool pooled at the corners of her mouth. Her eyelids flickered open as she took in her surroundings.

'How did it go?' I asked the nurse straight away.

'She was great,' she said without answering my question.

'But the MRI, how did it look?' JP pressed.

'The doctor will be around to see you shortly,' she said with a face that gave nothing away. More waiting and worrying; there seemed to be so much waiting.

'This isn't my bed, Mammy,' Robyn said, tugging on the taut linen.

'No, darling, you're in the hospital, remember?'

'But I'm not sick!' she protested.

'We all know that,' I said conspiratorially, 'but the doctor just wants to be extra sure.' I gave her hand a squeeze.

'Silly doctor,' she said, shaking her head. 'Can we go home now?'

'Soon, we just need to see the doctor for a minute before we go.'

'I never want to come here again.'

'I know, pet, it's all over now.' I rubbed her hand.

An hour later, we were still waiting to speak with the doctor. It felt interminable. Minutes felt like an eternity when it was the life of your precious daughter that hung in the balance. I just wanted to get her home, where she belonged, far away from this place. Every time a doctor came near, my stomach flipped – although I wanted to get it over with, I was also petrified of what they might say. In a perverse way, I wished I could hold them back forever.

'There's nothing wrong with her,' JP said once again as we both watched her do dance actions to some kids' show she was watching on his phone.

I really hoped he was right. I was swinging through waves of 'of course this will be fine, she's not sick' to desperate thoughts of 'what if...?' That was a place where I couldn't let my head go.

Before I could answer him, I saw the nurse from earlier on approaching us through the glass window facing on to the corridor. My heart tightened and I inhaled sharply. *Please let it be good news*, I begged internally. I tried to read her face for any giveaway signs, but it remained impassive.

'Mr and Mrs McIntyre, thank you for your patience.' She had a half-smile on her face. Surely, if it was bad news, she wouldn't smile, I thought.

I felt a renewed sense of optimism and I let myself breathe out again. I rolled my shoulders back and took a deep breath. Robyn was fine. The blood tests had said so.

'Why don't you both come with me, the doctors would like to talk to you alone. I will sit with Robyn for a few minutes,' she said, nodding towards the bed.

'What is it?' JP asked quickly.

'If you could both follow me down the corridor—'

'Can someone please just tell me what is going on?' I begged. Why did they need to take us into a different room? I felt the hairs on my arm stand to attention and my heart started to thump faster.

'Just come with me, Mrs McIntyre, and the doctor will explain everything.'

We followed her into a small room, where there was a team of doctors in white coats waiting for us – not just one person, like we had been expecting. There was a tiny window at one end, too high up to see out of, and a worn leatherette sofa ran the length of the room. The wall was covered in posters advertising counselling services and health warnings. A chest of toys stood in the corner and my eyes landed on a box of tissues that was sitting on the coffee table. Tissues meant tears. They wouldn't bring us here if it was good news, a voice said in my head. I took a deep breath, feeling it snag in my chest.

'What's wrong with Robyn?' JP asked as soon as we had closed the door behind us.

'I'm Dr Sharma,' one of the men began, 'and these are my colleagues, Dr French and Dr Stevens.' He paused. 'Mr and Mrs McIntyre, I think you should both sit down…'

12

A shiver flooded through me and my legs felt weak and jellylike. This wasn't good. The air felt as though it was being sucked out of my lungs and I couldn't replace it. I was spinning on a merry-go-round that I couldn't get off.

'We've carried out the scan on Robyn's brain,' Dr Sharma was saying now, and I felt my senses sharpen. 'There is no easy way to tell you this, but unfortunately the diagnosis isn't good. I'm sorry to tell you that your daughter has a diffuse intrinsic pontine glioma, or DIPG for short.'

'I'm sorry?' JP asked. His eyes were blinking rapidly, his forehead lines sitting down on his eyebrows.

'It's a very rare type of tumour that grows in the brainstem of young children. In Ireland, we only see on average three new cases every year. We're not sure exactly what causes it, but recent research suggests genetic mutations may have a role in the tumour formation.'

I just heard 'tumour' and tumour equalled cancer. Was he saying my daughter had *cancer*? It felt as though an air-raid siren was blaring in my head.

'Robyn has cancer?' I asked, the word getting stuck in my throat. How was I meant to use a terrifying word like that in the same sentence as my precious daughter?

'I'm afraid so. I have brought some scans to show you.'

He held up the MRI scans, black and white and grainy, and I wasn't altogether sure what I was looking at or even if I wanted to see. It reminded me of when Robyn was a baby and we looked at her ultrasound pictures, trying to make out whether we were looking at a leg or an arm. The consultant lifted another scan and then I saw it. A large white area contrasting against the darker image. There was no mistaking it. It was the size of a tennis ball, looming and menacing. I cupped my hands over my mouth and sucked in sharply. It felt as though there was no more air left in the room for me.

'This here is the tumour,' he continued, using a biro to point it out to us as if we could miss it. I couldn't believe that it had been cruelly growing inside my daughter like a silent invader doing damage. *She's going to fight this*, a voice inside me said suddenly. *Robyn is tough; she's going to get through this.* Cancer was not going to rob me of my beautiful daughter.

'So, what happens now? When can you operate? Get it the hell out of my daughter's brain,' JP asked.

I was grateful that at least one of us was capable of speaking and talking rationally to them because my head was spinning. I couldn't even try to articulate words at this time.

'Unfortunately, it is an inoperable tumour due to its location in the pons region of the brainstem. That's the area that controls breathing, eating – all the body's most basic functions. We can't access it and, even if we did, the damage we would do to such an important part of the brain would mean she would have no quality of life.'

'So, are you saying that we have to put her through chemo?' JP asked, scanning the faces of the medical team for answers.

I gulped. How could I subject my baby girl to that gruesome treatment? I had watched my own mother fight a battle with two rounds of chemotherapy, awful and raging, until she finally said the chemo was worse than the cancer and she didn't want any more treatment. She died six months later. That had been awful, but she was seventy-six, how could I let my four-year-old daughter go through the same ordeal? This wasn't what I wanted for my child, not by a long shot, but even in the minutes since this awful situation had been thrown upon us, I knew I would do everything in my power – even chemo – to help her beat it.

The doctor paused and chose his words carefully. 'Unfortunately, chemotherapy isn't an option for this type of tumour due to its location. The anticancer agents cannot cross the blood/brain barrier.'

I felt as though I was sinking, through the chair, through the floor, back down through the soil. I was far, far away from this tiny white room and this doctor with his hideous words.

'Well, what do we do then if she can't have surgery or chemo?' I heard JP asking, panic lacing his voice. His fight had left him, I could hear how delicately his words danced upon a knife-edge of fear.

'I'm sorry to have to tell you this, but DIPG is always fatal.'

No, no, no, no, no. The blow rained down upon me. Fatal? Robyn? This was all wrong. My daughter was back on the ward doing the dance moves to some YouTube video; she wasn't dying. I looked back at the scan on the table in front of us again. How had that been lurking inside my daughter's head and I had been unaware? Why hadn't I noticed it?

'But cancer isn't like when I was a kid, is it?' I heard JP asking. 'Survival rates are much higher nowadays.'

The consultant nodded his head in agreement. 'That's true for many kinds of paediatric cancers, but in the case of a DIPG, it is a terminal illness.'

'Surely in some other countries, they know more about it,' JP demanded. 'What about in America, they're probably years ahead of where we are?'

'Unfortunately, I wish I had better news for you, but there have been no survivors for this kind of tumour internationally. I'm sorry, I realise how devastating this must be for both of you.' His voice was kind but measured. He was used to delivering this kind of news and although it was clear that this was hard for him, he would go home tonight, maybe tell his wife about the couple to whom he had had to deliver a terminal diagnosis, and maybe his wife would purse her lips and shake her head in sympathy at life's cruelties, but then they would eat their dinner and it would be life as normal for them.

Just breathe, I told myself. Deep breaths. In and out. In and out. Tears pushed through and rolled down my face. I felt as though I had let Robyn down. Maybe if I had reacted quicker, when she was first sick. Or if I had noticed something earlier, we could have treated it differently and we would be getting better news here today. I was her mother; I was supposed to protect her. If I had found it sooner, if I had acted faster, this could have been different. I had to ask the question. 'Do you think if we had come to you earlier, things could have been different?' My voice was trembling, afraid of what he was going to say to me. If this was my fault, I would never be able to live with myself.

'With DIPG, even in the very early stages, it remains impossible to treat. Please don't blame yourself; most of my patients are much further along before their parents bring them to me. Even if we found it at the very earliest stage, I would still be giving you the same outcome today. It's a very fast-growing cancer.'

'But you have to do something for her!' JP was angry now. He was pointing his index finger at the team of consultants. 'You're doctors! You can't just leave her to die! We have to fight it!' He stood up and towered over the doctor who had delivered the news and I briefly wondered if he was going to lash out at the man who was shattering our lives with his words.

'The site of the tumour in DIPG patients makes it difficult to treat. We can offer radiation treatment to help prolong Robyn's life, but it is palliative care not a cure. You have to be aware that the tumour always comes back. You might buy yourselves a few months, but you need to decide whether you want to put Robyn through that for the short time she has left.' He explained it calmly, in a matter-of-fact way that told me he was used to delivering bad news. He had probably even been trained to do this in medical school.

'How long have we got?' I asked in a voice that didn't sound like my own.

'In my experience of DIPG, patients survive on average nine to twelve months post-diagnosis.'

The words were like a sucker punch in the gut. A few minutes ago, chemotherapy had seemed like the very worst option available to me, but now I would gladly take that option, I would have done anything at all to give my daughter a fighting chance.

'So, you're saying that no matter what we do, Robyn is going to *die*?' JP was shaking his head.

'I'm so sorry,' the doctor said. 'We'll give you some time on your own. We'll be outside if you need us.'

Then the team began to file out of the room. And that was the moment a part of me died.

13

The air was sucked from my lungs and I couldn't breathe. My brain had seized. It was too full of horror as JP and I walked wordlessly out to the car park. Neither of us could bear to speak to the other. What could we say? What words could we offer one another in the face of what we had just been told? I felt as though I was walking through a tunnel of mud. My legs were heavy and weak, one foot went in front of the other, but it was like I had no control over my body. I knew I couldn't see Robyn's sweet face just then, I thought I would break if I looked at her. I wouldn't be able to hold it together. I would dissolve like sugar in hot water and an avalanche of tears would burst forth from me.

The black words had poured into my eyes, my ears, my mouth, until I couldn't see, hear or speak. Everything was dark and blurry.

I was aware of people around us: trollies being pushed down corridors, patients sitting scrolling on their phones as they sat on the plastic waiting-room chairs, the nurses busy on their feet, the receptionist joking with her colleague about her holiday diet being gone out the window, but now they all took on an otherworldliness. There was a surreal quality to their interactions, like I was watching them on a black-and-white TV set, with the sound muted. My world had ended since walking into the hospital, and yet everything still went on as normal.

We continued out of the hospital until we reached a bicycle shelter and we both stopped walking. The full meaning of the doctor's words hit me with brutal force. It felt as though I was being repeatedly punched every time I tried to process what he had told us. He had said my daughter was going to die. *Bang.* She wouldn't survive this. *Bang.* The wind left my chest as the realisation hit me and I began to slide down against the plexiglass of the shelter until I was sitting on the damp concrete littered with discarded cigarette butts. I heard myself cry, a piercing wail, and it startled me. It didn't sound like me.

Things like this happened to other people. You watched their stories on a TV chat show, you cried with them at the pain of their loss and you squeezed your babies extra tightly that night, but this wasn't meant to happen to *me*.

I turned to JP. 'Tell me this isn't really happening?' I begged.

JP began to sob too and crouched down beside me on the ground. Then I knew it was real. That our reality was a nightmare.

I felt suffocated by the shock and grief. Suddenly I began retching, my whole stomach heaved as I was sick onto the ground beside me. Vomit spilled violently out of me until my stomach was empty.

'I'm sorry,' I whispered, feeling embarrassed as I began wiping my mouth with my hand. I rooted in my handbag for the packet of baby wipes that I always carried around with me.

'Hey, it's okay,' he said, putting his arm around me, and for a moment the familiarity of his touch was a balm; all the old hurts were temporarily suspended as I allowed myself just to be in his embrace.

'I never thought we would be facing something like this,' I whispered.

'They might have got it wrong, Sarah; scans always have shadows. By their very nature, they are full of light and shade. How many times have you read a story in the newspaper about people having their scans misread or two doctors giving different opinions on the same scan? They're notoriously hard to interpret.'

'They sounded pretty certain... you saw the size of the bloody thing.'

'Look, either way, we're not just going to take his word for it, we can get a second opinion. I'm going to research it – I'll find the best person in the field. There has to be treatment somewhere, even a clinical trial. Ireland isn't at the forefront of these things; I bet you they'll have something for her in the States. You'll see.'

How I longed for his blue-sky optimism; all I could see were black clouds shrouding my world from any light. I was sinking so far underneath the weight of my pessimism, I needed him to pull me along with him, no matter how futile it seemed in the face of the doctor's words.

I noticed that the leaves were starting to flourish on the trees around us, gone were the stark, bare branches, now replaced with green buds bursting with curled baby leaves. A lone gull caterwauled through the sky. Daffodils made a golden carpet in the flower beds around the hospital. I usually loved this time of year when the world began to emerge after a long winter. Bright spring sunlight hitting my cheeks with a tinge of warmth in its rays. It always spoke of the hope of better days to come, but today it felt mocking. How did everything keep going when my world had ended?

'What are we going to tell her?' I asked, looking fearfully in the direction of the hospital where, behind its walls, our daughter was being minded by a nurse and had no idea that her world was so perilous. I was her mother – I was the one who told her that everything would be okay. We were her protectors, JP and I – we were the ones who were meant to keep her safe.

'Nothing! Say nothing to her yet, please, Sarah. They might have made a mistake. I just need to get a plan together.' JP got up from the ground and leant forward onto one of the steel bike stands, gripping it with such ferocity that his knuckles turned white. 'I'm going to fix this. I promise you I'll do whatever it takes to protect her.'

I was grateful for his fight; I needed to cling to his strength. Whatever hurts had gone between us melted away because, like me, I knew that he would do everything that he possibly could to keep our precious daughter with us.

14

The street lights beyond the window cast a shadowy glow around the bedroom. I saw every hour on the clock on my bedside table as 2 a.m. became 3, and 3 became 4. The words from the day before kept tumbling around inside my head: 'tumour', 'inoperable', 'terminal'. My one overarching thought was: why us? Why had it landed on our doorstep? Why our Robyn? I didn't wish this diagnosis on any family, but why did it have to be *our* baby girl? Why couldn't it be some family in some faraway country that I would never hear about? Then I would feel gut-wrenching guilt for wishing this upon someone else.

We were told we could bring Robyn home with us and take time to let the diagnosis sink in. We had an appointment with her medical team in a few days to discuss palliative care options.

JP had followed Robyn and I back to the house in his car. Fiona had taken one look at me as I came through the door and knew something was wrong. Between everything that had happened, I had forgotten to call her from the hospital like I had promised. I had taken her upstairs to my bedroom, while JP stayed downstairs with the children, and told her the same devastating news we had just been told. I was still in a weird mixed state of disbelief, but I also knew deep within that this was now our truth.

'Oh, Sarah, no! Are you sure?' she had asked, shaking her head as I broke the news to her. She seemed certain that this must be an error. I knew how she felt because I had felt the same way in that claustrophobic little room as the medical team had told us.

I had looked up at the ceiling in a bid to stop myself from crying, but the tears still trickled down along my face.

'I'm sorry' was all I could manage. I don't know why, but I had felt the need to apologise. It was a strange thing, breaking bad news to people, because although this was my agony to bear, as Robyn's mother, I felt responsible for causing her this pain. And how were we supposed to prepare Harry for this? He adored his little sister. His world had already been shattered by JP's departure; how could he deal with this too? It was too much for a nine-year-old to process. I knew that over the next few days and weeks I would be shattering the lives of so many people who loved Robyn with this same news. I would be replaying this conversation with relations, friends, teachers, and guilt sat on top of my own heartbreak like oil atop a murky puddle.

I'd reached out and put my arms around Fiona and felt her trembling in my arms.

'I'm sorry, Sarah, I just don't know what to say to you...' she'd said in disbelief. She'd wiped her dripping nose with the back of her hand. 'I just don't believe it – beautiful Robyn. Are you sure?' she had asked once again.

I had swallowed back an impossibly large lump in my throat, then explained it to her carefully like the doctor had done for us, giving the bare facts without putting any meat on the skeleton, leaving no cause to be hopeful. I had needed her to get this because I knew I couldn't deal with it if she tried to tell me I was wrong or to give me false hope. I had watched as she digested all the information, exactly like I had done. The stages of denial, shock, anger all flitting through her eyes. And my heart broke, again and again and again. For Fiona, for JP, for myself, but mostly for my darling Robyn.

Eventually, at 6 a.m. I pulled back the duvet and climbed out of bed. I crept along the landing, taking care not to wake the kids. I tiptoed until I reached Robyn's door, then I gently pushed it open and went inside. The room was painted sunshine yellow, she had chosen the colour herself the summer before. Her night light scattered stars across the ceiling. Under the soft canopy that was draped above her bed, sleep caressed her small body. I moved closer until I was stroking her smooth skin and brushing her blonde curls back off her face. Her shallow breaths barely registered underneath the bed linen, so I placed my hand on her chest just to feel the reassuring rise and fall as she breathed. How could that menacing tumour hide behind such a beautiful façade? How could it so cruelly destroy the part of her that thought and loved, hoped and dreamed? The part of her that made her who she was – my Robyn.

I looked down at my daughter, she was so peaceful, so bliss-fully unaware of what lay ahead for her. I lifted her duvet and climbed in beside her, curling up into her warmth, and it felt as though my heart was being fractured into millions of tiny pieces.

* * *

JP and I walked around in a haze over the next few days and, after we got over the initial devastating shock that our daughter was terminally ill, we gathered again with the medical team led by Dr

Sharma to talk through the prognosis and the palliative treatments available to us, should we wish to go down that road.

I was so grateful for JP; he was able to talk to the doctors and ask all the questions that needed to be asked, while I was still in disbelief that this was happening. He asked them about clinical trials, but we were told that Robyn wasn't an eligible candidate as her particular type of tumour was very aggressive. They assured us that they would inform us should anything suitable arise in the future. I couldn't help thinking it was more of a platitude than a real cause to be hopeful. Dr Sharma was adamant that nobody survived a DIPG. Even a 1 per cent survival rate would have given me a lifebuoy to cling to, but we were being given nothing. He said most DIPG patients lived between nine and twelve months after diagnosis, but some died sooner. The figures were bleak; 90 per cent would die within the year and the remaining 10 per cent usually passed away within the second year post-diagnosis. He calmly explained to us in that time her quality of life would deteriorate rapidly. Firstly, she would lose her balance, then she wouldn't be able to walk. Her eyesight would go, her speech, her swallowing. Day by day, we would lose another bit of our precious daughter. Essentially, she would be locked in. Not only would we lose our daughter, but we would have to endure seeing her fade away before our eyes. Our darling girl was being robbed of her very essence. The thought of it was cruelly overwhelming. JP argued that at some point in time there would have to be a first survivor of DIPG and why couldn't it be Robyn? She had been our miracle baby once before, why not again? But the team quashed his bravado with serious yet sympathetic faces that said they had had this same conversation before with other parents, as they told us they weren't hopeful of finding a cure any time soon.

Radiotherapy was our only option, but that was merely buying us time – borrowing from the bank of mortality. The medical team were at pains to point out that this was palliative care and not a cure. It seemed every flicker of hope was quenched before the flame ever lit. And so, with nothing more that could be done, until we decided whether we wanted to start radiotherapy, we went home.

Every time I thought about the road ahead, my heart felt as though it was breaking all over again. I remembered when Robyn was a baby sleeping in her crib when sometimes she would be so still that I would have to put my hand on her chest for reassurance that she was alive. There was always that split-second worry, followed by a flood of relief whenever I felt her ribcage pull away from my hand as she drew breath into her tiny lungs, but there was a time looming ahead when her lungs would stop doing their job and those very worst fears would be realised. What would I do when my arms yearned for the weight of her? When my nose craved her smell and my fingertips needed to feel her warm skin underneath my own? How were we supposed to say goodbye to her? How could we ever let her go?

15

The following Saturday, we rose, and I made pancakes for breakfast. As the children ate, I sat at the table in a daze watching them. Harry and Robyn couldn't believe their luck as I let them spread layer after layer of Nutella on their pancakes and then heap on the marshmallows without any of my usual warnings about going easy on the sugar. I could see them looking at one another with raised eyebrows, wondering why I wasn't stopping them as they loaded spoons of Nutella straight from the jar into their mouths. I took a moment to look at Robyn, chocolate smeared all over her giddy face as she ate her pancakes. Except for her drooping eye, you would never know there was a thing wrong with her.

After a while, I heard the doorbell go and the kids ran into the hall. They knew their dad was calling over. Although JP still had a key, he obviously thought better of using it. He was coming over to see how Robyn was doing and we both knew that we also had to discuss the radiotherapy. We needed to make the decision sooner rather than later as we had been warned that the tumour could progress rapidly while we dithered, making our minds up.

'Daddy!' they cried when they opened the door.

'Hey, there,' he said.

'Come in,' I invited.

He stepped inside and took them up, one in each arm, and tickled them until they wriggled out of his grip.

I stood leaning against the frame of the kitchen door watching the sheer joy written all over their faces as JP played with them. I knew they were enjoying the recent thaw in what had been a tense few months between us, although they didn't know the reason why. Whenever he had come to see the children, they had always been exchanged on the driveway. I guessed that, to them, by having their dad back in the house there was some sense of having normality restored.

'How did you sleep?' JP asked as he followed me into the kitchen while the kids went into the sitting room to watch TV.

'I didn't,' I replied. My head was fuzzy and my eyes stinging from both the lack of sleep and the endless salty tears I had cried since the fateful day we got the news.

'Me neither,' he sighed. 'Will I make us a cuppa?'

'That would be great.' I flopped wearily down into a chair.

I watched as JP began filling the kettle and opening cupboard doors as if he had never left. He knew the teabags were kept in the tin to the right of the kettle and the mugs were in the press overhead. Everything had changed and yet some things just stayed the same.

'Here you go,' he said, placing the mug down on the table in front of me when it was ready and adding just a dash of milk, exactly how I liked it.

'Thanks,' I said, savouring its warmth.

He pulled out a chair and sat down at the table opposite me. 'How's she doing?' he asked, nodding in the direction of the sitting room.

'That's the thing, JP,' I said, shaking my head. 'She is perfect.

She ate four pancakes smothered in Nutella for breakfast! You'd never know that she had that monster lurking in her brain. I keep thinking that maybe they've got this wrong...'

He nodded. 'I keep doing that too...' he admitted. 'I finally told my parents...'

Aside from Fiona, we still hadn't told anybody else. It was as if we were too afraid to say it out loud because then it would become real. It was hard enough to absorb it ourselves without dealing with other people's reactions, but we both knew we couldn't hold back the tide forever.

'How did it go?' I asked. Once again, the strange sense of guilt that had snaked through me when I had told Fiona about Robyn's diagnosis prickled along my skin. I felt personally responsible for causing everybody this pain.

'As awful as you'd expect. I thought Dad was going to collapse. Mum seems to think that by getting Father Moran to say a mass for her that it's going to cure her,' he said sardonically.

'It's just her way of coping, JP,' I said softly. 'It's so hard to accept that there's nothing anybody can do. People need something to cling to.'

He paused. 'I googled it, y'know...' There was an unmistakable tremble in his voice.

I had deliberately stayed away from the internet; I was too afraid of what I might find there. I didn't have the strength to trawl through medical literature and face the full horror of what we were dealing with.

'And?' My eyes searched his face for hope. The only thing keeping me going was JP's insistence that he would find something; I was clinging to him doing something to fix this situation.

He shook his head and pinched the bridge of his nose, trying to fight back tears. 'It's not good news, Sarah...'

'Go on.'

'Dr Sharma was right, it's always fatal – no one has ever survived it.'

JP told me how he had gone back to the flat, poured himself a generous whiskey, then he had taken out his laptop and typed the letters DIPG into Google. He had clicked on to the first result, which had confirmed what Doctor Sharma had told him. He had clicked on to 'survival rates', his heart sinking as he had read through it. He had closed down that web page and went onto another one and it was equally grim reading. Eventually, he had closed down the laptop, and sank back against the sofa as hot tears streamed down his face.

My heart broke afresh; as much as Dr Sharma's pessimism had scared me, some small part of me had hoped he had been exaggerating. I had been counting on JP to find a small nugget of hope, a raft for us both to cling to.

'Nowhere? You're telling me that not one child anywhere in the whole world has ever survived this?' Tears pushed forward in my eyes. Just when I thought I couldn't possibly cry any more, there were always more tears to come.

JP shook his head. 'I'm sorry – Neil Armstrong's daughter died from a DIPG way back in 1962 and nothing has advanced since then,' he continued. 'Imagine, it's almost sixty years on and we're still no closer to finding a cure!'

'But why?' I shook my head angrily. 'I don't understand – why isn't anyone finding a cure? Why is nobody doing anything about this?'

'It seems that there aren't many research teams working on DIPG because it is such a rare type of cancer and the pharma companies tend to focus their efforts on the leukaemias and blastomas – more money to be made there,' he said with a tone as bitter as lemon. It wasn't like him to be cynical, but I didn't blame him, I was feeling the same way myself.

We both fell quiet, each suffering our own loss and acceptance of this cruellest disease.

'We need to talk about the radiotherapy,' JP broached. 'We can buy some more time and, who knows, maybe a miracle cure will be found in the meantime?'

'That's not going to happen, even if scientists found a cure right now, these things take years to come to fruition. It ll be too late for Robyn,' I said, wiping tears away.

'Well, I think we should try the radiation anyway,' JP continued.

'But shouldn't we think about the effects on her? She's only four – she's practically a baby. Is it worth putting her through it if the tumour always comes back?'

His face fell. 'Sarah, anything that gives us time is a no-brainer. We can get a few more months with her and by then there might be something else we can try, surely that's worth it?'

'That's not going to happen, JP. You heard what the doctor said, it just buys a few months, usually only around three. What about all the side effects? We'll basically be frying her brain. Not to mention the fact that she made me promise not to take her back to the hospital. Don't you think she's going to be going through enough? We have to think about what is best for her!'

He was aghast. 'Well, we're doing it,' he said, looking up at me.

'JP, you can't just make the decision for both of us! We need to think about her quality of life for the time she has left. Do we really want her last days to be spent going from hospital appointment to hospital appointment? Or do we want to try to make the time we have left with her as special as we can?'

'I can't believe we're even having this conversation!' He stood up from the table. His brow furrowed; his nostrils flared.

'You heard the side effects – nausea, exhaustion, pain, to name but a few! All the poking and prodding, injections and medicines. She hates needles! Not to mention the general anaesthetic that she would have to get every day while they were doing the treatment because she's too young to lie still – it's too much.'

'So, you're not going to give her a chance? You're just going to let her *die*?'

His words crushed me. Although I knew her illness was terminal, it still hadn't sunk in that Robyn was actually going to die. 'I just want what's best for Robyn.'

'And so do I!' he blazed.

'Sit back down, JP,' I said wearily. I was too exhausted to fight any more. 'Look, I'm not against it, anything that makes this easier on Robyn is a win in my book—'

'You heard what Dr Sharma said, in most cases the tumour disappears and allows the patient to have a normal quality of life for a few months. We can use that time to make memories before it comes back again.'

I crumpled as tears fell down my face. 'There's so much we'll never get to do with her,' I sobbed. 'She'll never have her first crush or know what it's like to kiss in the rain. She won't ever score the winning goal in a hockey match or stay up all night at a college party and then struggle into a lecture first thing the next morning. We won't get to cheer her on at her graduation or watch her become a mother.'

'I won't get to vet her new boyfriend or walk her down the aisle on her wedding day,' JP said sadly.

'She's being robbed of so many things,' I wept. Just four years old; a breathtakingly short time. If life could be divided into seasons, she hadn't even got out of spring.

'How are we meant to look her in the eye as her body fails her and we can't do anything to help?' JP asked.

'I don't know the answer to that.' I shook my head, battling tears. I had spent so many hours lying awake tormented by the same thought. The image of her beautiful, innocent face searching mine for reassurance that I couldn't give was terrifying. A stray tear fell down my cheek and I wiped it away quickly.

'And Harry,' JP continued, 'he's a smart kid, he's going to realise soon that something is up, that is if he hasn't already. What are we going to tell him?'

'I'm not sure,' I replied. I knew we needed to be honest with him, but right then I didn't have the energy to face it.

JP reached forward and put his arms around me. Although we had been through a lot over the last few months, we had years of togetherness that you couldn't erase that quickly.

'I promise you, Sarah, we'll make as many memories as we can for as long as she's able. From now on, we need to make every day count.' He gripped my hand in his and his touch spoke right down into my heart and soothed my broken soul.

Suddenly, the door from the living room opened and Robyn came in clutching Mr Bunny. Besides the slight drooping on one side of her face, she looked perfectly normal and healthy. You'd never know that she only had just months to live.

I straightened up, remembering where I was and all that we had been through.

'Mammy, is Daddy going to come back home to live with us now?' Robyn asked, looking from JP to me and back again. She had a big grin on her face, and I made a mental note to try to remember this one. I kept doing that now, trying to commit all her little details to memory, because my biggest fear was not being able to remember her.

'Eh, no, sweetie,' I said. 'Daddy still has to go back to his flat.'

'Come up here, pet,' JP said, reaching out for her.

She climbed up onto his knee, stuck her thumb in her mouth and buried her head into his neck. I watched them both, feeling a swell in my chest at their closeness. Every cuddle was now precious as we knew there was a finite number of them left. Since the diagnosis, every day felt like a countdown until we would reach the last one and I hated that. I hated that we were watching a clock. I wasn't ready yet to say goodbye. I didn't think I'd ever be ready.

HARRY

Everything is going wrong. I thought it was bad when Dad left, but it's even badder now. Mam had stopped crying for a few weeks, but now she keeps crying again and it's even worse than the last time. Her eyes are always red, and she is acting really weird, sometimes she keeps staring at me and Robyn and then she starts hugging us too tight and it's really squishy.

I was watching WWE and John Cena was slamming down Brock Lesnar and Mam came in and I thought she was going to get cross with me and make me turn it off because she doesn't let me watch things with fighting and guns and things like that, but she just said nothing, and I know this is strange, but I wanted her to tell me to turn it off. Then I was eating spoons of Nutella from the jar this morning and she never even said anything, so then when I put it on my pancake, I took out the marshmallows and started eating them straight out of the bag, even though we're not allowed to do that because the sugar is really bad for us, but she didn't even care. And I don't think it's Dad's fault now because Mam and Dad are friends again and he keeps coming over every day, so I think my plan to bring Dad home is starting to work, but Mam says he still has to live with crazy Megan so I have some more work to do.

I think it might be Robyn's fault that everyone is sad, she's being really weird too. I wanted to play chasing with her the other day, but she kept tripping over, even though there was nothing in the way, so I told Mam she kept falling over and then Mam started crying AGAIN!!! So then I felt bad for making her cry, so I stopped telling her and said to Robyn, 'Let's just watch TV.' I just want everyone to stop being weird so everything can go back to normal.

16

A few days later, I woke to hear the sound of Robyn retching in her bedroom once more. My heart sank as I ran into her room.

'It's okay, sweetheart,' I soothed, helping her out of the bed and taking off her soiled pyjamas. It was then that I noticed her eyes were crossing over. Even though Dr Sharma had warned us that this would happen, I didn't think it would be this soon. We had had a blissful few days since coming home from the hospital when, except for her drooping face, you wouldn't have known she was sick. In my more optimistic moments, I had wondered if they had made a mistake, but now here it was, a reminder that the tumour was still there, lying in wait like the menace that it was. I was frightened by how rapidly it was taking her from us. I wasn't ready yet, I needed more time.

'Stay there for a second while I get you clean clothes,' I said.

I went out onto the landing and dialled JP's number. Before he could say anything, I blurted out what had happened, and he said he'd be straight over. I heard another voice on the speaker then and I realised he was in the car. I guessed he was on his way to work. It was Megan saying something to him about being late.

He snapped back at her before quickly apologising to me and saying he would be with me soon.

'Where is she?' JP asked as soon as he arrived at the front door.

'She's upstairs,' I said. 'Harry is in the living room. I didn't bring him to school yet.' Harry was still going to school every day, but I had decided to keep Robyn at home with me. I wanted her with me all the time now. Her playschool teachers had been stunned when I had told them about her diagnosis. 'I don't want Harry to see her like this because what am I meant to say to him?' I shook my head. 'It's all happening too fast. I'm not ready to lose her yet, JP,' I whispered as tears choked my throat.

'Then we have to try radiotherapy, Sarah,' he begged.

I dug my thumbs into the familiar, ragged holes of my cardigan and pulled it tightly around my body. Sometimes I wondered if I wore this cardigan more as a comfort blanket than for warmth. Slipping my arms into its woollen sleeves was like a hug. This was happening, no matter how much I wished it wasn't, and it was stealing my precious daughter day by day unless we did something to call a temporary halt to it. I needed to keep Robyn with us for as long as I could; I needed to stop the clock, and if radiotherapy would do that, then what other choice did I have?

'Let's do it,' I agreed, hoping I was making the right decision by Robyn and not just for our own selfish reasons.

And so, just a week later, we found ourselves walking into the hospital for the first day of radiotherapy. People always say they hate the smell of hospitals, but I actually like it. I don't mind the clean odour of antiseptic; it's the sick people I hate seeing. People who are worse off than you, recovering from illnesses or surgeries or sometimes not recovering at all. Hospitals always feel like a warning to me of how fragile life can be. Usually, I would thank my lucky stars that my family was healthy, but now we were one of them – we were the people I once had pitied.

Busy people flew past us, nurses, doctors and other healthcare workers, running to and fro doing their jobs. Then there were others like us, walking at a slower pace, unsure of themselves and where they were going. As we walked through the corridors, stopping periodically to read the signs pointing the way to the radiology department, I was glad to have JP by my side.

The team had warned us that the Monday to Friday sessions for the next few weeks would be intense, not just on Robyn but on the whole family too. We were told to expect Robyn to feel tired and nauseous after her sessions, but there could be more serious side effects such as radiation necrosis, where the radiation could cause some of her brain cells to die, causing worsening neurological symptoms, like headaches and vomiting. Although Robyn would have her treatment and then return home each day afterwards, our life would revolve around this hospital ward.

We had worked out a routine where JP would come over to get Harry ready for school in the mornings while I brought Robyn into the hospital. After he had dropped Harry off at school, he would head on to work. We both knew that he wouldn't be able to come with us every day; he still needed to keep up appearances in the office, but as he worked close by the hospital, he would be able to drop in on his lunch break. It remained unspoken between us that JP would need time off further down the line, so for now this seemed to be the best option to keep all the balls in the air. I had organised a schedule between Fiona and JP's mother Joan to collect Harry from school every day and to stay with him until I got home from the hospital.

Joan and Richard were devastated by the diagnosis and were doing their best to be supportive despite everything that had happened between JP and me. Joan had even blessed Robyn with a relic of Padre Pio when she had come to see her the last time; she was convinced prayer was going to cure her.

I had also told my friends Linda and Mel and they had both been stunned and at a loss for words. And once again I had found myself apologising. They were parents too and I knew it was difficult to listen to me describing their worst nightmare. They were always calling and sending messages of support and I knew they were there for me if I needed them.

We had explained to Robyn that she needed to have special medicine to help make her feel better. She seemed happy enough, but I knew she was thinking of sweet-tasting medicines like Calpol and not big, scary radiotherapy machines. She didn't really understand it. We had already been in to have the radiation mask made and the simulation had been done. The mask would keep her perfectly still on the bench by fastening her to the bed so that only the tumour would get attacked during the radiation and the healthy parts of her brain would be protected.

Although the moulding technician had pretended that he was a magician to make the process a little less frightening for Robyn, I couldn't help but gasp when he had first held up the finished mask for us to look at. It reminded me of a cage being placed over her beautiful face. As an adult, I found the idea of it claustrophobic, so I could only imagine how Robyn felt about it all. A play therapist had gently explained to Robyn that it was a superhero mask to help with her special medicine, but her four-year-old eyes were full of scepticism, and I knew she wasn't buying it.

Because of her age, she would need a general anaesthetic every day to help her lie still for the radiation and I was dreading it. Dr Sharma had assured me that most children tolerated them well and that the effects would wear off fast each day, but even so, I was nervous. General anaesthetics were serious for an adult, let alone a child, but to have to put your child through one every day for several weeks in a row was horrifying. It was a reminder of how much our landscape had altered in such a short space of time.

'No, Mameeee, I don't want them to do this,' Robyn screamed as the anaesthetist bent over her, trying to find a vein to insert the IV cannula. She remembered how it had hurt from the last time. Her free hand was clinging to my jumper, she was pulling so tightly that it was almost choking me.

'Please, Robyn, we have to do it to help make you feel better,' I coaxed. 'Remember all those headaches and the way you've been getting sick in the mornings? Well, this is going to help stop all of that.'

'I'm sorry, sweetheart,' the anaesthetist apologised, screwing her face up in concentration as she studied Robyn's small hand. 'I'm having a hard time finding one. I need to try again.'

'Make them stop!' Robyn's whole face was red, snot ran down onto her top lip. She kept trying to swipe her arm away from their grip, but the nurse who was assisting had her pinned down tightly.

'We're just trying to help, sweetie, I promise,' the nurse tried to cajole. 'It'll be all over in a minute.'

My stomach churned.

Robyn turned her head to JP then. 'No, Daddy, make them stop! Tell them to stop!' She wrestled and lifted her tiny body off the bed as JP tried to hold her down. 'Mammy and Daddy, please... Tell them to stop it. I said please, Mammy!' She was looking at me, her small face full of hope that by using her best manners we might stop all of this, and I thought I might be sick. I felt as though I was betraying her. I was her mother. I was supposed to protect her, but I had signed the consent forms to allow this to happen. JP was so hell-bent on trying the radiotherapy, but I still wasn't convinced we were doing the right thing for our daughter and I wasn't sure I ever would be. Were we being selfish putting her through all of this just so we could have more time with her?

JP reached over and squeezed my hand tightly and I knew that he was struggling too.

Eventually, the anaesthetist cried, 'I've got it!' and soon the sedation began to work as the fight left her small body and she lay back onto the pillows as the anaesthetic took effect. I saw white prints mirroring her fingertips had been left behind on my skin. I automatically blessed myself as Robyn was wheeled in to start her radiotherapy.

'Why are you wasting time praying?' JP asked. 'Surely now, after everything that has happened, you can't believe in all that crap? I mean, what kind of a God would do this to the people he supposedly loves?' He paced around the floor.

I self-consciously lowered my hand again and wrapped my arms around myself. 'It gives me strength, okay? It gives me something to cling to when my whole world seems to be slipping away from me.'

He lowered his eyes to the floor. 'I'm sorry,' he apologised, shaking his head. 'I shouldn't have said that.'

We walked back silently together to the ward. I sat down on her empty bed, clutching Mr Bunny tightly to my chest, breathing in her smell. Rays of sunlight streamed in through the window; it was a beautiful spring day out there. On the way to the hospital, we had driven along the Strand Road, with the red-and-white-striped Poolbeg chimney stacks standing like candy canes in the distance, while the safe haven of Dún Laoghaire Harbour sheltered the far end of Dublin Bay. We had passed Sandymount Strand, where the tide was so far out that the endless honey-coloured sand seemed to stretch to infinity. We should have been out there letting Robyn run wild and free along the beach while she still could, I thought. We should have been treating her to ice cream sundaes while she was still able to eat. Instead, she was going to be trapped in a hospital day after day, looking at mint-green walls, being prodded and poked and dealing with the effects of a general anaesthetic. I kept asking myself whether we were doing the right thing? Was it fair to do this for the short time we had left with her? It would take its toll on an adult, let alone a four-year-old child.

'Are you okay?' JP asked.

'I don't think I can do this,' I whispered.

'Yes, you can, Sarah. The first day was always going to be tough. She'll be back with us again in no time.'

'I hate this though – it's not fair, JP. It's awful knowing what that tumour is doing to her tiny body, but then we're subjecting her to all of this too. The general anaesthetic, the radiation – it's too much for a four-year-old.' Although JP was doing his best to be a support, he didn't live with us any more, he wasn't going to be there when the radiation was too much for her small body to take and made her sick. He wasn't going to see the fear in her eyes as I drove her to the hospital every morning. He wasn't going see the full brutal impact of it all. But I would.

'I know it's hard, but we're doing the right thing; we can't give up on her.' He put his arm around me, and I sobbed and sobbed against his chest.

* * *

As soon as I saw the nurse wheeling Robyn back from radiotherapy, my heart soared. It was the same feeling as when she had been placed in my arms for the first time after she was born. That day, as the midwife had handed my precious daughter to me, wrapped up like a present in a white towelling blanket, I had felt like I had just been given the greatest gift.

'Mammy and Daddy,' Robyn croaked a short time later.

I sat up straight away and placed Mr Bunny beside her. 'Sweetheart, you're awake.'

'I'm sorry I made you sad, Mama.'

I quickly wiped my eyes as I felt guilt fill me up. 'No, sweetheart, you didn't – it's not your fault. Come here, I need a hug.'

I needed to keep my feelings in check, Robyn had enough going on without me upsetting her too. I needed to be strong for her no matter how awful it was at times. And it was awful, we were going through the darkest days of our life and the hardest part was knowing that there was worse to come. There was no light at the end of her tunnel.

JP filled the cup beside her bed with water and guided a straw towards her mouth. She took a sip and lay back down again.

'You did it, baby girl, I'm so proud of you.' I leant forward and kissed her forehead, her skin like silk against my lips.

She fell back asleep once more while her body tried to adjust. The nurse had said she might drift in and out for a little while.

'How are you feeling?' JP asked when she opened her eyes again a few minutes later.

'I don't like it here, Daddy.' She looked down and caught sight of the cannula in her hand. 'Ow, take it out!'

'It's okay, love,' JP reassured her.

'No, Mammy,' she screamed and started to claw at her hand. 'I don't like this place.'

'Shush, baby,' I soothed.

'I'm scared,' she sobbed, 'I want to go home to Harry.'

Each word she said broke my heart a little more. 'We'll be allowed home soon, pet, just once the nurses are happy,' I explained.

'Look, they gave you a sticker,' JP said to distract her. He took out the reward chart that was going to document her daily radiotherapy sessions where she would get a sticker for each one.

'Oh, it's a pink one.' Her face fell. 'Pink isn't my favourite colour. I want the lello one!'

'Well, maybe tomorrow you'll get a yellow one,' JP cajoled her.

'I'm not coming back here ever again!' she wailed.

I felt a stone sit in the pit of my stomach. 'Of course not, pet,' I promised in that vague way that parents do sometimes when you hope your child will forget. How was I going to explain to her that we had to come back again tomorrow and the next day and the day after that again? This place was going to become like a second home to us. Whenever my kids had something worrying them or scaring them, I was almost always able to fix it and if I couldn't, I could usually find the right words to soothe them, but this time I couldn't. There was nothing I could do to help her.

17

In the rear-view mirror, I watched as Robyn's eyes closed down, before jerking back open again, then they dropped down once more, until finally they were just too heavy for her to stay awake any longer as she fell asleep. She was clutching tightly to Mr Bunny in one hand and her reward chart from the hospital in her other. She wanted to show JP the glittery star the nurse had given her to mark the end of her first week of radiotherapy.

She was exhausted. It wasn't just the tumour that was being blasted, day after day a little more of her was wiped out too. She wasn't my usual sparkly daughter. I wasn't sure if it was the tumour or the treatment, perhaps it was a combination of both. I guessed having a daily general anaesthetic didn't help either. Even though she had dropped her daytime nap when she was two years old, now every day when we came home, she would fall into a deep sleep.

I was tired too. It had been a stressful week taking Robyn to the hospital every morning.

'Why are we here again?' she had asked as I drove into the

hospital car park for our second session. 'I want to go to playschool and see Lily!'

'We need to get more of your special medicine,' I had explained, helping her out of the car.

She had stopped dead, planting her feet on the ground. 'But I already did-ded it yesterday, Mammy! I was a good girl yesterday, why do we have to come back here again?' she'd protested. How I had longed to lift her up into my arms and run away from this hospital and the awfulness that lay ahead of her.

'We need to get the special medicine every day, sweetheart, I'm sorry.'

'No, Mammy, I'm not going.' She shook her head and folded her arms across her chest stubbornly.

I had tugged her arm gently, but she rooted her two feet firmly to the tarmac and refused to budge.

'I feel better now, I don't need any more medicine.'

'Please, Robyn, we can go to the toyshop afterwards,' I had bribed.

'NO!' she'd screamed. 'I'M NOT GOING BACK IN THERE!' Then she'd lain down on the ground and thrown a tantrum like I had never seen her do before. Her legs and arms flailed everywhere. I had always felt lucky that I had skipped the terrible twos, Robyn had been an easy toddler. Fiona had always joked that she'd make up for it as a teenager. I'd felt a stabbing through my heart as I thought of yet another thing we would never get to experience with her. I could see people were walking past and staring at us. I had felt like screaming at them to get lost, they didn't have a clue what was going on in her world.

I had taken a deep breath and bent down onto my hunkers to her. 'What is it, pet? Are you scared?'

'I TOLDED YOU THAT I'M NOT GOING IN THERE,' she'd screamed loudly into my face.

An older woman had walked past and tutted loudly at us.

'What?' I'd shouted after her. 'What's your problem?' I hadn't been able to help it. The words were out before I knew it.

'We wouldn't get away with that in my day.' She'd pursed her lips together in disapproval. 'She needs a good clip around the ear!'

Robyn had stopped her tantrum and looked up at me, suddenly fearful. She wasn't used to seeing me getting into confrontations with strangers.

'It's okay, I'll get up now, Mammy,' she had said obediently, already climbing up from the ground. She had taken my hand and we proceeded through the car park and into the hospital without another word. She had walked quietly into the hospital with me every morning since, and I hated the way she had so quickly become resigned to the fact that this was to be our new daily routine.

Even though it had only been a week, in a perverse sort of way, I had already got used to our daily hospital visits and had my own routine of sorts. After Robyn was wheeled down for her treatment, I would grab a takeaway coffee from the hospital coffee shop. I would have a chat with the girl working there while she frothed milk for my cappuccino and then I would carry it back to the ward to wait. I knew my way around now without having to stop and read the signs. I also knew that if I had to make a phone call, the reception on the ward was awful, but if you stood under the atrium in the hallway, the signal worked perfectly. I could imagine how we would feel institutionalised by the time we reached the end of the course of radiotherapy.

I was really looking forward to the weekend and having two days to ourselves without any hospital visits before we would start into the second week of her course. It was also St Patrick's Day that weekend and, although Robyn wouldn't be up to going into Dublin city centre to stand on O'Connell Street and watch the parade, I had bought green face paint and some silly shamrock-shaped hats, and I was going to throw a small party for the children at home.

I turned the nose of the car into the driveway, silenced the engine and, even though it felt cruel and went against all my motherly instincts, I woke Robyn up. I wanted her to eat something, it seemed as though she was surviving on sips of juice and thin air at the moment and I was worried about her. It was more important now than ever that she keep her nutrition and energy levels up. I was terrified she might catch a cold or a stomach bug because I knew her immune system would really struggle to fight off an infection. Each day when we came home from the hospital, I would make her favourite pancakes in the hope that I could coax her to eat a few bites. She needed all the strength she could get right now, her body needed nourishment.

'Are you hungry?' I asked.

She shook her head listlessly, too tired even to speak.

I carried her into the house and placed her down on one of the kitchen chairs. I set to work cracking the egg into a well in the flour and then poured in the milk, all the time whisking the mixture together. I poured the batter onto the hot pan, but when I turned around again, Robyn had fallen asleep with her cheek flattened against the table. I sighed, knowing she would sleep for the whole night now.

I scooped her up into my arms and carried her up the stairs. I placed her down on the bed and covered her with the duvet. I sat down on the edge and stroked her wan face.

'How's she doing?' a voice from behind me asked, causing me to jump.

I turned around and saw it was JP bringing Harry home. I hadn't heard them come in.

'Sorry, I hope I didn't frighten you – Harry let me in,' he added. 'I just wanted to see how she is today.'

'Hi there,' I said, straightening up. 'She's exhausted. She hasn't eaten a thing. I tried to make pancakes for her, but she was asleep before I had even finished making the first one.'

'The poor kid,' he mumbled. He rubbed his hands down over his face and I knew this was just as upsetting for him too. I guessed JP felt like he never really got to see her awake any more. Even when he dropped into the hospital on his lunch break, Robyn was usually still snoozing off the after-effects of the anaesthetic. 'Well, hopefully we'll find out soon that it has shrunk the bloody thing completely and it'll be worth it.'

Although it was still bright outside, I left her night light on because she hated the dark and then we both crept out of the room. I stopped on the landing and turned to JP.

'Do you think we're doing the right thing?' I asked, as I questioned our decision again for what felt like the millionth time. Right now, the side effects of the treatment, coupled with the cocktail of drugs that she was on, seemed far worse than any of the symptoms the tumour had caused. Were we being selfish and putting our needs to have more time with her ahead of her need to live the best life she could for the short time she had left? What kind of quality of life was this for Robyn when the poor child spent most of her time asleep? And so the questions kept looping around my head. I wished there was an answer to them because nobody ever seemed able to tell me the 'right' thing to do. I felt I was locked in a washing machine stuck on a cycle of guilt. It was eating me alive. Was it worth it? The question had been on my mind a lot lately, especially over the last few days as the cumulative effects of the radiotherapy, trips back and forth to the hospital, and the time spent waiting around on the ward, were all taking their toll on her.

'Don't you want as much time as possible with her?' JP raised his eyebrows at me incredulously.

'Of course I do, why are you even asking me that?' I snapped. I was tired and worried. I knew my patience was in limited supply. 'But we have to do right by her. She's completely wiped out; her little body and immune system must be under so much pressure.'

'She's just had a week of radiotherapy! Of course she's feeling out of sorts, Sarah. What do you expect?'

'But it's gruelling – if it is going to ruin her last few months, then we need to ask ourselves if it's worth it. We can't be selfish in this – I just need to make sure we are putting her first.'

JP shook his head at me. 'I can't believe you're even saying this, Sarah. What has got into you? We decided on this together!'

'I don't want to make this any harder on Robyn than it already is. Isn't it enough that this horrible thing is growing inside her brain? A general anaesthetic every day for five days in a row? That would take its toll on anyone, let alone a child already battling a brain tumour! She hates all of this. She's scared, JP, our little girl is so frightened, and I hate myself for not being able to fix it and take away her fears. I hate the fact that we are the ones putting her through this trauma.' Needles, cannulas and medicines had become daily parts of her life. But what was even worse was that now she wasn't even putting up a fight, it was like she just accepted it, resigned to the fact that nobody was going to listen to what she wanted or be her advocate and that broke my heart. I hated all the decisions that the DIPG diagnosis had thrown at us. Really hard, life-altering decisions and the worst part was there was no right or wrong answer.

'And you think I don't?' he blazed. 'Do you think I like watching my daughter going through all of this? Do you think I can't see the fear in her eyes as doctors and nurses loom over her? Don't you think I wish with every cell in my body that I could put myself in her shoes and take away all of the pain and the fear? But she is fighting a bloody brain tumour, Sarah! For some shitty reason, this awful thing has landed on our doorstep and we can either sit back, do nothing and watch her die or do all we can to fight back. I know what my decision is.'

'But it might not even work! This might all be for nothing!'

'We have to try everything!'

'But at what cost, JP? It's okay for you – you're not living here any more, you don't see how tired she is, how hard it is to wake her every morning. You don't see how much she's terrified of going to the hospital, even though she is trying her hardest to be brave. She doesn't eat; when she's not asleep, she's listless and lethargic; she's not herself, her spark has gone – she doesn't feel like our Robyn any more. I know she's dying, JP, but right now I feel as though we've already lost her.'

'How can you say that?' He was aghast. 'She's here – she's still with us.'

'I feel as though she is slipping through my fingers and I can't stop it happening.' I shook my head sadly.

'Look, she's exhausted, Sarah.' His tone was softer now. 'I know it's hard on her, and on you too, but let's just get to the end of these radiotherapy sessions and see if it has worked.' He pressed his hands on either side of my shoulders. 'Just hold firm. We're nearly there now.'

But it didn't feel like we were nearly there. In fact, the journey was only just beginning. And even when we did get there, would I be able to look Robyn in the eye and say it had all been worth it?

18

'See you tomorrow, Lisa, we're out of here. Another day down, only three more to go!' I called to one of the nurses as I packed up Robyn's bag to leave the hospital after yet another session of radiotherapy. I knew all the staff on a first-name basis by now, even the girl in the coffee shop that served me my double-strength cappuccino every morning.

We were nearly at the end of Robyn's course of radiotherapy and I was counting down the days until her last session. She was tired all the time and her appetite was non-existent. Easter had passed and she hadn't even attempted to open any of the eggs people had bought for her. It was heartbreaking to see my daughter become a shadow of her former self. Her cheeks had lost their colour and the sparkle in her eyes had vanished. Dr Sharma had also prescribed steroids to help manage her symptoms, which had caused Robyn to bloat, and she didn't look like herself any more. 'She doesn't look like me,' she had said, pointing at her reflection in the mirror, and my heart had been shredded. I was praying that the radiation would ease her symptoms so she would feel well enough for us to go and make memories with her until the tumour's inevitable return. Once we were finished in the hospital, I hoped life could get back to some kind of normal – whatever normal was when your daughter was terminally ill.

'When I'm better, I want to go to playschool to see Lily,' she had said. Her one wish was to see her friends again and I hoped she might be up for a visit once she had regained some of her strength.

We would find out after her next MRI whether the radiation had shrunk her tumour and I dearly hoped that putting her through all of this would be worth it in the end, that we would get more time.

She had been a trooper throughout her radiation therapy, and we owed it to her to do some fun stuff. I had so many things planned; I wanted to take her to the beach and let her feel the sea breeze on her skin and dip her toes in the cool water. I had briefly thought about taking a holiday of a lifetime to Disneyland Paris or Legoland, but I wasn't sure if she'd be up to it; even in the best of health, it would be a big undertaking for a four-year-old. Would she be here for her fifth birthday in September, or what about next Christmas? I couldn't bear to think that she wouldn't be. I was taking it day by day without looking too far ahead and, somehow, I was getting through it.

I was just putting Robyn's coat on her when my phone rang, and I saw the number for Harry's school flash up on the screen.

'Hi, Sarah, this is Ms O'Mara.'

'Ms O'Mara, is everything okay?' I asked quickly.

'I'm here with Harry. He said his aunt was supposed to be picking him up today, but nobody has arrived yet?'

Oh shit. Panic laced its way down my body. Fiona had told me she had a long-standing dental appointment for this afternoon that she couldn't cancel, and I had completely forgotten to see if

Joan was able to collect him instead. 'Oh my God, I'm so sorry,' I said. 'I'm at the hospital, but I'm just leaving now, and I should be there in half an hour.'

'Don't panic, I'll be here anyway doing my corrections. He can wait in the classroom with me and get a start on his homework.'

'Thank you so much, I'll be there as soon as I can,' I said, hanging up, feeling mortified. I turned to Robyn. 'We better run, sweetie, we forgot to collect Harry,' I said, reaching for her hand.

Robyn moved out of the ward as though weighed down with concrete. I tried my best to encourage her to hurry, but I was conscious that she was suffering from the after-effects of her radiotherapy and the general anaesthetic and was still quite drowsy.

'Come here, love.' I lifted her up in one arm, hauled the heavy bag with my other one, and ran as best I could towards the car park.

As we drove in the direction of Harry's school, it seemed as though we hit every set of traffic lights ever invented. I groaned as yet another green light changed to red just as I reached it. I slammed my palm against the steering wheel in frustration, willing it to change again. How could I have forgotten Harry? Jesus Christ, I knew I had a lot on my mind, but there was no excuse for leaving him stranded. He had effectively been side-lined over the last few weeks. Eventually, the lights turned green and we drove off again.

'I feel sick, Mammy,' Robyn said suddenly from the back seat.

Oh no, I groaned internally. I was driving faster than usual, and I guessed the motion was too much for her. I quickly scanned the roadside for a safe place to stop the car, but it was too late as she vomited all over herself. I pulled over into a gateway, got out and cleaned her up as best I could, but I was going to be even more delayed getting to the school now.

By the time I reached the school, Robyn had dozed off again and I didn't have the heart to wake her, so I left her strapped into her seat and hurried into the school building. I ran down the corridor towards Harry's classroom. Colourful artwork decorated the walls, and under normal circumstances I would have stopped to admire it, but today I didn't have time.

'I'm so sorry,' I apologised as I ran through the door when I reached his classroom. 'I was in the hospital and there was a mix-up – I promise it won't happen again.'

'Hey, don't worry at all, it happens more than you'd think,' Ms O'Mara said kindly. 'Harry mentioned his sister is in hospital?' she continued in an enquiring tone, but I didn't trust myself to explain what was going on, especially with Harry in the room with us.

I nodded. 'Yes, she is, unfortunately.' I looked at Harry's tear-stained face and felt hot tears spring into my own eyes. 'I'm so sorry, little man,' I said, pulling him into a bear of a hug.

We said goodbye and, after more harried apologies, we walked back out to the car.

'I got a fright, Mam,' Harry said. 'I thought something happened to you or Robyn in the hospital.'

I knew he was starting to suspect something was going on. Harry was beginning to pick up on things and now he was starting to worry. He had already been asking why Robyn looked so bloated and why either Fiona or his grandmother had to collect him from school now instead of me. I was trying to protect him from it all, but he was getting anxious and maybe the time had come to tell him that Robyn was sick, but what was I going to say? He was a child; he would assume she would get the right medicine to get better. How on earth was I going to tell him that there was no medicine left to help her? I could barely get my own head around it.

'I'm so sorry, Harry, Fiona had to go to the dentist today and I completely forgot all about it.'

'What's that smell?' he asked, scrunching up his nose as he climbed into the back seat of the car.

'Robyn got sick,' I sighed.

'Urggh. It stinks.'

'Hiya, Harry,' Robyn said, waking up at the sound of her brother's voice.

'Why are her eyes all funny?' Harry asked.

The crossing of her eyes had become even more pronounced. I hated seeing her face like this, it was all wrong. My beautiful baby girl's face looked contorted.

'Stop, Harry,' I warned.

'But they are,' he continued.

'My eyes are not funny,' Robyn said indignantly.

In the rear-view mirror, I saw Harry raise his eyes and look out the window and we drove the rest of the way in silence.

We got home and after I had bathed Robyn and coaxed her to eat a tiny square of toast, I put her into bed cuddling Mr Bunny. I made Harry a plate of pasta and then I headed outside to clean Robyn's car seat and the upholstery of my car before the vomit dried in.

When I was finished, I came back inside and flopped down wearily onto the sofa beside Harry. I was exhausted. I could feel my eyes closing with tiredness.

'What you watching?' I asked.

'It's Liverpool v. Man U.'

'Cool.'

'Can you make me a hot chocolate, please, Mam?'

'In a minute,' I replied, making no effort to move. I felt as though I was melting into the sofa and I honestly didn't think my legs would ever be able to move off it.

'It's not fair,' Harry started.

'What isn't?' I said, opening my eyes again.

'You keep saying "In a minute" whenever I ask you to do something, but then you always forget to do it. You're always saying you're too tired or else you're too busy with Robyn.' His small face was growing more exasperated by the second. 'First Dad left, then Robyn keeps needing check-ups and you're always in the hospital. You never take me or collect me from school any more. I never get to have my friends over. I haven't been to football training in ages because everyone is "too busy", and Robyn is "too tired". He put his index fingers in the air and made invisible air quotes. 'We never go anywhere together any more. I hate it.'

He was right; as hard as it was to hear what he was saying, he was right. Harry had been neglected over the last few weeks. Although Joan and Fiona were doing their best to keep things as normal as possible for Harry, I knew it wasn't the same. I was juggling this all wrong, I was so focused on putting all my time and energy into Robyn, I was forgetting about my other child who needed me. Although JP tried to help out, I was effectively solo parenting; there was nobody to tag-team with when I was too tired to function at the end of a long day. It all fell squarely on my shoulders.

'Harry, I'm sorry, I had no idea you were feeling like this. I know we probably haven't been tuned into you lately, but Dad and I have had stuff on our mind...'

'What stuff?'

'Well, you know all those hospital trips with Robyn?'

'Uh-huh.'

'She's sick, Harry.'

'Duh.'

'Do you know what's wrong with her?'

He shrugged his shoulders.

'Well, there is something bad growing in her brain.'

'Is that why her eyes look a bit weird?'

'Yeah.'

'So what? Can't you just give her medicine?' Despite his bravado, I could see worry lurking in his eyes.

'Well, that's what all the hospital trips are about. She has to go and get her medicine there. We've only three more sessions left and after that then we won't have to go to the hospital every day and things will settle down again. Now, how about I go make you that hot chocolate?'

He perked up instantly, our conversation quickly forgotten. 'Can I have extra marshmallows?'

'I think that can be arranged.' I stood up and ruffled his hair. I knew I wasn't being completely honest with him, but I wasn't ready yet to have that discussion. I would need JP with me for that one. I knew we couldn't put it off forever, it was looming ahead in the distance, like a train hurtling down the tracks towards us.

HARRY

They forgot to collect me from school today and I was really worried that something bad had happened, like maybe the whole family were in a car crash and I was going to have to go live in an orphanage or else the house went on fire and the firemen couldn't save them in time. Teacher said I shouldn't worry and that it was okay, that it was just a mix-up and that someone would be there really soon, but I was still scared. She brought me into the staffroom, which was really weird because we're never allowed to go in there. She gave me a chocolate hobnob and then we went back to the classroom and she let me help her cut out things and even though I was still in school, it wasn't that bad. Then Mam came running into the classroom and she was hugging me, and I was a bit embarrassed in front of teacher, but I was still happy to see her because I didn't have to go and live in an orphanage any more.

The car was so disgusting because Robyn got sick in it and I had to hold my nose the whole way home so I couldn't smell it. Now Mam is being extra nice to me because she forgot to collect me. She let me stay up late to watch the whole Liverpool match instead of making me go to bed at half-time and Liverpool beat Man U 2–0! Firmino scored a cracker. Go on the Pool! She even said I can have Jamie O'Connor over for a play date. She said Robyn just has to go to hospital three more times and then she will be able to take me to school again and collect me the way she used to and not forget about me. When she was tucking me up in bed tonight, I asked her when Robyn was going to get better, but her voice went all funny, and I think she was going to cry so I told her not to be sad because the doctors are giving Robyn the medicine to fix her and then everything will be okay again.

19

My head was fuzzy: the result of the combination of worry and no sleep. I rose early, flicked the switch on the kettle and made myself a strong coffee. While the rest of the house slept on, I was sitting at the kitchen table clasping the hot mug between my hands, but I wasn't drinking it. Instead, I stirred my spoon around and around, creating a vortex in the black liquid. The house was silent apart from the hum of the fridge and the odd rattle of a pipe somewhere in the heating system.

It was the day we would get the results of Robyn's MRI scan – the one when we would be told whether the radiation therapy had worked or not, and I was worried to distraction. I had spent the night being tossed and turned by insomnia before finally admitting defeat and getting out of bed. I had prayed to a God I wasn't sure I really believed in, to please let it be good news, over and over. *Please let it all have been worth it.*

Despite having completed her gruelling course of radiotherapy, Robyn's symptoms hadn't eased like Dr Sharma had said they might, and I was scared. Her eyes were still crossing over and her left side had grown much weaker, which caused her to walk with a limp, but nonetheless, I was still clinging to the hope that we would get good news at our appointment later on.

'How are you doing?' Fiona asked as she came into the kitchen that morning. She was going to stay with Robyn while JP and I went to the hospital to meet Dr Sharma. I was going to drop Harry at school and then meet JP at the hospital.

I shrugged my shoulders.

'I know it's a stupid question,' she apologised. She turned to Robyn. 'I thought we'd bake some fairy cupcakes, what do you think, Robyn?'

'Can I lick the bowl, Auntie Fiona?' Robyn asked, smiling, but her face was lopsided. Its perfect symmetry was gone. Her speech was starting to get slurred now too, and I felt my heart squeeze as if someone had placed their hands around it and wrung it out. It was so hard seeing the tumour changing my baby girl like this.

'Course you can!' Fiona replied. 'Then we'll curl up, stuff our faces and watch back-to-back episodes of *Paw Patrol*, how does that sound?'

'Thanks, Fi,' I said, reaching up to give her a kiss on the cheek.

She squeezed my hand. 'Good luck.'

I nodded. 'Thanks. Let's go, Harry,' I said, grabbing my bag to head out the door.

'Why did Fiona say "good luck"?' Harry asked as I reversed out of the driveway.

'Well, today is the day that we find out if Robyn's medicine has done its job.'

'I don't think it has, Mammy, her eyes are still wonky and now she can't even walk properly,' he said matter-of-factly.

Tears pushed into my eyes as Harry voiced my worst fears.

'Do you have Gaelic football after school today?' I asked to distract him.

He shook his head. 'You know that's not on for the next two weeks. We got a note, remember?'

'Oh, sorry, I forgot that.'

'You forget everything,' he sighed and rolled his eyes.

When we reached the school, I kissed him at the gate, even though he squirmed away from me. Then I continued on to the hospital.

I met JP in the hospital foyer like we had arranged. We didn't speak as we made our way to Dr Sharma's rooms. I knew we were each too wrapped up in our own worries and fears.

'JP, Sarah,' Dr Sharma said a short while later, shaking our hands as he showed us into his office. 'Good to see you both again. Take a seat.'

We did as he instructed and sat down in the two leather armchairs opposite his desk. We had become so familiar with this room over the last few weeks. I looked at the photograph of him and, I guessed, his wife and sons which stood in a silver frame on top of his desk. One of the young men in the picture was wearing a graduation cloak and a mortar board. For some reason, that picture always reassured me; Dr Sharma was a family man, he knew what it was like to love a child and I knew he would put himself in my shoes and take the best care he possibly could with mine.

'Now, I know you've probably been waiting anxiously for these results, so I won't delay.' He inhaled sharply and I saw his eyes dart away from us. 'I have seen the images from Robyn's MRI, but it isn't good news, I'm afraid... Unfortunately, the tumour hasn't abated as much as we would have hoped. It seems that it is a very aggressive type and is unresponsive to the radiation treatment.' He opened a file that was sitting on his desk and showed us the scans of her brain. The tumour was plainly obvious to see, and I felt the air leave my lungs.

'So, what are you saying?' JP asked.

'As we explained before embarking on the treatment, radiation works to shrink the tumour in roughly 80 per cent of DIPG cases, but you're one of the unlucky ones. I'm so sorry, I can't imagine how disappointed you both must feel here today.'

It felt as though I was sinking under water, a current was pulling me down to a place where everything was muffled and slow. When we had first been told our daughter would die, it was as if there was a buffer there, it was almost like my brain had refused to believe the news we were being delivered, but now there was nothing. Time was up. This was happening.

JP stood up off his chair and exhaled loudly. 'You need to do something.' He was panicked, his words came out thick and fast.

'I'm so sorry, there's nothing more we can offer you,' Dr Sharma said. 'I don't think it would be fair to Robyn to carry out any more radiotherapy when I wouldn't be hopeful that it would offer any more benefits. You mentioned that some of the symptoms have worsened in the last few days—'

'But you can't just sit back and watch her die!' JP was aghast. 'You can't just give up on her – you're her doctor!' He stabbed his finger accusingly at Dr Sharma. 'You took an oath to help save lives. You have an obligation. You have to do something!'

'I'm so sorry,' Dr Sharma replied.

The guilt assailed me like a smack in the face. I had put my daughter through all of that radiation, poisoning her body, and for what? I had watched her get distressed by needles, watched her cave to exhaustion, nausea, growing weaker by the day, but I had told myself it would be worth it because we would get a brief reprieve from the tumour. But it was all for nothing.

'Can I ask you something?' I asked.

'Of course, Sarah.'

'How long have we got?' My voice sounded small and faraway

as though I was at one end of the tunnel and Dr Sharma was at the other end.

'It isn't an exact science... but I have seen patients live for several more months with this type of tumour and I've seen patients deteriorate rapidly. Unfortunately, I can't give you a definitive answer.'

'But what should we do?' JP blazed. 'We can't just do nothing! If this was your child, what would you do?'

Dr Sharma paused thoughtfully and steepled his hands together. 'Taking everything into account, if it was my daughter, I think I'd take her home and cherish the time we had left together.'

* * *

We left Dr Sharma's room and walked back out towards the car park. I thought it was strange that I didn't cry. It was as though my body was too broken to make tears. Was it the shock or had I already accepted that Robyn was going to die? Then the guilt got me, what kind of a mother gives up on her own daughter?

'Come on, I can't let you drive yourself. I'll take you home,' JP said as we found ourselves lost and broken in the hospital car park once more.

'But what about my car?'

'We'll sort it out later, don't worry.'

I sat in JP's BMW without argument. I didn't care about the logistics of collecting my car at another time; I was just glad to have someone take control. I don't think I could have driven myself or I would have been a danger on the roads. I noticed a long blonde hair clinging to the seat. It was obviously Megan's. I plucked it up, rolled down the window and watched it sail out onto the air.

'They can't just give up on her.' JP slammed his palm against the steering wheel. 'There has to be something we can do.'

I knew he was in shock at the outcome of the MRI, but I think deep down I had known coming into the hospital that morning that it wasn't going to be good news. I had seen my baby fading away, one tiny piece at a time. Maybe it was a mother's instinct.

We both fell silent then, each lost inside our own heads. We hit traffic coming up to the East-Link Toll Bridge and we crawled along, moving just a few metres until we'd stop again. I watched frustrated drivers sigh and talk hands-free into their phones in the cars beside me. There was a time when heavy traffic would work me up too, but now getting annoyed by traffic seemed so trivial compared to my worries. How I wished that was the worst thing in my day.

JP's phone rang as we crossed the wide mouth of the River Liffey and Megan's voice filled the car speaker. She sounded young and airy and carefree. It was so at odds to the way my head felt right now.

'What time will you be home?' she asked.

'I'll call you back, I can't really talk right now,' JP said quickly.

'It's a simple question!' she barked. 'I'm going out tonight with the girls.'

'Well, enjoy it.'

She sighed heavily. 'That's why I was wondering when you'll be home, can you give me a lift to Claire's house?'

'I'll call you back later, Megan, okay?' he said and then he pressed the end-call button.

'How's it all going?' I asked. I couldn't help myself.

He shrugged. 'Megan is...' He paused. 'Well, she's younger, y'know?' he said eventually. He looked across at me in the passenger seat. 'My head's all over the place lately,' he added, as if that explained everything.

* * *

Eventually, JP pulled up outside our old home and silenced the engine. I stared at the house where we had welcomed both our children, the house that was full of memories at every turn. This was the place where we had returned home from honeymoon and JP had swooped me over the threshold and very nearly dropped me because we were laughing so much. This was the place where we had both shed so many tears when pregnancy test after pregnancy test was negative, but where we had squealed and danced around the room when we saw two pink lines on the test that was to be Harry and then Robyn too. This was the place where I had paced the floorboards feeling tired down to my bones as I soothed fractious newborn babies and it was the place where JP would come home from work and surprise us all with a takeaway on a Friday evening. This was the house I had put so much time and love into, to make it not just a house, but a home.

A few years back JP had arrived home with a glossy marketing brochure for a new development that was being constructed along the seafront in Malahide. We had gone along to the show house and, as we had walked around the property, which was far more spacious than our own, with its tasteful interiors and views across Dublin Bay, JP had wanted us to put down a deposit there and then, but I had been more reticent. In the end, I had told him that I couldn't leave our home simply because it was *our* home. He had laughed and I knew he thought I was being ridiculous, but the truth was so much happiness and joy echoed between the walls of our house and I couldn't bear to think of another family living there amongst our memories, no matter how silly that might have sounded.

We both stayed sitting in the car; we needed time to gather

ourselves before seeing Robyn. I knew seeing her was going to kill me. That's when it all would become real.

Eventually, I climbed out of the car and began walking up the path. JP followed after me. It felt as though I was pulling my legs through wet concrete with every step. I stood on the doorstep for a moment looking at my door with its sunny yellow paint and wondered how I was supposed to look Robyn in the eye now.

'How're things?' I said to Fiona when we went inside. The heavenly smell of baking filled the air.

'We had a great morning.' Fiona nodded in the direction of the living room where, through the glass, I saw Robyn was watching *Paw Patrol* wrapped up in a blanket. 'I think she's tired, but she's a trooper. So how did it go?'

I shook my head, unable to voice what we had just been told.

Fiona's face collapsed and she bit down hard on her lip. 'Oh, Sarah,' she said, throwing her arms around me as I released the tears and sobbed into her shoulder.

Suddenly, a blonde head stuck around the door frame. I choked back tears when I saw her sweet, innocent face.

'Hi, Mammy and Daddy,' she said, smiling at us both. 'I made-ded you a cupcake!'

My heart sank to the floor, this was the cruellest thing. She was my world.

I looked at Fiona and JP and we all had tears in our eyes as we struggled to keep it together. I walked over and lifted her up into my arms and breathed her in. She smelled of icing sugar and marshmallows. I motioned for JP to come over and the three of us enveloped one another into a hug.

HARRY

I hate Jamie O'Connor. He's so mean. He came over to my house today and we were playing FIFA on the PlayStation and I was Liverpool because it's my PlayStation and he had to be Chelsea and I was winning 4–0. Then he said he was going home because he didn't win. And I said he was just a sore loser and then he said, 'Well, anyway your sister is a weirdo.' He said, 'She looks really funny, like this,' and he started pulling his eyes with his fingers and doing an impression of Robyn and it wasn't very nice because I know she looks really weird and her face is all crooked and it looks like it's falling down on one side and sometimes I don't know where her eyes are looking, but Mam said you're not allowed to say that out loud because it's mean. So, I got really mad and the white dots came in my eyes, I couldn't help it and I ran at him and tackled him on the sofa and then Mam came in and saw what was going on and she shouted at me to stop. Then she told me to say sorry to Jamie, but he started it, so I said, 'I'm not saying sorry to him.' Mam asked me what happened, but I couldn't tell her because I knew it would make her sad, so then she told me to shake hands with him, but I wouldn't do it, so she called Jamie's mam to come collect him and then she sent me to my room even though it was all his fault because he started it.

20

Scientists say that time is an illusion, that in reality everything that has ever been or ever will be is happening simultaneously right now at this very moment, but when time is cruelly snatched away from you, you know that time is a very real, tangible thing.

In the days after we were told that the radiation therapy hadn't worked, I found myself making daily pleas with God, bargaining with him, telling him things I would do if he could just give me more time. I knew there would never come a time when I would be ready to say goodbye to my darling daughter, but it certainly wasn't now.

In the end, we just kept going. Because that's what you do when you don't know what else to do, you just keep going. I thought of the movie *Finding Nemo* that we had watched with the kids on TV a few months ago. At one stage, Dory had said to Marlin: 'Just keep swimming.' The kids had loved saying it over and over again for weeks afterwards. Well, that's what we had to do right now, *just keep swimming*.

The last days of April would soon be pushed out by the long, heady days of May. Late-evening birdsong and the sound of children's laughter playing on the green outside filtered in through the open windows. Then there was the plinky music of the ice cream van as it came around every evening or the upbeat songs on TV advertising family holidays – everywhere there seemed to be reminders of happier, carefree times and what we were losing. I would see a mother scolding a child in the supermarket because they wanted sweets and I longed to tell them that it didn't matter, just buy them the sweets, because life was too fragile. I would give anything to go back to those days again.

JP was spending a lot of time at the house with us. His job had told him to take as much time off as he needed, but I wondered how his absence at home was going down with Megan. He never said much about her and I didn't ask. Sometimes he would bring Joan and Richard over too and they would sit and help Robyn with a jigsaw or play with her *Frozen* dolls. We tried to do something small together as a family every day. We let her decide what she wanted to do, and it was usually a trip to Malahide Castle to see the butterflies in the Butterfly House or a walk along the beach with an ice cream on the way home. They were always simple, ordinary things, but as the warm sunlight hit her cheeks, a smile would spread across her face. One day, she had decided that she wanted to go to playschool to see Lily, so I had taken her in, and she had sat doing circle time with the other children while I stayed at the back of the classroom letting her have her independence with her friends. My heart had twisted looking at all the other children who had already grown up so much in the time that Robyn had been absent. They would all start school together in September, a day that Robyn should have had too. We should be buying her uniform and letting her choose her school bag, but those milestones were being snatched away from us.

Her legs had grown progressively weaker and now she wasn't really able to walk any more. I had taken her old buggy out of the garage and JP would push her along. Her speech had become difficult to understand and it broke my heart when she was trying to tell me something and I wasn't able to decipher what she was saying. I knew it frustrated her too because I could see a sheen of anger in her eyes which completely broke my heart. The worst part about all of this was that she understood everything, her mind was still perfectly fine.

I could see Harry was struggling to accept these changes in his little sister too.

'Why can't Robyn talk properly?' he had asked me one day.

I still hadn't been able to bring myself to tell him that Robyn was dying. I was worried that once we told him, things would change between them and I wanted him to have a normal relationship with his sister for as long as he could. His world was going to alter so much, he was going to learn the agony of losing a loved one at an age where no child should have to experience that pain. I couldn't even begin to imagine how the loss of his younger sister would shape the man that Harry would grow into in the future. But I also knew we couldn't put it off for much longer.

One evening, I had just tucked up Harry and Robyn in their beds and was finally sitting down after cleaning the kitchen when I heard the doorbell go. I saw it was JP in the security peephole. He still flitted between disbelief and anger, whereas, although I couldn't say I was ready for what was coming down the tracks towards us, I guessed I had reached acceptance. He was still hell-bent on doing something. He spent his nights trawling the internet for anything to keep our daughter with us.

'JP?' I said in surprise as I opened the door. He had been over to see the children earlier in the day, so I hadn't been expecting him.

'I need to talk to you,' he said, blustering inside.

'What's wrong?' I asked.

'I think I might have found something, Sarah...'

'What do you mean?'

'A cure for Robyn.'

Instead of feeling hopeful, my heart sank as if it had been poured with lead. I was used to hearing him tell me about different alternative therapies that he had found on the internet and usually he agreed with me that they were a bunch of quackery.

'It's a treatment being pioneered by doctors in Arizona in the US,' he continued.

'Arizona?' I repeated, full of scepticism.

'They have developed this protocol using a combination of intra-arterial chemotherapy and immunotherapy and it's having good results.'

I looked at him blankly.

'They basically inject chemotherapy agents through the artery in her leg and it leads directly into the brain,' he explained.

This sounded different and he had my attention. 'But why didn't Dr Sharma tell us about this if it's saving lives?' I couldn't believe our medical team would have overlooked any realistic options. They had always fought hard to give Robyn every chance without allowing us to raise our hopes.

'Exactly! They just gave up on her. Took the easy option and left her to die.'

My head was spinning. 'But has it worked? Has it saved people?' I felt my heart rise, but I warned it to be cautious. It couldn't survive being crushed any more.

'Well, it's an ongoing trial... there are kids from all over the world being treated there at the moment. I looked up the parents' stories and although nobody has beaten it yet, they seem to be getting more time.'

My heart fell again down to the floor. 'But if nobody has survived it, JP, then why would you even consider it?' I was angry at him for giving me false hope that I couldn't deal with right now. 'Radiotherapy didn't do its job because her tumour is so aggressive, you don't know that this will work either and I'm not using Robyn as a guinea pig.'

'But it might, Sarah! Even if there's only a tiny chance, we have to try it—'

'JP, stop it! You're looking for a miracle that doesn't exist. Nobody is experimenting on my child. They could kill her even faster if they made a mistake or got the dosage or the drugs wrong. I want to do all I can to make sure her last days aren't full of hospitals and needles, you saw how much she hated the radiotherapy. I want her with me all the time – I'm not putting her on a plane to America.'

'You're giving up on her,' he shouted at me angrily.

I felt white-hot fury burning through my body. 'No, I'm not! If it was you or I that was sick, we could choose to go down the path of experimental treatment, but she's our daughter, we have a duty to protect her and make her last days as easy as possible for her.'

'I just don't get you at all, Sarah,' he said, shaking his head in exasperation. 'Why won't you do something that gives her a fighting chance?'

'Don't you see? It's because I love her that I'm doing this. It doesn't give her a fighting chance – it just prolongs the agony for her, the misery for us. You heard what Doctor Sharma said – nobody has survived it! You need to accept it, JP, this is happening. We are going to lose her. Our baby is going to die.'

'Somebody is going to have to beat this disease sometime, it could be Robyn! There has to be a first DIPG survivor! And even if it doesn't cure her, if it just buys us a few more months, then surely that is better than nothing at all. Why can't you see this?'

'Because I'm her mother!'

'Oh, please! That's bullshit, just because you gave birth to her doesn't put you on a higher parenting pedestal!'

'When you're a mother you learn to put other people's needs before your own and that's what I'm doing right now.'

21

The knots in my shoulders had grown impossibly tight. They ached and burned. I took a deep breath and rolled them backwards, trying to ease them out. JP's words had really rattled me. How could he say those things? Even though I rarely drank at home, I walked over to the fridge and poured myself a generous glass of white wine. Then I sat down at the kitchen table and opened up my laptop. Although I had deliberately avoided searching the internet since the day we had got Robyn's diagnosis, I needed to see for myself what he was talking about. I knew that if there was any hope at all of this treatment JP mentioned working, then I owed it to Robyn to research it further.

I took a large sip of wine and typed the words 'DIPG' and 'Arizona' into Google. Immediately I was met with hits for the same clinic that JP had spoken about. I clicked on to the first link and read down the page. The doctors claimed to have treated several children with DIPG and that some of them had shown evidence of being tumour-free on their subsequent scans. I fell down a rabbit hole as I clicked on to page after page. Many of the parents of the children had written blogs about their treatment journey and as I read their stories, where they shared their innermost hopes and fears, I couldn't help but be drawn into their lives. They were ordinary people just like we were until the cruel monster had invaded their world. I read on with burning hope that they had defied the odds and had had a happy ending – not just for their sake but for my own selfish reasons too. There were photos of a family celebrating a scan showing their child being tumour-free, but then there was an update three months later showing that the tumour had in fact come back and their child was now 'resting in the arms of the angels'. Tears streamed down my face as I clicked through page after page reading similar stories, hoping someone, somewhere, might have beaten the odds, but none of these kids had survived. It was exactly as Dr Sharma had warned, the tumour always came back. It always won.

The one thing JP hadn't mentioned was that there was great scepticism towards the clinic in the wider medical community. Although some people praised the doctors as heroes, many more hailed them as modern-day snake oil salesmen. Each treatment cost hundreds of thousands of dollars and the doctors had never submitted their data for peer review or published their protocols in medical journals. There was also talk of their dubious 'tumour-free' scans, not to mention the significant distress it caused for the patients and their families. I felt crushed reading the stories of families who had sold their home or used their life savings to give their child a fighting chance. There were many who had even used the savings of their extended families too, in a bid to raise funds for the treatment, only to still lose their child anyway. My heart broke for these desperate people who would do anything to save their child, they didn't deserve to be treated this way. Disregarding the cost, at best the doctors' therapy was unaccredited and at worst they were charlatans taking advantage of vulnerable people. How could JP think this was the right option for Robyn?

I closed my laptop and tears streamed down my face at the hopelessness of it all.

Robyn was falling through the air, falling, falling, falling. An arc of water droplets cascaded off her small body. JP tossed her up again and her laughter bounced off the water and echoed under the low vaulted roof. Her whole face shone, and water glistened like jewels on her hair as JP caught her once more and wrapped her in close against his chest.

JP had called over earlier like he usually did, and we had taken the kids to the swimming pool, but things had changed between us after our argument the day before. The recent thaw in our relationship had cooled once more, and things were strained between us again. Although we were still speaking to one another, it was purely for the sake of Harry and Robyn. The tension between us was so thick, I felt as if I could cut through its sinewy girth with scissors.

I felt water rain down upon me and I realised Robyn had splashed me. I saw the mischievous spark in her eyes and my heart soared. I dragged my hands through the water and watched as it arced over her small body as I splashed her back.

'This means war,' Harry said, and suddenly water assailed me from every direction as we had a water fight.

I used to come to the pool with the children every week when Harry was doing his swimming lessons. While Harry was in his class, I would grab a coffee in the café outside and Robyn would have juice and a cookie. How I longed for our old life again.

Those ordinary days where nothing remarkable ever happened seemed blissful now. Where once I would have thought they were mundane, now I realised they were the most beautiful of all. Joy was in the simple, everyday moments, like a shared smile or the warmth of a hug, but we were usually too unaware of the fragility of life at moments like that to appreciate just how lucky we were.

After we had towelled off and dressed, we grabbed a snack in the café, before driving home together again in my car. We pulled up at the house and JP carried Robyn inside. She couldn't walk unaided now and although we hadn't got a wheelchair for her yet, I knew those days weren't too far ahead.

'Are you staying for a while, Dad?' Harry asked.

'I can't, son, I've to collect Megan from work.'

Harry's face fell. I knew he was enjoying seeing more of his dad, nothing made him happier than when the four of us were together.

'I'll see you both tomorrow, okay?' he added.

I walked out to the front door with JP. He stepped outside before turning back to me on the doorstep.

'I'm sorry about yesterday... what I said... I was out of order.'

'You were.'

He shook his head. 'I'm desperate, Sarah – we need to do this or else she's going to die! We need to try this treatment. It's our only hope.'

'I looked the clinic up, JP, and there's no way I'm sending her off to Arizona to be treated by a bunch of quacks!'

'But it's all we've got! Her doctors here have failed her, we have to go further afield. Even if there's a 1 per cent chance, we have to try it...'

'No child has ever survived it, JP – not one.'

'Those doctors, they're on to something though – who knows, Robyn could be the first.'

'And if I agreed to it, how would you even fund it?'

'Well, we could sell the house...' he said tentatively.

I shook my head in disbelief. 'Besides it being the most ludicrous thing you've ever suggested, after we had paid off the mortgage, we still wouldn't come near to covering the costs.'

'Well, I was thinking... we could fundraise...'

'And spend the short time we have left with Robyn busy and preoccupied with organising all of that?'

'Well, I could do it.'

I shook my head and sighed heavily. 'This is madness, JP. Complete and utter madness!' I shivered. Although summer was around the corner, the evenings were still cool.

'You're the one who's mad, I can't believe you won't try every avenue to help her. I can't let my daughter die knowing there might have been something I could have done to save her. I could never live with myself and I don't know how you will either!'

'Believe me, if there was a viable cure, I'd be the first in line, but there isn't—'

'What kind of mother are you? You need to put her first and fight for her. We brought her into this world, we're her parents, we need to do everything that we can to stop her leaving it. She's too young to decide for herself – we're her voice – you can't just give up on her!'

I felt rage rising up like a spectre inside me, coursing through my veins. I should have known his apology meant nothing. His words were so cruel, and I couldn't believe he was saying them. I was her mother who loved her beyond words. Did he really think that by accepting she was dying that I was giving up on her? I would never, ever accept her death, but I couldn't argue with the doctors and science. I imagined myself in ten years from now, twenty years, even fifty years, still feeling so cheated at the hand life dealt us. But I had to put Robyn first and make her last days with us as special as I could. Tears were coursing down my face.

'At what cost, JP? Is it fair to put her through that ordeal when it's not going to change the outcome? The end result is going to be the same – we're still going to lose our baby girl!'

22

Streaks of red met circles of green and vivid smudges of blue. Robyn was using her fingers to paint a picture of a garden. She dipped her index finger into the yellow paint and circled it around the page to make a sun as bright as the May sunlight streaming in through the patio glass. Every piece of artwork she did was cherished; whereas before after a brief stint of being displayed on the fridge I might have chucked some of it in the recycling bin, now I treasured everything. She enjoyed doing arts and crafts, and although her left hand was losing power, I knew it was important to let her do those things while she still could.

My phone rang, I checked and saw it was Fiona. I dipped my fingers into the muddy water to wash off the paint and lifted the phone.

'Hi, Fi,' I answered.

'Eh, Sarah, are you at home?'

'Yeah, why?'

'Put on *Good Morning Ireland*.'

'Why?' I said, going into the living room and searching for the remote.

'Because JP is on it.'

'*What*?'

I located the remote underneath a cushion and quickly flicked on the TV to hear the presenter saying, 'Up next we have a dad who is desperate to save his terminally ill daughter, you won't want to miss his heartbreaking story.' Then an image of Robyn wearing a straw sun hat and a blue dress that had been taken on holiday last year flashed up on the screen. *What the hell?* I felt anger charge around my body. How dare he? How dare he do this to Robyn? This wasn't his story to tell.

I watched as the glossy blonde presenter leaned forward in her chair towards JP, her brows creased in concern. 'JP, tell us about your four-year-old daughter, Robyn.'

I listened as he described our daughter, full of fun and mischief, and then recalled the awful day of Robyn's diagnosis and the prognosis given to us by the hospital. He explained that her only hope of survival was an experimental treatment offered in the US and how he was fundraising to pay for it. As I heard him tell Robyn's story, I could feel my anger grow with every word that left his mouth. The way he was telling it made it sound as though this treatment was going to cure her, but he wasn't telling the full story.

'If she doesn't get this treatment she will die,' he said before an image of a JustGiving page flashed up on the screen, and I suddenly realised this was JP's method of fundraising. A banner ran along the bottom showing messages being sent into the show from viewers watching at home. They were streaming in from all around the country, congratulating him on his courage and wishing him and Robyn well.

'Thank you for coming and telling your story here today, JP,' the presenter said as she wrapped up the interview. 'I think I can speak for everyone when I say you have the whole country behind you, and we wish you and Robyn all the best with her treatment.'

'Are you still there?' Fiona asked.

I had forgotten I was still on the phone to her. 'I can't believe he did that!'

'There's more, Sarah. There are features on him in both the *Irish Times* and the *Irish Independent* today.'

'What is he trying to do? Does he think if he raises the money that he's going to get me to change my mind?'

'You know this is just his way of dealing with it, Sarah, this is his way of trying to stay in control of his grief.'

'But he's making a hugely stressful time unbearable. We're at loggerheads, which isn't helping Robyn.' I sighed heavily and squeezed my eyes shut. 'It's such a mess. I just want everything to be as peaceful as possible for her – not this craziness.'

'I know you do,' Fiona agreed.

I called JP straight after I had hung up from Fiona. He didn't reply so I rang him again twenty minutes later, but there was still no reply. Eventually I saw his number on my screen as he called me back.

'What the hell was that about?' I blasted immediately before he even had time to speak. 'I can't believe you've gone on national TV and put our private life up there for the whole world to see! All the school mums – our neighbours – every Tom, Dick and Harry in north County Dublin will know what's going on! You can't just steamroll me into this, JP! You're crazy even doing this!'

'Well, judging by the reaction from the viewers and the dona-tions that are flooding into the page, you're the one who is crazy by not even wanting to try something that might save her—'

'But that's because you didn't give the other side of the story, you didn't tell them that the treatment won't even work! You made it look as though money was the only obstacle stopping Robyn from getting better. You can throw all the money you want at it, but it won't cure her, JP!' I blazed.

'She's too young to decide for herself – we're her voice, Sarah!'

Through the glass, I could see Robyn looking at me from the kitchen and her eyes were wide with concern. She wasn't used to hearing me raise my voice. 'I have to go,' I said, hanging up the phone before he could say anything more.

'It's okay, Robyn,' I soothed, going into the kitchen. 'It was just someone trying to sell me cheaper electricity.'

She went back to painting her flower while I used my phone to google JP's 'Help Save Robyn' JustGiving page. Even though it had only just gone live within the last twenty-four hours; I couldn't believe he had already managed to raise €61,183. He was well on his way to his target of €300,000. What would happen if he reached it? What would we do then? I wasn't going to change my mind, especially after everything I had read about the clinic, and I didn't he think he would back down either.

I scrolled down through the donations, enthralled. Some people had left comments below their donation like 'You're in our thoughts and prayers' or 'Keep fighting the fight, little Robyn'. Strangers who had seen his appeal on the TV or read about it in the newspapers and had taken our story into their hearts. People we didn't know and would probably never meet were lighting candles and praying for our little girl. I was gobsmacked to see one anonymous person had donated a whopping €5,000. Tears sprang into my eyes at people's generosity, and it was all for a little girl they would never know.

So many people seemed to be supporting JP that it was hard not to doubt myself. Was he right? I was starting to ask myself some difficult questions. Shouldn't I be exhausting every possible avenue to save my child, even if the odds weren't that great, isn't that what any loving parent would do? Maybe I was making the wrong call here. And I couldn't get this wrong, the stakes were too high; our daughter's life was hanging in the balance.

HARRY

Today was the worst day ever. Nobody would let me share their colours in school. I forgot my pencil case and I asked everyone on my table, but nobody would let me use their Twistables, so I had to ask teacher for a loan of her colours, but they're all really old and broken so my picture turned out the baddest in the whole class. Then nobody would play with me in the yard either and when we had a popcorn party after lunch because teacher said we were really good all week, nobody would let me put my hand in the box and I asked why and then Jamie said that his mam saw my dad on the TV, but I said, 'no she didn't 'cos my dad wasn't on the TV,' and he said, 'yes he was' and that I have germs and I said, 'no I don't because I always wash my hands with soap after the toilet.' And he said that I have the 'cancer germs'. Granny had cancer and I know it's when people get really sick, but I didn't know what Jamie was talking about, so then I said nothing. He's not my friend any more because he keeps saying mean things. Teacher asked me if I was okay, but I just said I didn't like popcorn any more.

Robyn's eyes drooped to a close as I stroked her golden hair back off her face. Her body needed more sleep now as it tried its hardest to fight back. I could see the tumour was stealing her energy and she had fallen into a routine of having a long nap every afternoon.

When she was asleep, I came downstairs and saw an envelope sitting on the mat in the hall. I opened it to see it was a card from one of our neighbours to say she was thinking of us. Recently, casseroles and lasagnes had magically started appearing on our doorstep, and I was receiving messages of support from friends I hadn't heard from in years. Although I was touched by everyone's kindness, I knew it was all because of JP's television appearance. Everyone now knew about Robyn's illness.

When JP called to the house to see her that day, I could barely look at him. Things were very strained between us after his publicity stunt on national television, so even though I was an hour early, I said I was going to collect Harry from school while he stayed behind to mind Robyn.

I went into the little café around the corner from Harry's

school to pass the time and ordered a cappuccino. Usually, I would have a mental battle with myself as I tried to summon the willpower not to order a slice of cake too, but as I looked at them displayed through the glass counter that day, none of them appealed to me. Just like Robyn, I too had lost my appetite lately from all the stress and worry. Nothing tasted good any more. I knew I had lost weight; clothes that were previously too tight now hung off my body.

I carried my cappuccino and sat down in a quiet corner. I lifted the mug to my lips and sipped my coffee and even it tasted tarry and smoky. I took my phone out to check JP's fundraising page once more. I had been keeping an eye on it since he had made his TV appeal, but I nearly dropped the phone when I saw it was now in excess of €160,000. Just days after his television appearance, he was over halfway there. There were hundreds of comments now and I read through some of the recent ones with tears in my eyes. The kindness of strangers was so touching – despite everything that had happened to me, it was plain to see there was so much goodness in the world, but these people couldn't save Robyn no matter how well intentioned they were.

I put my phone face down on the table and sighed. I was doing the right thing – I knew I was. And yet, and yet... The whole thing was crazy, but in my weaker moments I wondered if perhaps I was the crazy one? People from all over Ireland, some from abroad too, were supporting JP, but they didn't see into our home where our daughter was very sick and growing weaker by the day. The strength in her left side had completely gone now and she would tire easily. Her speech could be hard to understand, and sometimes she resorted to pointing with her right hand to tell me what she wanted. She was finding it difficult to swallow too, so I had started puréeing all her food like I had when she was a baby. Instead of moving on and gaining more independence, my daughter was moving backwards through time. The awful thing was that I knew she was frustrated by the changes in her body. Even if I changed my mind, I wasn't sure she would survive the flight to the US, let alone the gruelling treatment being offered over there.

With ten minutes to go until Harry finished school, I went up to the counter and bought a cookie for him before leaving the café. As I walked around to the old red-brick building, the smell of freshly mowed grass filled my nostrils and the hum of lawn-mowers played in the background. Those smells and sounds always reminded me of studying for exams when I was in college. Even now they signalled that summertime was just around the corner. I usually loved the slower pace of life that the school holi-days brought – late rising in the mornings, lazy breakfasts followed by a day clear of the usual routines where we could do whatever we wanted. We would jump into the car and head to Portmarnock beach for the day, followed by fish and chips wrapped in newspaper on the way home, or sometimes we would take a picnic to the Phoenix Park, but now I was dreading the shift in time. It was hard to look forward to anything any more. Time was our nemesis.

When I reached the school, I looked around where all the other parents were gathered at the railings. It had been so long since I had been here.

'Sarah,' I heard a voice call from behind after a moment.

I turned to see Jennifer, the mother of a little girl in Harry's class, making her way over to me. I didn't know her well, but we had met at school concerts and birthday parties over the years. I waited for her to reach me.

'I haven't seen you here in ages. How've you been?' She lowered her eyes to the ground. 'I heard about Robyn – I'm so sorry.'

'Thanks, Jennifer.'

'If there's anything I can do, just let me know.' She gripped my arm.

'I appreciate that.'

'There's Ava coming now, I'd better go,' she said. 'I'm thinking of you, Sarah.'

At a time when I felt the whole world was against me, now more than ever, every gesture of support meant so much.

I soon saw Harry coming towards me in the distance. His face broke into a wide grin when he saw me waiting for him at the railings. It was usually JP or Fiona who collected him these days because I hated leaving Robyn. I felt my heart soar for my first-born child.

'How was school?' I asked, putting my arm around him when he reached me, and I was glad he didn't bat it away like he usually did.

'Good. I made this for Robyn...' He held out a misshapen piece of pottery that I guessed was meant to be a unicorn.

'Wow, Harry, that's amazing, she will love that.' I felt a lump catch in my throat, he adored his little sister. 'Did you get much homework?' I asked as we walked back to where I had parked my car.

'Yeah, loads,' he groaned.

'I got you a cookie,' I said, holding out the brown paper bag for him.

'Cool! Thanks, Mam,' he said, taking it from me.

We climbed into the car and put on our seat belts. I had just pulled out into the traffic when I heard Harry call me from the back seat.

'Mam?'

'Yes, love?'

'Does Robyn have cancer?' he asked through a mouthful of cookie.

I nearly crashed the car. 'Where did you hear that?' I tried to keep my voice level.

'Jamie O'Connor said that Robyn has cancer. His mam saw it on the TV.'

I felt my shoulders climb up to my ears. Bloody JP! I hadn't even considered that this might be one of the implications of his media campaign. I knew word about Robyn's condition had got out there, but I didn't expect the children in school to be talking about it. I would need to have a word with his teacher.

'Do you know what cancer is, Harry?' I began.

'Yeah, it's what Granny died of,' he stated matter-of-factly.

I winced. I wasn't ready yet to have this conversation with him, especially as I was driving along the road. Should I pull over, I wondered? But I knew if I did that then it would alarm him, and he would know it was serious. I felt my anger grow at JP. This was all his fault, and I was left dealing with the consequences.

'Well, your body is made of good cells, but sometimes bad cells grow there too and when that happens it's called cancer,' I explained.

'So does Robyn have it, Mam?' he asked, impatient at my long-winded explanation.

I felt as though we were running over ice and I was waiting for a crack. The realisation that his sister was going to die would hit him any minute now and I wasn't ready for it. My fingers clenched tighter around the steering wheel. 'Well, the reason she was going into the hospital every day was that they have a special machine there that can zap the bad cells,' I continued.

'So, is it like a Nerf gun then?'

'Well, yeah, I suppose it is.' I was holding my breath, waiting for whatever he would say next.

'Cool,' he said, turning to look out the window. 'Can I play FIFA when I get home?'

'Sure,' I said, breathing out a sigh of relief as my shoulders came back down from my ears. For now, I was glad to have escaped the discussion, but I knew it was looming on the horizon. There was a day coming soon where we would have to tell Harry and destroy his world forever.

24

I silenced the alarm before it even had time to go off. It had nearly become a habit now, as I was awake before it every morning. I slept fitfully these days. I would lie awake feeling so overwhelmed for the future, so terrified by what was coming for me. It felt like a brick was being pushed down upon my chest. I would try to recall Robyn's face to make sure I could remember every detail of its beauty and sometimes the image wouldn't come to me and I would feel panicked and sit up gasping for air. I was terrified I wouldn't be able to remember her exactly the way she was.

I planted a kiss on her silky curls and left her to sleep on while I climbed out of bed to wake Harry for school. Robyn was now sleeping in bed with me every night, for no particular reason other than I wanted to cuddle her close to me for as long as I still could. I wrapped my dressing gown around me and swung my head around the door of Harry's bedroom. Pieces of Lego, Match Attax cards and dirty socks were strewn around the floor. I would need to tackle it later.

'Come on, love, it's time to get up.'

His voice came out muffled beneath the duvet, 'I don't want to go to school, Mam.'

'You know you have to. It won't be long until the summer holidays, so it's only for a few more weeks,' I cajoled. We were now in late May and he only had a little over a month left before the school year was finished.

'I'm not going!' He pulled the duvet up over his head.

'Why not?' I asked, coming into the room and sitting down onto the edge of his bed. 'What's wrong?'

'I'm not feeling well...'

My breath hitched in my chest. I knew kids got sick all the time but after everything we were going through with Robyn, I couldn't help but jump to the worst-case scenario. I pulled the duvet down from around his head and placed my hand on his forehead. 'You don't seem to have a temperature. Is it your tummy?'

He nodded.

'Do you feel sick?'

'Yeah.'

'Okay, well, perhaps we'll keep you at home today and see how you are.' Maybe he was brewing something or maybe he wasn't sick at all, but if he really didn't feel like going into school today, I was happy to let him hang out with us at home. We all needed a day to chill out once in a while.

He quickly got out of bed and bounded down the stairs after me.

'I thought you were supposed to be sick?' I said.

'I am!' He instantly started to rub his tummy.

'Hmm.' I tried to hide a smile. I knew Harry was out of sorts with everything going on with Robyn so he probably wanted some attention, who could blame him? Whereas it once would have been important to me that Harry never miss school unless he was really ill, now I had a new perspective on life. In the grand scheme of things, it didn't matter if he pulled a sickie now and again. I texted JP to tell him Harry was taking a sick day, so he didn't need to collect him that morning.

Robyn woke a while later and, after breakfast, I took the king-size duvet off my bed and let the two of them snuggle up on the sofa underneath it while they watched cartoons. I took out my phone and took a photo of them with their faces peeping out from beneath it, smiling up at me with big cheesy grins. These were the moments I treasured the most, things like this, the ordinary, simple joy of seeing my two babies snuggled together as they watched TV. And then I would remember the awfulness that was coming down the tracks and feel a weight pulling me down, almost pushing me through the floor and I didn't think I could bear the sadness. I felt panicky; a tightness and breathlessness seized my chest whenever I thought about what the future held for us.

I had gone to one counselling session recommended to me by the hospital. As if counselling was going to be able to fix the pain in my heart of losing my daughter. I had gone along anyway, feeling that I ought to at least try it, but I knew after one session I wouldn't be going back. It seemed like another non-essential item on a to-do list and I was ruthlessly chopping non-essential items from my life. Robyn's diagnosis had made me greedy with my time. I didn't want to do anything that took me away from her. The one thing I had taken from the session was that I needed to focus on the everyday joys. The counsellor had told me to stay in the moment and not to let my thoughts race ahead. I was trying hard to focus on the positives, and right now Robyn was here with us and that's what I needed to remember and take each day as it came.

I took a deep breath inwards right down into my ribcage and

exhaled slowly outwards like I had been taught to do. *Focus on the now, Sarah*, I told myself. And right now, my two most favourite people in the world were curled up together, giggling at the TV screen.

* * *

The next morning, when I tried to wake Harry for school, he tried the same trick again, but I knew I had to be firm with him. I didn't mind a day here and there, but he needed to go to school, it wasn't going to help anyone if he fell behind. I coaxed him out of bed, made his breakfast and persuaded him to dress himself before JP arrived to collect him.

'Your dad's here,' I called out when the doorbell sounded before nine.

'Please, Mam, I don't want to go,' he begged as I went out to answer the door.

'What's got into him?' JP asked as he came into the kitchen.

'Beats me,' I muttered.

Things were still difficult between us. I was keeping an eye on his JustGiving page and I knew he had managed to raise over €250,000 so far – an astronomical amount of money. He was nearly there. As I watched the donations creeping higher, it felt like a countdown, but to what I wasn't entirely sure. What was he going to do once he reached the target? The question loomed ominously in my mind all the time and I hated that I was spending precious moments that I had left with Robyn worrying about it.

Harry was clinging to my leg. 'Please, Mam, don't make me go.' He hadn't behaved like this since he was a toddler. Harry was always the child who ran happily into school. Even on day one of Junior Infants, he had waved JP and me off enthusiastically, while other kids cried and begged their parents not to leave them. I had already spoken to his teacher, Ms O'Mara, and told her about Robyn's diagnosis and she had promised she would keep a very close eye on him, but maybe I needed to talk to her again.

'Do you want me to take you?' I offered, thinking he might just need some time alone with me.

He shook his head. 'I don't want to go, Mam, please, can I stay at home with you and Robyn again?'

'Oh, sweetheart, you have to go.' I felt guilty for allowing him to stay home the day before. I had thought it was a nice treat for him, but maybe I had given him the wrong message and now he thought he could skip school whenever he wanted to.

'Come on, son, let's go.' JP eventually managed to prise him off my legs.

Harry bent down and gave Robyn a kiss before JP led him out to his car, his head hung as though he had the weight of the world on his young shoulders.

I felt so upset for the rest of the morning as I moved around tidying up the kitchen after breakfast. I carried a basket of laundry into the utility room and began loading it into the machine. I knew all kids had off-days, but it was so unlike Harry. I needed to be more attentive to him, we had all be so focused on Robyn that we had neglected him. Sometimes being a parent felt like you needed to be a chef, taxi driver, nurse, counselling service, acrobatic juggler and a professional mind reader all rolled into one. And even if you managed to pull all of that off, you would still get it wrong.

25

JP and I sat at the kitchen table as we both helped Robyn to twist pipe cleaners together.

'That's a great snowman,' I said.

'It's-snot sshnowman, it's ola bear,' she corrected. Her speech was becoming increasingly slurred and I found myself straining to make out the words.

'Of course it's a polar bear – silly me!'

Things were fraught between JP and me, but for Robyn's sake, I was glad we had been putting on a united front and pretending that everything was fine whenever she was around. We would sit, one on either side of her, and help her to peel back a sticker or to glue pieces of paper together. JP was still angry that I wouldn't agree to the treatment in Arizona, however we both knew we needed to be able to put our differences aside whenever Robyn was around, but there was no denying that his JustGiving page was the huge elephant in the room. I was keeping an eye on the fundraising page, which was teetering dangerously close to the target of €300,000 and it felt like time was ticking on a bomb. Although I would never admit it to JP, sometimes when I looked at her, I questioned whether I was doing the right thing at all. Was I making the correct decision for her? But then I thought of the science and the opinions of her medical team. I remembered the fear in her eyes every time she had to go to the hospital and knew that I couldn't put her through all of that again. I knew I was doing the right thing by Robyn, but yet I couldn't help but wonder, *what if…*

'I'd better go collect Harry,' JP said, looking at the clock after a while.

While he was gone, I tucked Robyn up in bed for her nap. I came back downstairs and began chopping apples to make a purée for her.

Less than thirty minutes later, I heard the front door slam shut and I silenced the blender. 'How was your day, sweetheart?' I called out to Harry. 'I'm in the kitchen.'

He appeared a moment later and I knew as soon as I saw him that something was up. His little face was red, and his eyes swollen with tears. Although Harry hadn't mentioned Robyn's cancer since our conversation in the car, he did seem to be quite unsettled lately. His tears going to school that morning – something which had never happened before – didn't sit well with me. I wasn't sure if it was his way of reacting to the news and he just wasn't able to verbalise it. Or could he sense that there was more that we weren't telling him? Maybe he understood more than we were giving him credit for. I didn't want to push it with him either, in case he wasn't ready yet for that conversation. Perhaps he needed to come to the realisation in his own time. I exhaled heavily. It was so hard to know the right thing to say or do – there was no parenting manual for what we were going through.

'Bad,' he replied.

I looked at JP in bewilderment.

'Hey, what's happened?' I said, bending down to him on my hunkers.

He buried his face into my shoulder and began to sob.

'Something happened in school today,' JP began. 'Ms O'Mara asked to have a word with me when I picked him up.'

My heart fell. It had been on my list to call Ms O'Mara to talk about my concerns for Harry, but I just hadn't got around to it.

'What is it, Harry? What happened?' I asked, but he wouldn't meet my eyes and began to sob harder.

'Apparently Harry hit another boy in the class today,' JP said. 'Some boy called Jamie O'Connor?'

'What?' I was shocked; it was so out of character for him. He wasn't an aggressive boy. But then I remembered the incident where he had tackled Jamie right here in our living room. I had been stunned by that outburst. Maybe there was something more going on here... 'Did you do that, Harry?' I asked.

He pulled his head out from my shoulder, looked up at me and nodded fearfully.

'But why would you do that?'

'He told everyone not to play with me.'

I was taken aback. 'Why did he do that?'

'Because Robyn is sick, and he said I might spread the germs and that everyone was going to die if they played with me. I didn't mean to hit him, but I got really mad and I couldn't help it. Then he ran off and told teacher on me.'

I felt white-hot fury build inside me, but I needed to stay calm for Harry's sake.

'I'm sorry, Mammy,' he added as he began to sob again.

'Well, you did the right thing if you ask me,' JP said, butting in.

'JP!' I swung around to him.

'What?'

'You can't tell a child it's okay to hit someone!'

'Well, if this Jamie O'Connor thinks it's okay to spread lies around school maybe a punch is exactly what the little shit needs.'

Harry looked shocked by his dad's use of bad language.

'Tone it down,' I said to him. 'This isn't helping, and you'll wake Robyn.'

Then I turned back to Harry. 'Look, what Jamie said is wrong. Cancer isn't caused by germs – you can't catch it off other people. Robyn can't make other people sick; do you understand what I'm saying?'

'Yes, Mam.'

'Is this why you didn't want to go to school yesterday and today?'

He nodded. 'He keeps telling everyone not to let me have a loan of their colours or not to touch me.'

'Why didn't you say something, Harry?'

'Because I didn't want to make you sadder, Mam.'

A wave of guilt upended me. I should have realised what was going on sooner, my intuition should have told me that something had happened to him in school.

'Oh, Harry, you poor thing. He shouldn't be saying things like that, no wonder you lost your temper. I'll go into Ms O'Mara tomorrow and have a word.' I wrapped my arms around my son and in my head, for the millionth time, cursed stupid, bloody cancer and the havoc it was wreaking on all our lives.

Just then my phone rang, I straightened up and walked over to pick it up off the table. I saw that it was Jamie O'Connor's mother, Belinda. *She doesn't hang around*, I thought grimly. I knew where this conversation was going.

'It's the boy's mother,' I mouthed at JP before hitting the answer button.

'Belinda?' I said, answering the call.

'Hi, Sarah, I guess you probably know why I'm calling – Ms O'Mara said she would have a word.'

'Yes,' I said. 'She did.'

'Harry gave Jamie a black eye today in school...'

'Yes, I believe there was an altercation.'

'I'm sure we're both on the same page when I say nine-year-olds shouldn't be punching one another, Sarah. I know you have a lot on your plate right now, but I can't let my child be bullied, no matter how much I feel sorry for you...'

I didn't want her patronising sympathy.

'I'm sure you understand,' she continued. 'If the situation was reversed, you'd feel exactly the same—'

'Did Jamie tell you that he told the other children not to play with Harry or share their crayons with him in case they all caught the germs he is carrying from his sister's *contagious* brain tumour and they all got cancer too?'

She gasped. I could almost hear her choking on my words. 'I-I really don't think Jamie would say something like that, Sarah—'

'Are you calling Harry a liar?'

'N-no, of course I'm not,' she stuttered.

'Good!' I said.

'I'll talk to him, Sarah – I'm sure there are wires crossed somewhere...'

'Great, and maybe you could explain to your child that cancer isn't a contagious disease while you're at it.' Then I hung up.

My heart was racing.

I turned around to see JP and Harry were both staring at me open-mouthed. It was so unlike me to be confrontational, but it was as if this tumour had invaded me too and turned me into somebody I didn't recognise. I was no longer fearful of things that would have sent me into a flap a couple of months ago, probably because the very worst thing that could happen was happening. Robyn's cancer had unleashed something wild and furious inside me and I couldn't rein it in. I didn't care what people thought of me, the only thing that mattered was protecting my family.

'Did I really just do that?' I asked, shaking my head.

JP came over and high-fived me. 'The stupid cow deserved it.'

Harry looked from me to his dad in confusion, wondering why we were behaving like this.

I started to laugh then, the giggles kept coming, bubbling up inside me and they wouldn't stop. I felt manic. Hysterical. The laughter frothed over until tears streamed down my face and I wasn't sure if they were happy or sad tears.

HARRY

I didn't want to go to stupid school today, but Mam made me go. I wanted to stay at home with Robyn snuggled up on the sofa like we did the day before and watch Frozen *again because that's her favourite movie. Even though it's for girls, it's not too bad. Robyn can't really do much stuff any more but we can still watch the TV together and I like that. The reason that I didn't want to go to school is because Jamie O'Connor keeps being mean to me. In the yard at break time he tolded the whole class not to play with me or they would get the cancer germs too. Then I got the white dots in my eyes again because he keeps doing it and this time I couldn't help it, I boxed him, and his glasses broke, then I got in big trouble and was sent to the principal's office and everybody knows you only go there when you are in REALLY BIG TROUBLE. I was really, really scared. Mrs Maloney the principal said she had to speak to my parents because children are not allowed to hit one another in school. I was so worried when Dad collected me and Ms O'Mara tolded him what I done, but when I told Mam and Dad the truth, they didn't get cross with me, which was really strange. Then Dad said Mrs O'Connor was a stupid cow and then Mam started laughing and she wouldn't stop, even though she always tells me it's not nice to call people names. It was so weird because she was crying too and I didn't know you could laugh and cry at the same time, but that's what Mam was doing.*

26

We were running along the sand on Malahide beach towards the water's edge. I was chasing after Robyn, her legs moving gracefully through the air as she plunged into the Irish Sea. She squealed as the cool water rushed around her ankles. She turned around to me and grinned.

'Come on, Mammy,' she called. Her head was tilted back towards the sky and sunlight hit the apples of her cheeks.

'Okay, I'm coming, sweetheart.'

I ran in after her and screamed with shock from the chill of the water against my skin.

Robyn was laughing at me and she reached out her hand to take mine. I stretched to take her small hand in my own, but I couldn't find it. I was searching for her hand, but there was nothing there.

I woke with a start with my palm searching the bed until it landed on her small body sleeping beside me, clutching onto Mr Bunny. And then I remembered my cruel reality and my heart hit the floor.

Whenever I did manage to sleep, I had a blissful few seconds when I first woke where I would forget. In those seconds, Robyn wasn't sick. I could breathe, I could dream of the future, but then I would remember, and reality slammed into me all over again just like it did on the very first day in that tiny white hospital room and it broke me afresh all over again. There was always a trade-off – the price for those few seconds of ecstasy between sleep and wakefulness was at the expense of remembering.

The dream wouldn't leave me for the rest of the morning as I tidied up the kitchen and loaded the washing machine. It had seemed so real. Her smile. Her legs working properly once again. I could still feel the coolness of the water against my skin, the tangle of brown seaweed between my feet. Robyn had seemed so light, so carefree. So happy. The way she used to before our lives had descended into this maelstrom.

The doorbell went and pulled me back to reality. I went out to the hall and when I answered it, I saw that my mother-in-law, Joan, was standing on the doorstep.

'Sarah,' she said curtly, as I pulled back the door.

'Come in, Joan,' I said. She and Richard had been calling to the house a lot since Robyn had got her diagnosis, but today I saw that she was alone. Robyn was upstairs having a nap and Harry was at school, so I felt bad that this would be a wasted trip.

'Can I get you a tea or coffee?' I offered as she made her way into the living room and sat down neatly on the sofa, keeping her handbag clasped upon her knees.

She shook her head. 'No, thank you, I won't be staying long.' There was a caustic edge to her tone, and I had a feeling that this was more than just a social call. 'Where's Robyn?'

'Upstairs having a nap. She gets tired so easily these days,' I sighed.

Joan nodded. She lifted the silver-framed photo of a pudgy-cheeked Robyn on her christening day that sat on the coffee table beside her up into her hands. She brought it towards her face and I saw tears glistening in her eyes as she studied it. 'I still can't believe it...' she whispered.

Joan's initial reaction to Robyn's diagnosis was disbelief, and anguish had followed soon after. Although we had never been particularly close, I knew this was devastating for her. She adored Robyn; after losing her only daughter tragically as a child, when Robyn was born, she had been overjoyed to have a granddaughter. She used to buy her the most ridiculous pink, frilly dresses with matching hair-bows that JP and I would dutifully dress her in whenever we were visiting but would remove straight away as soon as we had left. I knew it wasn't just JP and I who were hurting right now. This was hard on so many people, the repercussions of what we were dealing with spread like ripples across a pond. So many people loved her.

'Me neither,' I admitted.

'Look, Sarah, the reason I called here today is because I want to talk to you about the clinic in America...' she began.

I felt my heart stop. 'I see... did JP put you up to coming here?'

She shook her head. 'Of course not, but he said that you're not in agreement with him... and I honestly couldn't believe what he was telling me! Is it true, Sarah?'

'If you mean that I won't let JP take her there for the treatment then, yes, it is true.' As the money he had raised climbed ever higher, JP and I had been arguing about it constantly.

She placed the photo back down onto the table. 'I know this isn't a nice situation for anyone, but I can't understand why you wouldn't take any chance you get to save her! Miracles happen all over the world every day, but you have to grab on to them – you have to believe and be open to them.'

'The treatment doesn't bloody work!' I snapped. I was tired and frustrated by having to explain myself. Why was nobody listening to me? 'JP isn't telling you the full story! Despite all their claims, the doctors there still haven't saved one child!'

'Calm down, Sarah, we're all on the same side here – we just want what's best for Robyn.'

I nodded. 'That's all I want too, Joan.'

'Well then, why on earth are you being so difficult?'

'Why can't you see that I'm doing this out of love for her? You're a mother too, Joan, and you also know the pain of losing a child.'

'I do. That's why I can't understand any of this.' She shook her head. 'If I could have had a chance to save my Ellen, no matter how small, I'd have taken it with both hands.'

'But what kind of a mother would I be if I ripped her away from her home, the one place where she feels safe and loved and sent her off to endure god only knows what kind of treatment in a strange country?'

'Please, Sarah, as Robyn's grandmother, I'm begging you – I've already lost a child, I can't bear to lose her too...' Her voice choked, and tears shone in her eyes.

'And you think I can? Do you think this is easy for me? Do you know how it feels to look into her eyes and see fear and not be able to do anything to help her? I'm telling you, if I believed there was something, *anything,* that would cure her, I'd do it in a heartbeat, but I won't send her off to the other side of the world like some kind of lab rat, I won't do it to her.' Did she honestly think that I was okay with all of this, that I would just leave Robyn to die if there was a realistic treatment option available? Did my mother-in-law know me at all? Could she really think so lowly of me?

'I know the last five months haven't been easy for you. I know John-Paul has made mistakes, but please just listen to what he is saying – give Robyn a chance to beat this disease.'

'If JP can show me a child who has beaten this thing, I'll be the first in line, but until then Robyn is staying at home where she belongs!'

'Why on earth won't you take this lifeline to save her – no matter how small the chances are – it's still a chance more than she has right now!'

It was the same question that kept me awake during the long hours of the night when the street lights cast shadows across my ceiling. It seemed nobody else agreed with me and it made me doubt my own judgement. Was I making the right choice? Whenever I looked across at Robyn's face, while she slept curled up beside me, her small chest rising and falling in slow, even beats, I knew I had to get this right. She was relying on me. She trusted me to protect her. But what if I was standing in the way of saving her life?

'How can you just give up on your own daughter?' Joan demanded.

Suddenly I was consumed with fury. Her words had ripped me open and scooped me out until there was nothing left any more. It was clear that no matter what I said or what arguments I put forward that I wasn't going to able to reason with her. I had had enough. I was so tired; I was broken and defeated and didn't have the energy to pour into fighting any more. I stood up, indicating that I was finished with this conversation.

She stood up too, still clutching her handbag. She began heading towards the door before stopping and turning back to face me. Her eyes burned into mine.

'What kind of a mother just leaves her child to die?' she said, shaking her head sadly at me.

27

JP was upstairs with Harry and Robyn reading them a bedtime story, while I was downstairs tidying up the playroom after the mess of the day. As I knelt amongst the discarded pieces of a jigsaw, blocks of Lego and the scattered pieces of a tea set, I couldn't help but feel a strange sense of unease. JP's behaviour since he had arrived that evening was baffling me. Instead of coming through the door with anger burning in his eyes as had been his way for the last few weeks, he had actually greeted me with a smile on his face, which in itself was unsettling because it had been a long time since he had smiled at me. He had swung Harry around and lifted Robyn up into the air until her face spread into a grin. Our recent acrimony seemed to have been forgotten.

Although I hated to be cynical, given our different stances about the clinic in Arizona, I couldn't help but feel wary. It was only days since his mother had come and pleaded with me to let JP take Robyn to the US. I had called him afterwards and we had had a huge argument. He denied knowing that Joan was going to call over, but I didn't believe a word that came out of his mouth any more and warned him never to send his mother round to do his bidding again. After I had hung up, I had called Fiona to tell her what had happened. She had come straight over with a bottle of wine and as we had sat up drinking it, I questioned my decision for the millionth time. What if I was wrong? It seemed the whole world was on JP's side. But I knew deep down that I was doing this out of love for Robyn.

I heard his footsteps descending the stairs now and I felt my heart start to beat faster, although I wasn't quite sure why.

'I have some news,' he began, as he rounded the playroom doorway. His voice was tentative, but there was an urgency behind it that he just couldn't mask. 'I wanted to wait until the kids were in bed,' he added. I noticed that he wasn't meeting my eye.

Here it was. I had had a feeling in my bones that there was something he wanted to say, something potentially explosive. He had been treading delicately as if trying to avoid buried landmines ever since he had arrived.

'Oh yeah?' I felt my chest tighten and I picked myself up from the floor.

'Well, it's good news actually...' I watched as he took a deep breath inwards. 'The clinic has accepted Robyn on to their treatment programme.'

'Woah, JP.' I raised my palms to slow him down. 'I've already told you that I'm not sending her there.'

'But I have the money almost raised, I reckon we should hit the target by tomorrow if the donations keep coming in the way they have been and now she has a place on their programme – what else could you possibly want?'

I had been checking his JustGiving page too and I knew he was right. Now the only obstacle in his way was me. He had obviously thought that once he had everything lined up, I would finally give in, like I had with the radiotherapy, but even if it cost nothing, I still wouldn't consent to Robyn travelling halfway across the world to subject her to some dubious treatment.

'Of course they've accepted her!' I snapped. 'They just want your money and they don't care where it comes from, they'd accept a dog off the street if you'd pay them for it!'

'Come on, Sarah,' he begged, clasping his palms together as if in prayer. 'I have the money – we can actually do this – we can get on a plane and get more time with our daughter. Don't overthink it, just say yes.'

'It's not about the money, JP – it was never about the money.' I shook my head, feeling my exasperation grow with every word that left his mouth. He just wasn't listening to me. It was as though he couldn't hear – or perhaps didn't want to hear – what I had been saying. 'It's about what's best for Robyn. I told you already, I won't do it – there's no way I'm putting her on a plane to be subjected to some unproven treatment, how can you even think it's an option?'

'How can you think it's not?' he blazed. His earlier smiley demeanour was rapidly slipping away. 'I just don't get you.' He shook his head.

'What about her quality of life for the time she has left? Is that not important to you?'

'She can't walk, she can barely talk – where is the quality of life in that?'

'I just want what's best for Robyn. I'm sorry, JP, I can't do it to her – it's too big a risk and, besides, she hates hospitals.'

'So, you think that leaving her to die is what's best for her?' he burst out. 'You're not going to fight for her?'

'When are you going to realise that it's false hope? Dr Sharma would have told us if there was any realistic chance of saving her!'

I thought of what he said to us at our last appointment: 'Take her home and cherish the time you have left together.'

'Doctors get it wrong all the time. Dr Sharma is old-school and narrow-minded. Just because it's a relatively new treatment doesn't mean it isn't worth pursuing. Doctors from around the world are travelling to the clinic to learn more – they wouldn't do that if they weren't impressed by the results the doctors are achieving there.'

'You're deluding yourself; you only have to read the stories of the other children they have treated there – it doesn't work, JP! Robyn doesn't need any more hospitals; she just needs to be at home surrounded by the people who love her.'

'I don't understand you, Sarah. The whole country is behind me, I'm getting wishes from people I don't even know, there are people from all over the place saying prayers and novenas for me. If everyone else can see this is the right thing to do – people who don't even know our daughter – how can you, as her mother, not see it?'

'I am doing it out of love.'

'Give her a chance, Sarah, I'm begging you, please, even if it's miniscule, it's still a chance – it's more than we've got right now. Remember the month Harry was conceived, the clinic told us that the transfer was unlikely to be successful and we weren't going to risk it, but then we thought, let's just try... and lo and behold, just when we had given up hope, we discovered you were pregnant. Miracles happen when you least expect them. Give her a chance. Don't make her pay for what's happened between us.'

It was as if someone had placed a hot poker on my skin and now white rage was burning through my body. He actually thought that the decision not to let Robyn go to Arizona was my way of trying to get revenge on him. Could he be any more self-obsessed?

'You think that's what this is about? You think I'm doing this to get back at you?'

'Well, aren't you?'

I shook my head at his audacity. 'That's low, even coming from you. I would never, ever play roulette with my daughter's life just to get back at you. You might have broken my heart, but you didn't break me, JP! I love that child beyond anything in this world.'

How could he think like that? Surely, he knew me well enough to know that from the moment my children had been born, they had been my sun, moon and stars. Every breath I took was for them.

'Do you remember the day Robyn was born?' His tone was softer now and I wondered where he was leading me.

'Of course I do!' I said, feeling irritated by his change of tack.

'Well, when she was placed into my arms that day, she looked up at me with inky dark eyes, blinking at me full of curiosity. Those eyes – I'll never forget them – she looked like an old soul, as though she had been here before, and as I held my tiny miracle daughter, I made a promise to her, Sarah. I swore I would do everything in my power to protect her. So, if you're not going to fight for her, then I have to do it.'

'JP, sometimes loving someone means letting them go,' I whispered, shaking my head sadly.

'Not in my book it doesn't. I will do whatever it takes to save her. I will travel across the world – nothing is going to stop me – not money, not doctors, not even you. I'm not going to rest until my daughter is on that plane to the States.'

28

JP was standing opposite me and the ground was separating along a fault line between us, Robyn was stuck in the middle and she was going to fall in between the cracks unless one of us pulled her across to our side. The gap was growing, and we needed to act quickly, but my arms wouldn't work as I tried to pull her back. 'You can save her, Sarah – if you want to,' JP was saying. 'Just take the step.' But I was paralysed. 'Just take the step,' he repeated.

I woke up sweating. The words were ringing in my ears. *Just take the step.* But no, I couldn't... How could I do it to her? And yet everyone else seemed to think I was crazy. That I couldn't possibly love her if I wasn't willing to at least try the treatment in Arizona. But they only had JP's version of events, nobody seemed willing to hear the truth that nothing was going to save our precious child.

The dream played on my mind for the rest of the morning. *Just take the step,* echoed through my brain.

'You look exhausted,' Fiona said later that morning as she came through the door with bracelets jangling on her arm. It was as if she couldn't decide which one to wear in the morning so she threw the lot on so none of them would feel left out. 'Did you not sleep again?'

'I spend so long lying awake at night wondering how I'm going to get through all of this and then, when I eventually do sleep, I'm tormented by nightmares. So, I don't know which is better – to lie awake and think about my real nightmare or be haunted by imaginary ones.'

She followed me into the kitchen where Robyn was sitting at the table.

'Come up and see your Auntie Fi,' she said, lifting Robyn up. 'I brought some glitter and I thought we might make a snow globe today, what do you reckon?'

Robyn did her best to nod her head.

We lined up bottles of food colourings for her to choose one to dilute through the water. She used her right hand to point to the yellow. She pointed to a figurine of Olaf from *Frozen* that Fiona had brought too that we were going to stick inside the lid of an old jam jar and then we were going to fill it with the coloured water mixed with glitter.

I thought of last night's nightmare again and felt a shiver. Robyn trusted me to get this right, I had to make the right decision.

Suddenly Fiona upended the pot of glitter all over my head and I was brought back to the moment as it rained down all around us, some of it landing like freckles upon Robyn's face. Robyn smiled but only the right side of her mouth moved now.

'Let's get a selfie,' Fiona said. She angled her phone and we stuck our glitter-covered heads in beside Robyn's. Fiona pouted with duck-lips while Robyn and I grinned at the camera. All these little memories were so precious. How I wished I could take them from my head and store them in a glass box to keep them safe.

Just then the doorbell rang, and I went to answer it. I pulled back the door to see the postman.

'I need you to sign for this,' he said, handing me a plush cream envelope.

I signed my name where he indicated, mildly curious about what it might contain, and shut the door after him. I tore my index finger down beneath the gummed seal and unfolded the letter printed on thick cream paper inside. The logo at the top read:

Simon Jones & Company Solicitors

My heart stopped as I read it. I stood in the hallway stunned. At first, I thought it must be some kind of mistake, that the letter had been sent to the wrong person. I was about to run after the postman and tell him that there had been a mix-up, but when I checked it once more to make sure my eyes weren't playing tricks on me, it was definitely my name that was at the top of it. Words flew up at me from the page: 'summons', 'court', 'respondent'. My legs were weak, and I knew they might give way. I had to place my hand on the bannister to steady myself. I felt sick to the pit of my stomach.

'Fiona?' I called.

'What is it? What's wrong?' she said, joining me in the hall.

'This is insane. How *dare* he?' The words tumbled out of my mouth. 'JP – he's filed legal proceedings – he wants to take me to court to force me to take Robyn to Arizona for the treatment.'

'What the hell?' she said, grabbing the piece of paper from my hands and reading it. She slapped it down against her thigh when she had finished. 'He's crazy! What on earth is he thinking? Initiating a court case at a time like this? This is the last thing either of you need!'

'I just can't believe he would do this,' I said, shaking my head. 'I mean I knew he wasn't going to back down easily, but I never thought he would resort to taking me to court.' I was incredulous that he could even think of doing something like this.

'You've got to fight him, there's no way a judge would ever agree with him!'

My head was spinning, and I was struggling to process what this meant for us.

We went back into the kitchen and sat down at the table. I noticed Robyn was watching us, and I could see worry shading her eyes. I knew she was wondering what was going on. The guilt crawled its way inside me, sludging through my body. I needed to keep calm in front of her. Did I want her last days tainted with an upset mother?

Fiona and I looked at one another and we both fell quiet.

What the hell was going to happen now? Why would he do this? Was I meant to put time and energy into finding a solicitor to represent me? Time was my most precious commodity, but it was rapidly running out on me and I didn't want to have to use what little I had left in that way. And what if the judge agreed with him, what then? I would have no choice but do it to my little girl.

I was scared. I didn't want to be dragged into a legal battle, but as Robyn's mother, I knew had to fight JP every step of the way to protect her. My world was spinning out of control and I didn't know how to make it stop. I was already climbing the biggest mountain by facing the death of my daughter, but now it seemed there were more mountains to be climbed and I was tired, I couldn't see how I would ever surmount them.

* * *

Later that day, JP collected Harry from school and when I saw his car pull up in the driveway, I went out to meet them clutching the letter tightly. It was a warm June day, but I still shivered. I felt cold all the time lately. I told Harry to go inside and I'd follow him in in a minute. I didn't want him to hear what I was about to say.

'Okay, Mam,' he sang. Over the last few days, I was relieved that Harry seemed to be much happier in himself going to school since the incident with Jamie O'Connor had been dealt with. The teacher had spoken to the class and educated them on the facts about cancer. Jamie hadn't mentioned Robyn's cancer again and whatever Belinda had said to her son had obviously worked.

'What the hell are you playing at?' I said, waving the letter at JP as soon as Harry had closed the door behind him. I now understood what people meant when they said they were seeing red because in that moment as the blood pounded through my veins and pulsed in my ears, it was the only colour I could see.

Instantly, JP looked sheepish. 'I'm sorry, Sarah, I don't want to go down the legal route any more than you do – but I have to fight for her. We have the funds raised – we're ready to go.'

I shook my head. 'I never thought you would stoop so low. Don't you think we've enough on our plate right now without bringing solicitors and judges into it too?'

'We're being tossed a lifeline, why won't you take it?' he begged. 'I know you love those kids just as much as I do so I don't get why this is difficult for you. We owe it to her to at least try!'

'I won't consent to her being taken to the US, JP. You heard the prognosis the same as I did, she is going to die – no matter what we do – it's out of our hands. She's too weak – the flight alone would be too much for her!'

'You're leaving me with no choice, Sarah!' he threatened. 'Why can't you see it's our only hope?'

'Why can't you see that it won't work. We're losing her, JP, and you need to accept it.' Why didn't he get this? He was hell-bent on trying to save her, I was beginning to wonder if it was some kind of misplaced attempt to make up for his sister's death all those years ago, but he was trying to regain control of something that was uncontrollable.

'I will never, *ever* accept it, Sarah!' He stormed down the driveway before turning back to me. 'How can you possibly say you love her if you won't fight to save her?' Then he climbed into his car, slammed the door behind him and reversed out of the driveway.

29

I pulled the car up outside an elegant three-story-over-basement Georgian townhouse in leafy Ballsbridge where the offices of Geraldine Horan, who was now apparently engaged as my solicitor, were located. I didn't have my own solicitor, so Linda had suggested that I contact a woman she knew from her tennis club and had arranged the meeting for me to discuss it all. As my eyes took in the imposing red-bricked building with clematis bursting from the façade, I couldn't help but shudder – if this was where Geraldine had chosen to locate her practice, I hated to think what her fees might be.

I climbed the granite steps leading to the front door and walked over thick wool carpet as I made my way into the reception area. After a few minutes waiting, I was shown into her office.

I looked around the room where heavy leather-bound tomes sat in an antique mahogany case and certificates calligraphed in Latin decorated the walls. Files were piled up on the desk before me and even on the floor around the desk like miniature tower blocks.

As I sat down in the chair where Geraldine had told me to

take a seat, I felt shell-shocked. How had I ended up here? What had we become? Was this really my life? It felt like I was living in a movie with a cast of actors.

After JP had left us, I thought that his affair was the worst thing he could ever do to me, but this betrayal was so much worse. I hated that this was stealing precious time both mentally and physically from me. I didn't want to engage in fighting, I just wanted to spend as much time as possible with my daughter.

'Do you understand me, Sarah?' Geraldine was saying as she twiddled her pen between her fingers.

I nodded even though I hadn't heard a word she said. She was talking to me in alien legal terms. She threw out words like 'applicant', 'respondent', 'proceedings', 'high court' with wild abandon, forgetting that this was my life, *my daughter*, we were fighting over.

'The burden of proof will fall with JP's team and if a judge finds that it is in Robyn's best interest to receive this treatment and that there is a significant chance she can beat it, he or she may rule in favour of JP. This case all hinges on his team's medical evidence.'

'Dr Sharma said that nobody has ever beaten it, not anywhere in the world. It doesn't get more clear-cut than that.'

'Okay, Sarah, that is good.' She began to write something in her notebook before pausing as she realised her mistake. 'I mean, it's not good for you or your daughter obviously... but it's good for our case...' She looked mildly embarrassed.

I groaned internally. It all boiled down to legal point-scoring, nobody cared about the terminally ill child at the heart of it all.

She continued, 'We will need a report from Robyn's doctor... this... em... Dr Sharma you mentioned. Do you think he would be willing to testify for us as an expert medical witness?'

'I – eh – I'm not sure...' I admitted. I thought of Dr Sharma busy on the ward saving lives. He wouldn't want to be dragged into this mess. Even I didn't want to be dragged into this mess.

'JP will need to have expert medical witnesses too and if the treatment is as experimental as you describe, then finding a credible one will be his biggest challenge,' she continued. 'Of course, the judge may request an independent witness also, to make a recommendation to the court.'

I nodded and made monosyllabic replies as required. I just wanted to run away. I would have rather stuck my head under a duvet and never come out again than deal with all of it, but to give her credit, Geraldine Horan was proving efficient and to the point.

'If we can get evidence from Dr Sharma supporting our position then we will have a really strong case.'

'And if we don't?'

She paused. 'Let's just cross that bridge when we come to it, Sarah...'

I nodded because I didn't want to let my mind go there either; the scenario that JP might win this and force me to allow Robyn to travel to the States was unbearable – it would rip what little was left of our family apart.

'It's also worth bearing in mind that a case like this will naturally attract a lot of media attention. Although it will be held *in camera* as Robyn is a minor, there will be media coverage. This type of case, especially when it is between two parents, will be fodder for journalists, so you need to be prepared for the impact of that on your life.'

I gulped. Although JP had already stoked the media fire with his television appearance, I hadn't even considered that our story might be inked across the tabloids too. I hated the thought of our innermost battles being pored over by the press. Would people think I was an uncaring, or worse still, a neglectful mother?

'Now, Sarah,' Geraldine cleared her throat before continuing, 'we also have to discuss the matter of costs, as you know legal battles can be expensive and in a case like this...' she paused, 'if the judge rules against you... your costs could be substantial. Is this something you are prepared for?'

I shook my head in disbelief at the injustice of it all. 'But I didn't ask for any of this!' I cried. 'JP started it all!' Anger sparked within me. This seemed so wrong. Where the hell was I supposed to get that kind of money? I didn't have savings. I knew Fiona would help me out if I asked, but it wasn't fair to drag her into this. And it wasn't just the money, it was the time he was stealing from me too. This meeting was only just the beginning, there would be more meetings, and then the court hearing itself. I had to stop my head reminding me that every hour spent apart from Robyn was one less spent with her and it was all JP's fault.

'Unfair though it may seem, unfortunately it is a harsh reality and one that you must be aware of. If you wish to defend your choice to abstain from the treatment in the US that JP wishes to pursue, then I'm afraid you don't have any other option.'

I drove home in a daze. In the distance, sunlight glinted off the Spire as the car stopped and started in the city-centre traffic. When I reached the house, Fiona, who had been staying with Robyn and Harry for the afternoon, opened the front door to me and wordlessly I trudged into the kitchen. I felt defeated before the battle had even begun.

'Well? How did it go?' she asked.

'Awful, there were so many things I didn't realise. If I lose, as well as subjecting Robyn to the treatment, I could have to pay JP's legal costs as well as my own. Where would I even get that kind of money?'

'But that's hardly fair!'

'Geraldine said that's the risk I run if I want to defend myself.'

'Well, you have to do it,' she stated matter-of-factly.

'Every time I doubt myself and wonder if I'm the one who's got it wrong, I think of Robyn's face whenever she had to have a cannula put in or all the times that she was so sick after her radiotherapy and I know I can't put her through any more. I have to fight for her, Fiona, she's been through enough, I cannot put her on that plane...'

'Come on,' Fiona said, opening the fridge and taking out a bottle of white wine. 'I think you could use this.'

'I probably shouldn't even drink, I'll just end up crying.'

'Well, maybe that's what you need.'

She went to the drawer and found a corkscrew. Even though it was only five o'clock, I didn't protest as she opened the bottle and poured two large glasses.

'I just don't know how I ended up here,' I said, shaking my head. 'How did I go from having everything I ever wanted – a husband and two beautiful children – how the hell did I go from having a happy family – because we were happy, Fiona – no matter what JP says, we *were* happy – to losing everything?'

She placed her hand over mine. We both knew she had no words that could console me. 'I've no answer for that except that life is cruel, but you're strong, Sarah. You're much stronger than you give yourself credit for.'

I shook my head and took a sip of my wine. 'I'm not though – people say that to me all the time, the nurses in the hospital, Linda and Mel, my neighbours or people I bump into in the supermarket, but they don't really know what I'm like inside here.' I jabbed a finger at my chest. 'I'm so scared, Fiona, I'm terrified. I'm afraid of the court case, I'm afraid of what will happen to Robyn, but most of all I'm so scared for the future without her. You know back when we were trying to conceive, I always thought my biggest challenge was to get pregnant. I thought once that happened, I could relax, but then when I discovered I was pregnant with Harry, I realised that I was petrified of something going wrong and all I wanted was to get through the pregnancy and have my baby arrive safely. I was sure all my worries would be over once my baby was here and then Harry was born and as soon as that newborn is placed into your arms, it's like you've just opened up a door leading to a chasm of unfathomable depths which is full of new fears and you realise then that your real worries are only just beginning. It's like you've just exposed your Achilles heel to the world because you feel so vulnerable. And suddenly there are so many more sad stories on the TV because you've opened your eyes up to just how fragile life is because how could you possibly survive if anything should happen to this tiny new person who is now your whole heart? And now it's happened to me – my biggest fears will be realised – my daughter is going to die, but I'm still frightened. I'm a wimp. I just can't imagine my life without her in it.' I shook my head as if it would reorder the chaos inside it, rejig my worries and give me clarity. 'Do you know something? Sometimes when I look at her, I can see the fear in her eyes that she can't voice and it gets me right here.' I thumped my fist against my solar plexus.

'Oh, Sarah,' Fiona gasped.

'I'm so tired, Fiona,' I sighed. 'I'm frightened and tired.'

Fiona placed her hand over mine on the table. 'I believe in you, you're not alone. I will support you every step of the way. You need to fight for her, Sarah, this is where you need to dig deep. And even if the whole world seems to be against you – you're her mother and you know her better than anyone.'

30

June sunlight warmed my face and the smell of the hops from the Guinness brewery across the Liffey filled my nostrils as I climbed the steps of the court. The hum of hushed chatter murmured around as I followed Geraldine into the courtroom. I saw JP standing, emboldened by his legal team, while I took a seat beside Geraldine at our table. He was dressed in a navy-blue suit with a crisp white shirt beneath and sunglasses perched casually on top of his head. I noticed he was carrying a large file, making me immediately feel underprepared as I held onto my handbag which contained just my purse, phone and a few tatty hair bobbins. Although we were doing our best to put on a united front when we were with the children, his visits to the house in the days leading up to the hearing had become increasingly strained. I looked across to him – my eyes boring into him, begging him to stop all of this madness – but he wouldn't meet my gaze. He knew he could withdraw his application at any time, and we could walk away from this, but right now I resented him. The *in camera* restrictions meant only family members could attend and I noticed his parents, Joan and Richard, were sitting a few rows behind him. Fiona was staying at home to take care of Robyn, so it was just me on my own against the world, or so it felt.

I watched Geraldine move briskly and efficiently as she removed her papers from her tan leather briefcase before flicking it shut again in a swift move. She was wearing a plum-coloured power suit that gave her an air of business. She seemed calm and composed. She was always so unflappable, I wondered what it would take to ruffle her feathers?

I took out my phone to make sure it was silenced and saw I had messages from both Linda and Mel wishing me luck. I replied with a quick 'thank you' and then put my phone back in my bag.

'Are you okay?' Geraldine asked me. 'Remember the report from Dr Sharma is really strong – it will be very hard for JP's team to argue against it. They'll have to come up with something all-singing and all-dancing to beat it.'

I winced. She was so fired up to win this case and I was grateful for that – that's what I was paying her to do after all, but there were real people behind this, real people with real feelings and a little girl who wasn't going to survive. Geraldine had practically whooped when she had received the medical report from Dr Sharma and I knew to her it was like having a grenade stored in our arsenal. His report had been unequivocal and bleak in his outlook for Robyn. It had been hard to read his words, knowing it was my daughter he was talking about.

'Let's hope Judge Williams sees sense and dismisses this application entirely,' Geraldine continued with confidence. When I had heard it was a male judge, my heart had sunk. I had somehow hoped that a female judge, who might even be a mother herself, would have more sympathy for my case.

'And if he doesn't?' I asked, my eyes searching her face for answers. Geraldine never seemed to think of the alternatives.

'Well, then things are going to move up a gear, but let's not think about that just yet,' she said.

A clerk stood up and ordered, 'Silence in court. All rise,' and I saw Judge Williams entering the courtroom. I gulped. I had expected him to be wearing a wig, but his salt-and-pepper grey hair was neatly cropped, and he wore a simple black gown with white collar. If it weren't for the fact that he entered at the top of the courtroom, on a raised platform, I wouldn't have picked him out as the judge. He looked normal, like he could be my father or a man you would meet in the supermarket.

I followed what everybody else was doing and rose as he took his seat. I had never been in a courtroom before; everyone else around me seemed to know the protocol. It was all so formal. Geraldine had told me to address the judge as simply 'Judge' and only to speak when spoken to, but I was so terrified I was going to say or do something wrong.

'Here we go,' Geraldine whispered as the judge shuffled his papers in front of him as if we were about to watch a match kick-off or a movie in the cinema.

Oh God, I thought as my stomach somersaulted, wondering what lay ahead for us that morning.

'An application under the Guardianship of Infants Act in the matter of McIntyre v. McIntyre,' the clerk called out from the bench beneath Judge Williams.

The judge put on his reading glasses as he looked through the details of the case in front of him.

'I have read the application papers before me. Can the respondent's solicitor, Ms Horan, approach the bench, please?'

Geraldine coolly walked towards the top of the room. I held my breath. My hands grew clammy and my heart started to race. I wished I felt half as confident as she looked.

'The case before you today concerns four-year-old Robyn

McIntyre who is the daughter of Mr and Mrs McIntyre. The couple also has a nine-year-old son,' Geraldine explained.

'The couple is estranged, is this correct?' Judge Williams asked.

'Yes, Judge, Mr McIntyre left the family home a few months prior to Robyn's diagnosis,' Geraldine replied.

'My client is in daily contact with his children and remains a committed and loving father,' JP's solicitor interrupted.

Geraldine continued unperturbed. 'Robyn was diagnosed with a terminal brain tumour earlier this year. Unfortunately, it is both inoperable and incurable—'

'Objection,' JP's solicitor interrupted once more.

'Continue, Ms Horan,' Judge Williams ordered.

I shot a look over at JP's table, where he was clearly not pleased as he began furiously scribbling something on his notepad.

'The particular type of brain tumour that Mr and Mrs McIntyre's daughter has has a zero per cent survival rate – I reiterate, no child anywhere in the world has ever survived this type of cancer. As you can imagine, it is a devastating diagnosis for any parent to receive. Robyn's medical team in the Dublin children's hospital, headed by Dr Sharma, has always been adamant that she will not survive. We have filed an expert report from Dr Sharma in support of our position.'

Judge Williams riffled through the papers and began reading Dr Sharma's report. 'Dr Sharma cites irreversible progression?' he asked.

'That's correct, Judge,' Geraldine nodded. 'The applicant, Robyn's father, Mr John-Paul McIntyre, wishes to pursue treatment in the United States against the advice of Robyn's medical team in the Dublin children's hospital and also against the wishes of the child's mother, the respondent, Sarah McIntyre. The clinic

John-Paul wishes to use is trying an experimental and unproven regimen. The doctors in question have never submitted their procedures for peer review nor have they allowed the wider medical community to examine their research. At best, the treatment may buy Robyn more time, although this is debatable as she has previously responded poorly to radiotherapy, therefore it is highly unlikely. Again, I repeat, nobody, not in this clinic or elsewhere in the world, has *ever* survived this type of brain tumour. As well as significant side effects and the risks this experimental treatment would pose to such a sick child, Robyn is too weak to travel. My client wishes not to subject her daughter to an unproven regime where the prospect of cure still remains nil. It is ultimately not in Robyn McIntyre's best interests to pursue this treatment and we ask today in the first instance that the application be struck out.'

I exhaled slowly; Geraldine had made an articulate argument.

Judge Williams steepled his fingers together thoughtfully. I studied his face to try and read it, but it gave nothing away.

'And the applicant's solicitor, Mr O'Reilly, what do you have to say?'

'My client is Robyn's father,' JP's solicitor began. 'My client loves his daughter very much so you can imagine how devastating this diagnosis has been for him.'

My knuckles grew white gripping on to the railing in front of me. JP's solicitor was making it sound as though he was the only one suffering here.

'Robyn's medical team in the Dublin children's hospital have offered only palliative treatment, even though there is a treatment centre in Arizona that is seeing good results and is at the early stages of a cure. My client is seeking a court order compelling Sarah McIntyre to allow Robyn to travel to the US for curative treatment. Time is of the utmost importance as any delays in withholding consent will have dire consequences on her prospect of survival. We have included documentation from the clinic with their proposed treatment plan for Robyn and case studies of previous patients.'

'But it is my understanding from the testimony that Dr Sharma has provided that this type of tumour is incurable?' the judge argued.

'Dr Sharma has remained close-minded to the potential for life-saving treatment offered by the clinic in question simply because the doctors have eschewed established medical protocol. Although the clinic is having good outcomes with children internationally, there remains a bias from the medical community recognising the life-saving advances that these doctors are achieving—'

'Judge, with all due respect, they have not cured a single patient,' Geraldine interjected.

JP's solicitor continued unruffled. 'We argue that if there is a chance, no matter how small, of this clinic saving or even extending Robyn's lifespan, then it is in her best interests to try it. Judge, we are asking you to take a leap of faith and we respectfully request that the application be upheld here today.'

Judge Williams pushed his reading glasses up from the bridge of his nose, looked down at the papers before him and began scanning through them once again. The courtroom fell silent as he considered what he had been told and I found myself holding my breath. *He has to dismiss it*, I prayed. The evidence was there before in him in black and white.

Judge Williams eventually peered over the top of his glasses as he spoke to us. 'Although the applicant has provided detail of the proposed treatment, he has not provided evidence that this treatment is in the child's best interest. Application adjourned pending expert testimony from the applicant in support of his position. I also wish to appoint an independent medical witness to review this case and make a recommendation to the court. Due to the time-critical nature involved, the case is adjourned for seven days.'

I felt the air being sucked out of my lungs. The case wasn't over today like I had prayed, instead it was growing legs and I now had to endure another week of this stress and worry. It seemed the battle had only just begun.

31

That night, after I had tucked the children up in bed, I flopped down onto the sofa. My head was thumping and every bone in my body ached with pure exhaustion. I was deflated and defeated. I was half-watching the RTÉ News when the words 'In a landmark case set to grip the country...' caught my attention. I immediately reached for the remote and turned up the volume. I listened as they described the court hearing that had taken place earlier that day.

Although the media were not allowed to identify us, it was shocking to hear the most private details from our life being beamed into people's homes across Ireland. Even though Geraldine had warned me that there would be public interest in the case, I hadn't even considered that it would be featured on prime-time TV. To everyone else, this was a person in a faraway place that they would never meet, but this was *my* life being pawed over by all the media outlets.

In bed as I felt the shallow rise and fall of Robyn's chest underneath my palm, I couldn't help but worry. Who knew what kind of crackpot JP would find to testify that travelling to Arizona was the best option for Robyn? I had already learnt the hard way that he would stop at nothing in his quest. As I had been leaving the courtroom earlier, Geraldine had set up another meeting for the following morning to go through everything before our next court date. I just wished this could all be over.

The next morning, JP arrived to collect Harry for school, but he didn't even come into the house like he usually would. Instead, he stayed sitting in his car until I sent Harry out to him.

'Why isn't Dad coming in?' Harry asked me in puzzlement.

'You're running a bit late, so he doesn't really have time,' I said, thinking on the spot. 'Grab your coat and bag, pet.'

'No, I'm not, Mam,' he said, looking at the clock on the kitchen wall. 'What's going on? First, Dad moves out and he never came into our house any more, then he was coming back in and now he's not coming in again?'

'Of course your dad can come in, you know he's always welcome here.'

'But then why don't you tell him that?'

'Come on, Harry, we don't have time now, your dad is in a hurry. Just grab your stuff and head out to the car.'

'Fine,' he huffed, dragging his feet down the hallway.

I hated that we were reduced to this, but I couldn't even look at JP, let alone talk to him right now.

After Harry had left, I sighed and made myself a coffee. I switched on the TV while I waited on Robyn to wake up. She was sleeping in a little later every day. She tired very easily and seemed to spend a lot of the day either asleep or watching TV on the sofa. As I flicked through the channels, I caught the panel on *Good Morning Ireland* discussing the case. One of the panellists was saying if it was her daughter, she would try everything, no matter how hopeless the situation, and the rest of them all nodded along in agreement. It seemed as though everyone was adamant that if there was even the smallest hope of the treatment working, we ought to try it because that's what any normal, loving parent would do if it was their child.

Once again, a part of me started to question my decision; what if I was wrong here? Was there a grain of truth in JP's accusation; was I digging my heels in just to get back at him? But no… I would never do that to our daughter.

Just then I was interrupted by the doorbell. I knew it would be Fiona. She was going to look after Robyn while I went to meet Geraldine once again.

'How did you sleep?' she asked, hugging me tightly as soon as she stepped inside the door.

I shook my head. 'Do you ever wish you could just go to bed and never wake up again?'

'Don't lose hope,' Fiona said. 'The judge has to listen to both sides – he wouldn't be doing his job properly if he didn't. That's why he has ordered an independent medical report. And there's no way JP will be able to get anyone to testify that travelling to Arizona is in Robyn's best interests.'

'But I'm so scared that he is going to find some batshit-crazy doctor that will, and he'll twist the whole thing in his favour and what then? Do I have to consent to her being shipped off to the US knowing that it could kill her? And what if this independent medical witness asks for her to be subjected to more tests or they want to examine her, how could I put her through that?'

'You have to have faith in the justice system, the judge will do his due diligence and if there is even a whiff of bullshit, he won't entertain it, Sarah, he can't.'

'Yeah,' I said, sighing, 'you're right.' But secretly I was scared.

'Have you seen what they're saying about me?' I asked her, jerking my elbow towards the TV as she followed me into the living room where the panel were still in deep discussion about Robyn's case.

She nodded. 'I couldn't avoid it, to be honest.' She picked up the remote and turned off the TV. 'Don't listen to any more, Sarah,' she urged. 'They don't know you, they don't know what's really going on. They only know the version that the media is painting to them. Anyone that does know you knows you're a great mother – the best of the best. Robyn's medical team are in agreement with you and that says it all.'

'I love you, Fi,' I said, throwing my arms around her. I was so glad to have her support right then.

A while later, I kissed Robyn goodbye, then I set off to meet Geraldine. As I drove along the coast road towards Ballsbridge, they were even discussing it on the radio and, although Fiona had warned me not to, I couldn't help but listen as callers rang in to the show to give their tuppence worth. I listened to their opinions of me and what they would do if Robyn was their daughter. It was torturous to hear them dissecting my life as if they knew my child and were medical experts themselves. Not once was Dr Sharma's report mentioned or the fact that I had the backing of Robyn's entire medical team. My dad's old saying, 'never let the truth stand in the way of a good story', was never so apt. I felt my knuckles clench ever tighter around the steering wheel.

Eventually, when I nearly ploughed into the back of a car that had stopped suddenly in front of me – because I was so enraged by a caller who professed that I was clearly a very selfish woman as any mother worth her salt would do whatever it took to cure their child's cancer – I had to turn off the radio and drive the rest of the way in silence.

I pulled up on a side street near Geraldine's office and parked. Gulls loitered on a nearby rooftop, squawking as I walked down the footpath. I passed a newspaper kiosk, where ink screamed from the front pages at me. The headline from the *Irish People* read:

MOTHER DENIES CHILD LIFESAVING TREATMENT

and the *Irish Daily News* went with:

MOTHER REFUSES TREATMENT FOR DYING DAUGHTER

Even though I knew I shouldn't look at them, I found myself lifting a copy off the stand and reading through it. I felt hot tears spring into my eyes reading such hurtful, hateful words.

The parents, who cannot be named for legal reasons to protect the identity of their child, are on opposing sides...

'Love, this isn't a library.' The seller stuck his head out through the hatch, interrupting my thoughts. 'That'll be two-twenty, please...' He held out his hand for payment.

I fumbled in my purse for the change, then I continued on towards Geraldine's office clutching my newspaper. I climbed the steps and walked into the reception and when I was eventually shown into her office, I went in without saying a word and placed the headline face up on her desk. She took it up and read it.

'This is just one of many,' I said. 'I can't escape it. I'm being portrayed as a monster, like what kind of parent would just let their child die?'

'I did see it on the news last night,' Geraldine admitted.

'But what they're saying isn't true. It's being twisted – they're only giving one side of the story. I love her more than anyone will ever be able to put into words.'

'We can seek an injunction against media coverage?' Geraldine suggested.

I sat down in the chair opposite her and held my head in my hands. That just felt like getting more entrenched and I was already in far deeper than I ever wanted to be. All these meetings about the case and all the space in my head that was being taken up by these legal proceedings, they were all robbing me of something far greater than my sanity – they were stealing time. I could withstand the vicious portrayal of me by the media, I could deal with the stress, I could deal with the worries for the future, I could even deal with bloody JP, but I could not deal with any more time being stolen away from me, time that I could be spending with Robyn. The whole thing was a mess and what was awful was that while we were scoring legal points, my daughter was growing sicker by the day. 'No,' I said, 'I just want to get this whole thing over with as soon as possible.'

* * *

When I got home that afternoon. I put my bag down quickly and followed Fiona into the living room where Robyn was watching TV.

'How was she?' I asked, sitting down beside her. I lifted her up onto my knee, drinking her in. 'Come here, Robby-Roo, I need a cuddle.'

She smiled her gorgeous smile at me. Even though now only the right side of her face moved, that smile could make my heart explode in my chest. I cradled her in my arms. I breathed in the heavenly smell of velvet-soft skin on the back of her neck combined with the strawberry shampoo that we used on her hair.

'Actually, she's only just woken up,' Fiona said. 'She was asleep for most of the afternoon.'

My heart sank. She was sleeping so much lately, and I didn't like to think what this meant for us. We had an appointment with Dr Sharma later that week to get the results on her latest MRI, and although my legal battles were terrifying enough, I was far more petrified of what lay ahead of us when we met him.

The Irish News Online Edition

The Daily Opinion

The topic being discussed across dinner tables and at workplace water coolers all over Ireland this week is that of a four-year-old girl who is at the centre of a landmark case that has gripped the country.

The child, who cannot be named for legal reasons, is suffering from a DIPG (diffuse intrinsic pontine glioma), a rare type of brain tumour usually only found in young children. The child has been given a terminal diagnosis from her medical team in the Dublin children's hospital and has undergone extensive palliative radiotherapy, which can sometimes give DIPG patients more time, but it was unsuccessful, and it is believed that the child hasn't long left to live.

However, the child's father has found new hope in the form of a clinic in Arizona, where doctors have shown they can extend the lifespan of children with this very disease. Although the treatment is still in its infancy, the father argues that they are seeing good success rates and have even managed to extend the life of several of the patients who have travelled from around the world to be treated there. He believes the team in Arizona are close to a breakthrough in curing this disease and wants his daughter to travel there for urgent treatment. The mother of the child in question will not give her consent and instead wishes the child to live out the short time that she has left in the comfort of her own home surrounded by those who love her. It is believed that the couple, who are estranged, also have an older child.

The father has issued proceedings seeking a court order to allow him to take his daughter to the US against the wishes of his wife, but Judge

Williams has requested the father present medical evidence supporting his application that the clinic in Arizona offers real hope for the child and he has also sought an independent medical witness report. The case has been adjourned for seven days. Nobody was available for comment.

It's hard not to empathise with both sides at the heart of this tragic story; it doesn't get more tense than a case where it's Mother v. Father and the stakes are your child. Doctors deal with these devastating choices every day, they advise their patients in their expert opinion, but it is only an opinion and ultimately the hard choices are made by loved ones when the patient can't use their own voice. These are difficult decisions for any loving parent – when do you say stop? When is enough treatment enough? When do you turn off a life support machine? When is it time to switch from curative to palliative care? When does the right to quality of life trump the right to life? This is real life, there is no clear cut-off point or rule book. These are decisions of the heart.

Nobody can predict how Judge Williams will rule at the upcoming hearing but as this child's life hangs in the balance, one thing is certain: a nation holds its breath.

So, we ask the question, would you take any hope offered, no matter how small, or allow your child to die peacefully?

Comments:

Rosemary Lavelle: What kind of a mother would give up on her child? The child needs medical treatment to save her life, and it beggars belief that a mother wouldn't want to do that! I hope she gets the treatment she needs. Poor innocent little girl stuck in the middle of all this madness. She calls herself a mother – she doesn't know the meaning of unconditional love.

JuliaMcKeown: Even if it was a 0.0000000000001 per cent chance to save my child, I'd take it.

MamOf5: A mother knows her child best. Let her spend her final days at home with her family. Leave these people alone, their suffering enough.

Anonymous: Sum ppl arent fit 2b parents. Karma will get u bitch!

John Doe: Maybe the mother has good reason. We don't know the full story. Maybe it it's the choice between spending her last months in a foreign hospital or in her loving care at home, then she could be right. Nobody has the right to judge without knowing the full facts.

Mona Lisa: Well if it was my child, I'd take any bit of hope I could get.

PugLove: Well said @JohnDoe.

The Real Truth: The dad is right. Big pharma companies hold all the power. The doctors in this country are all corupt, pharma companies are lining there pockets and they don't want to cure there patients – less €€€ in it for them.

EDSHEERAN: @The Real Truth *Yawn* More conspiracy theory bullshit.

Florian Jones: @EDSHEERAN @The Real Truth is right, you should educate yourself on the corruption of big pharma. Read *The Great Corporate Secret*.

EDSHEERAN: @Florian Jones Get Real!

SDP: @EDSHEERAN Uh-oh here come the tinfoil hat brigade ...

Kelly O'Farrell: My Mam had stage 4 cancer and was given no hope by her doctors so she went to a homeopathist and was cured. People need to try alternatives instead of just the traditional treatments. Doctors aren't always right.

Liam Donovan: Once again the rights of the mother supersede the rights of the father in this country.

PhoebeBuffay: @Liam Donovan Says who? The judge hasn't even made a decision yet!!!!

KatieG: God Bless them.

Peter Piper: Having lost a loved one to a brain tumour there has to be a point you stop fighting and accept what is happening. I've seen what a brain tumour does, it takes your personality, your movement, everything. Its a sad situation, but let them spend her last days peacefully.

SomewhereOverTheRainbow: My sister had a brain tumour when she was seven. She is now 34, married with two kids. Give the child the treatment.

Pigeon: That poor child, her life is in her mother's hands, a mother who doesn't love her enough to fight for her. Good luck to her daddy, your in my prayers.

32

The rain was teeming down and, on the patio outside, puddles joined together to make increasingly larger ones. It was the kind of summer's day that, in a previous life, we would have spent holed up inside the house playing board games, but instead, JP, Harry, Robyn and I were all sitting around the table looking awkward. JP was cuddling Robyn on his knee at one end of the table, while I sat beside Harry at the other end.

JP had contacted me by text message after our court hearing to ask if he could come to see Robyn and I had told him that he was welcome to see her any time he wanted. I meant it; I would never use our daughter as a pawn. Her whole face lit up whenever he came through the door and I knew she needed her dad too. No matter how much I resented him right then, he didn't deserve to miss out on these last days with her. I could never, and would never, deprive either of them of such a basic need.

He wouldn't look me in the eye when I opened the door to him. We never talked – it was as if we were beyond words now. I usually left the house during his visits; sometimes Fiona and I would go for a walk or I'd take Harry for an ice cream or just go to a supermarket and browse the aisles to kill time because I couldn't bear to be anywhere near him, but on this particular day, the torrential downpour outside had rendered me housebound. Every time I looked at him, my anger burned inside so hard that it felt like a physical pain in my chest. I resented him so much because he didn't have to do this; he could stop it at any time, and yet he chose to plough on regardless, sending shrapnel flying in his wake. I couldn't believe that this man I had once loved so much was putting me through hell, but I would keep walking over the hot coals for Robyn if that's what I had to do.

We were just days away from our next court hearing where it would be decided whether Robyn should travel to the US like JP desired or whether she would live out her last days peacefully in the comfort of her own home as was my wish. I wasn't sleeping or eating. My stomach was permanently knotted, anxiety gnawed through me like an earthworm through soil. As I looked across the table at JP, I guessed from the dark circles hanging beneath his eyes, he wasn't faring much better. What would I do if the judge granted him permission to take Robyn to Arizona? How could I, as her mother, who loved her right down to the marrow of my bones, let her board a flight knowing that a gruelling regime awaited her? I imagined myself running across the tarmac and lying down in front of the plane if that's what it took to stop JP. Or if he lost, would he be capable of doing something crazy, like snatching her and taking her abroad anyway? These were the worries that kept me awake at night.

'So, how's school going?' JP asked Harry, cutting through the quiet.

'S'okay.'

'Only two more weeks until you're finished for the whole summer,' I remarked.

Harry shrugged his shoulders.

'Where are you going on your tour this year?' JP tried again.

'Urrrrgh,' Harry groaned eventually, as we continued to drag word after word from him. 'Why won't you just talk to each other?'

'Sorry?'

'You both keep talking to me, but you're not talking to one another and it's really weird.'

JP and I shifted awkwardly. I knew that despite our differences neither of us wanted Harry getting upset about what was happening between us.

'Would you like a cuppa?' I offered JP for Harry's sake. It was the first time I had spoken directly to him since the day I had learnt about the court proceedings.

'That would be great, thanks,' he mumbled.

I stood up from the table, boiled the kettle and began making two mugs of tea.

'A spoonful of sugar and a dash of milk,' I said, putting the mug in front of him when it was made. For as long as I had known JP, he had always drunk his tea the same way.

'Thanks, Sarah.' He half-smiled at me.

We both fell quiet again and sat there in charged silence staring at our mugs until Harry sighed heavily. 'You're doing it again!' he cried in frustration. 'Jeez, you're both acting so strange, just stop it already and talk to one another!'

I pushed back my chair and stood up from the table. 'Look, Robyn needs a bath and I could use a hand,' I said for the sake of something to do. In recent weeks, as her mobility had declined, bathing Robyn had become a two-person job. Usually, I got Fiona to help me.

'Sure,' JP said, jumping up after me, relieved to have something to do.

* * *

JP cradled Robyn's body while I sloshed the water gently around her. She was smiling and I knew she was enjoying the sensation of bathing in the warm water. She couldn't tell me how her body was feeling, but I hoped it was soothing away any aches or pains that she might have. I couldn't help but remember the day Robyn was born, JP had offered to give her her first bath because I had been too weak after my caesarean section. With great confidence, he had taken her to the nursery and begun to wash her, until he remembered just how slippery a new baby was in water. He had had to call out to a passing nurse to intervene. An ashen-faced and suitably chastised JP had returned to my bedside afterwards. We had laughed so hard about it at the time.

'Remember that time in the hospital when you gave her her first bath?' I couldn't help but smile at the memory.

JP laughed then, the corners of his eyes crinkling like sunrays. 'I had forgotten about that. She was so tiny and slippery. It was like trying to hold on to a bar of soap in a swimming pool.'

I felt tears push forward into my eyes as I remembered. These days, happy memories were always quickly obliterated by sorrow. Although I loved recalling better times with our family, reminiscing could also be a cruel taunt of all that we had lost and were still losing. We both looked down at our beautiful daughter, floating weightless in the warm water, grinning up at us with those perfect baby teeth on display. I knew that despite everything that had happened between us, we were just two people who loved our daughter very, very much.

33

JP and I were barely able to look at one another as we went into the hospital for our appointment with Dr Sharma later that week. JP had insisted on being there, claiming he had some questions that he needed to ask. I knew JP thought that I was using Dr Sharma for my own needs to build a case against him – he just couldn't accept what we had been told. We had both been warned by our legal teams not to mention the proceedings in case we prejudiced our case. JP still had the money sitting there in the JustGiving account and he was just waiting for the green light to use it. We only had days until our next hearing with Judge Williams and, although JP and I never discussed it whenever we saw each other, I had noticed subtle changes in him. His demeanour didn't seem to be as confident as it had been previously. Geraldine had mentioned that perhaps his team were having difficulty getting their medical evidence to stack up after all, but it still didn't allay my fears.

We'd met one another in the car park and, rather than use the buggy, JP carried Robyn in his arms from the car into the hospital. As we neared the doors, I watched her body stiffen and her eyes widened with fear. Anxiety pressed down on top of me until it felt as though it was suffocating me. 'It's only a short visit today, sweetheart, I promise we'll be back at home before you know it.'

After a while, Dr Sharma came around and did his assessment on Robyn. I tried to read him as he made notes, for any clues to what he was thinking.

'Now, JP and Sarah, if you'd both like to follow me,' he said when he was finished.

We left Robyn in the care of a nurse, while we followed him down the corridor to his office. When we reached the door, I let Dr Sharma go ahead for a moment while I held back to talk to JP.

'Just promise me we won't have any dramas,' I warned before we went inside.

'I'm entitled to ask questions, Sarah!' he retorted.

We went inside and Dr Sharma gestured for us to sit down.

'So how's Robyn been doing?' he asked.

'She's doing good,' JP answered straight away.

I felt enraged, that was a blatant lie! I shot him a look, but he wouldn't meet my eyes. I was sure Dr Sharma could feel the charge of tension in the room between us. The anger was so palpable you could chop through it. I cut across JP and filled Dr Sharma in on her decline since our last appointment as he listened carefully, taking notes here and there. Out of the corner of my eye, I could see JP's face was clouded in anger as I spoke.

'And how are her pain levels?' Dr Sharma continued.

'She seems to be doing okay,' I said. 'We're managing so far with paracetamol and ibuprofen.'

He nodded.

'I wanted to ask you about the treatment clinic in Arizona,' JP began when I had finished. 'The doctors there have had good outcomes with other DIPG patients...'

'I'm aware of the clinic you're talking about, yes...'

'Well then, why aren't we trying it for Robyn?' JP demanded.

'The clinic you are talking about appears to be using a protocol of intra-arterial chemotherapy and some other methods – I say appear to be because they have never published their data or submitted it for peer review, nor will they let other medical professionals examine their work. They have had similar success rates to children undergoing palliative radiotherapy – the tumour may regress temporarily, but it always comes back. And the answer to the million-dollar question is that none of the patients they have treated have survived.' He shook his head. 'I'm afraid I couldn't recommend it as a treatment option.'

'But some of the people got extra time with their children, so even if it doesn't cure her, there's a chance we could have more time with her, isn't there?' JP protested.

'From my assessment today, Robyn is very weak, JP. Even if you decided to embark on this highly experimental treatment, you would need a medical professional to certify her as fit to fly and I can't see anyone willing to sanction that at this stage. The other option would be an air ambulance but, cost aside, assuming you had the funds in place, in my honest opinion, to be quite frank about it, I don't know if she would even survive the flight.'

'But if it was your daughter, wouldn't you want to try it?' JP tried again, unwilling to accept what Dr Sharma was telling him.

'In my medical opinion, going by the tumour progression in her last MRI, she doesn't have much time left. As well as a medical professional, I'm a father too, JP, so I can imagine how awful this is for you to hear, but if Robyn was my daughter, I would take her home and spend our last days peacefully together.'

There it was, laid out in the starkest of terms. Beside me, I watched as the words assailed JP like bullets. His face fell as his last hope was snatched away. It came like a crushing blow. Whereas I had already started to accept that we would lose Robyn, he was only reaching that place now. I realised then just how deeply in denial he had been. His belief that he would be able to save her had been so strong and, despite everything that had happened between us in recent weeks, I couldn't help but feel sorry for him.

'How long are we talking?' JP asked and I could hear a crack in his voice where despair threatened to rush through.

'I would estimate you have just weeks left with Robyn.'

We both gasped as it felt like a sucker punch right into our stomachs.

Weeks. Weeks. Weeks. The word looped around inside my head. Weeks was what you used to count down to Christmas or towards your summer holiday, not your daughter's life. It was so close. Although I had known this day would come, it still felt like a shock.

'I know this is a tough question for parents to think about, but I have to ask it, have you thought about your preferences for end-of-life care?'

We both looked back at him dumbfounded. My stomach lurched. *Oh God.* I had been so busy worrying about losing her that I hadn't allowed myself to think about her death. Where would it happen? What would it be like? I had held my mother's hand as her chest rattled before she had taken her last breath and quite frankly it had been terrifying. Even though she had had seventy-six years of life experience behind her, she had still been scared, but Robyn was too young to understand what was happening to her. Suddenly, I was panicked at the thought of this happening to Robyn and the air seemed to have left my lungs. My hands grew clammy and the room seemed to be spinning around me. *Just concentrate on breathing*, I told myself. *In. Out. In. Out.*

'It's okay, Sarah,' Dr Sharma said, obviously noticing my distress. 'You won't be on your own, you will have support through this. Have you thought about whether you would prefer Robyn to go into a hospice or if you would like her to be at home?'

'At home.' JP and I both looked at one another and answered in unison and I was glad that at least we were united on this.

'Okay, well then, you will link in with St Theresa's Hospice in your area and they will guide you through this. I'm so sorry, JP and Sarah, both as Robyn's doctor and on a personal level. I'm very sorry medical science has let you both down, but hopefully a cure will be found in the not-too-distant future.'

I nodded, not trusting myself to speak. I heard JP swallow a lump in his throat as Dr Sharma shook both of our hands and then we left his room for the last time. As we walked out into the corridor towards the room where Robyn was waiting for us with a nurse, it hit me all over again; the injustice and frustration of the situation rained down upon me. We were on mile twenty-six of our marathon and I wasn't sure I could keep going any more.

JP suddenly stopped dead in the middle of the floor and a man muttered impatiently as he had to swerve to the left to avoid him. I could see tears were streaming down his face. The bricks that had built his wall of anger had now been torn down and he was left crushed and broken amongst the debris.

'I-I-I don't want to give up on her.' He turned to me sobbing with every word that left his mouth. 'I ca-can't believe this is happening, Sarah,' he said, shaking his head in disbelief.

Tears fell down my own face as I saw his heartache mirror my own. Betrayals, legal battles and hurtful words were cast aside as I walked over and put my arms around him. We stood sobbing in the corridor as people continued to walk past us, each wrapped up in their own lives while ours had just ended. JP clung on to me and I held on to him just as tightly because I knew we were both afraid that if we let go, we would drown underneath the weight of all of this.

34

Rain ran down the windscreen as the wipers screeched to clear it again. JP was driving us home and I sat in the back seat with Robyn, who had fallen asleep before we had even pulled out of the hospital car park. It reminded me of the day we had brought her home from hospital as a newborn. I had had Harry in his toddler seat on one side of me and Robyn in her infant seat on the other and, as JP had driven along, being extra cautious when pulling out of junctions and taking care over the speed ramps, I had sat in between them both feeling so happy and full of gratitude that after all the years of yearning for a baby, here I was with the two most beautiful children in the world. JP had turned around at one point when we were stopped at traffic lights and smiled at the three of us together in the back seat and I don't think I had ever felt a contentedness like it.

Beyond the drizzle-spattered window, I saw a family with a roof box and bikes stacked on a rack on the back of their car, obviously on their way to catch the ferry for a holiday on the continent, and my breath caught. Everywhere I looked, there were painful reminders of all we were losing. Although Robyn was the one who was ill, we too would be dying a slow, lingering death as we tried to live our lives without her. How could we possibly survive it? Would I look at Robyn's classmates every year as they moved up through the school feeling angry and cheated because she should be there too? Would I be able to walk through the girls' clothing section in a department store knowing my daughter would never get to grow into those sizes? How was I meant to look at her friends, watching them year after year, graduate, get married and even have children, knowing that we had been robbed of all that? What would I say whenever people asked me how many children I had? Would I say one or two? If I said, 'I had two children, but one died', then I was opening up a discussion that nobody wanted to have, whereas if I said 'one', it would be easier to close down the painful conversation. But I didn't want to betray Robyn by pretending she never existed – I wanted her memory to live on forever. I wanted people to know that although she didn't live for a long time that I was her mother and I loved her, and she would always be my child even when I didn't get to hold her any more.

When we pulled up at the house, JP opened the back door of the car and gently lifted Robyn up in his arms. He carried her up the driveway and Harry came running out to meet us.

'Hi, Robyn,' Harry cried. 'We got you this in the toyshop,' he said, showing her an Elsa doll. 'Fiona took me earlier. I picked it myself,' he said proudly.

She opened her eyes briefly, but closed them again and I could see the confusion on his small face as he tried to understand why her reaction was so muted.

'She's just a bit tired,' I assured him. The trip to the hospital had wiped her out. Every little thing took so much out of her now. I felt an overwhelming need to cry and bawl and scream at the unjustness of it all. It wasn't just JP and I who were losing

Robyn, but Harry too and Fiona. Joan and Richard, her little friend Lily. So many people loved her and would be broken by this.

'Shall I carry her up to bed?' JP asked.

I nodded. 'She's exhausted.'

I followed them up the stairs and JP automatically went to go into Robyn's old room.

'She sleeps in our room now,' I said. 'I mean, *my* room,' I mumbled, feeling my face grow hot and wanting the ground to swallow me up at the mention of the bed we had once shared together.

I opened the door for him, and he lifted her into our ex-marital bed and tucked her up underneath the duvet. A piece of my heart broke as I watched her sink down onto the pillow, her eyes closing almost instantly. We were going to have to endure seeing more little pieces of our daughter vanish until one day she would be gone altogether, and it seemed to be the cruellest torture.

JP kissed her on the forehead, and we crept out of the room and stood on the landing. Neither of us were ready to go back down the stairs to face Harry yet and put on a mask to reassure him that everything was okay.

'Oh God, Sarah, we're really going to lose her...' JP said as tears filled his eyes. 'I'm not ready,' he whispered. His whole body began to shake as sobs wracked him once more.

I put my arm around his shoulder and guided him into Robyn's bedroom so nobody would hear us. I closed the door behind us and we both sat down on the side of her bed. Her soft toys and dolls all sat on her bed and her princess costumes hung on the coat stand in the corner of the room. 'I know,' I said. 'I'm not ready either, I don't think I ever will be. I feel so angry and cheated and robbed. It's all so unfair. The whole bloody lot of it.

I'm angry at God for giving us this child only to take her away four years later. Why would he do that?'

Tears now streamed freely down his face. 'You can't possibly still believe in God after this?'

'I don't know any more...' I admitted.

'Why us? Why is our Robyn being taken? I didn't think this could happen to someone I loved – I thought my love was enough – like this couldn't possibly happen to us. You know when you hear a family talking about something like this happening to them on the radio and you think how horrible it is and you think about them for a few minutes afterwards, but we're not meant to *be* the family!'

'Believe me, I've spent so many nights lying awake thinking the exact same things, but I've come to the conclusion that there's no explanation, it is just crap.'

'Mam? Dad?' we heard Harry call from downstairs. 'What are you doing up there?

'We better go down to him,' I said.

We both took a moment to gather ourselves, then inhaling deeply, we descended the stairs.

'So,' I said, pulling Harry into a bear of a hug when I went into the living room. 'How've you been today? I've missed you.'

'But you were only gone for a few hours,' Harry said.

'Yeah, but I'm still allowed to miss you,' I said, ruffling his hair. 'It's a mother's prerogative.'

'I'm going to head off,' Fiona said. She knew that we needed time together as a family. I had called her before we left the hospital and told her what Dr Sharma had told us.

'Thank you, Fiona,' I said, feeling my voice choke. 'I don't know what I'd do without you holding the fort and taking such good care of Harry.' Even though she had her own life to live, she had been like a mother and father to him over the last few months while JP and I were taking care of Robyn.

'You don't need to thank me, you know I love those kids as if they were my own,' she said with sadness filling her eyes as I walked her out to the door.

I nodded. 'Well, still, thank you.'

She pulled me into a tight hug. 'I love you, sis.' Then she headed outside to her car.

I went back inside, where it was just myself, JP and Harry left in the kitchen. I knew we needed normality for Harry's sake. 'Who's hungry?' I asked. 'Shall we get a takeout?'

'Yes!' Harry said, punching the air with excitement. 'Can you stay, Dad? We can get Dominos?'

'Of course I can stay.' JP paused. 'I mean, only if you're sure you don't mind...' he added, turning to me.

'Of course, we'd like that, wouldn't we, Harry?'

Harry nodded eagerly and I knew he was enjoying having his parents acting normal together again after the months of tension.

When the food arrived, we put on a movie and the three of us sat on the sofa, one of us on either side of Harry while we ate triangles of pizza. JP and I took turns to check on Robyn, but she was in a deep sleep since we had come back from the hospital.

'Who wants the last slice?' I asked.

'I'm too full,' Harry said, rubbing his tummy. 'We can keep it for Robyn when she wakes up.'

'That's a lovely idea.' I didn't tell him that Robyn couldn't chew pizza any more.

'Mammy?' Harry continued.

'Yes, love?'

'When will Robyn get better?' he asked.

I looked at JP and he looked back at me. I knew we were both thinking the same thing. What were we meant to tell him? What were the right words to say? I had googled it: 'How do you tell your child their sister is dying?' Like there was ever going to be any useful advice, but I just needed some help to navigate a path through this.

'Bedtime,' JP announced, standing up off the sofa.

'Can Dad tuck me up, Mammy. Please?' Harry asked.

I was relieved that JP's distraction tactic had worked. I knew I couldn't keep putting off telling Harry, but after the day we had had, I just couldn't face it that night. I needed more time.

I looked at JP.

'Can I?' he asked.

'Work away.'

JP and Harry disappeared upstairs while I began cleaning up after the takeaway, folding down the pizza boxes and squashing them into the recycling bin. When I was finished, I poured myself a glass of cool white wine. My shoulders were burning with knots and, as I took a sip of the wine, I tried to massage them with one hand.

'Did he go off all right?' I asked as JP returned back downstairs about ten minutes later.

'He was out like a light.' He paused. 'Thanks for this evening, Sarah, I hadn't realised how much I had missed this – I want you to know that I really appreciate it, especially after everything that has happened over the last while...'

I had to admit, despite everything that had taken place that day, it had been a lovely evening. It brought me back to happier times when we would all sit around together on a Saturday night. I had once taken that simple joy of family movie nights for granted without realising that one day it would be snatched away from me. I didn't know then that they were my best days, but now, as I realised they were finite, I appreciated every second of them.

'Well, it does the kids good to spend time with you, they love having you here,' I mumbled, taken aback by his admission. 'I've just opened a bottle of wine. Do you want a glass, or do you need to get back to Megan?'

'I'd murder one,' he said.

I poured him a glass and we went back into the living room and sat down.

JP fell quiet and I got the impression that there was more he wanted to say. He rubbed his thumb down through the condensation on the outside of the glass and then back up along the track again.

'I just wanted to say that I'm sorry, Sarah,' he said eventually. 'I'm going to call my solicitor first thing tomorrow morning and stop the proceedings. I'm sorry for putting you through it all, but I was desperate. I wasn't ready to let her go without a fight – I'm still not...' His voice wavered.

I felt relief flood through me. I had no more energy left to fight. Thank God, he had finally seen sense and accepted that we were not going to win this battle no matter how much we wished we could. 'Thank you,' I whispered. 'Although I didn't agree with what you were doing, JP, I loved that you weren't willing to let her go without a fight...'

'Why are we being put through this?' He held his head in his hands. 'I know I've made mistakes, but why should Robyn be paying for what I've done? I should be the one dying, not a four-year-old!' He looked up at me, his eyes were still red and his face raw and blotchy from all the tears earlier on.

'You think this is your fault?' I was intrigued by his logic.

'Well, isn't it? Isn't it all down to karma or something...?'

'That's not how it works – there's no man in the sky with justice scales, saying because JP left his family, his daughter is going to die.'

He shook his head. 'I'm just trying to make sense of it all and I can't – I don't understand why this is happening to us – I still can't believe it…'

'Life dealt us a really shitty hand, but we need to cherish each day we have left and take it all in. Yes, she is dying – but right now she is living. She is alive, there is air in her lungs and, believe it or not, as hard as it may be to accept it, these are our best days – these are the days that we are going to look back on when our hearts are sore and broken, the days when she was still with us. The days when *us* meant four people and not three. These are the ones we will yearn for when grief seems too much to bear, when we long for her touch, the smell of her skin fresh from sleep, the feeling of her pudgy arms around our necks.'

'How are you able to think like that? Like you can see the bigger picture and I can just see blackness.'

'I've had my fair share of black days too, but that's when I have to remind myself of what we have right now. I'm taking it day by day. Every day she is here is a good one in my book and I'm not looking beyond that because, to be honest, it's terrifying if I allow my head to go there. We've an awful journey ahead of us and we're going to need to be able to lean on one another. There will be days when I don't have the strength and I will need you to lead the way and there will be days when I'll have to keep the ship afloat.'

He nodded. 'You always know the right thing to say. You always did…'

I felt my face flush at the reference to our past. We were interrupted by his phone ringing, jolting us out of the moment. He picked it up off the sofa, checked the screen before pressing the end-call button and sighing.

'Look, JP, let's not waste any more time being angry with one another, the past is in the past, deal?'

He nodded. 'You're right. As usual. I'm done fighting,' he sighed.

His phone started to ring again and this time he picked up. I could hear Megan's voice screeching and shouting down the line to him before he had even had time to say hello.

He hung up on her and rubbed his hands down over his face. 'I'd better head off,' he said, standing up abruptly. He had only taken a few sips of his wine, so I knew he would be okay to drive.

'Yeah, of course.' I got up too and walked him out to the hall. I didn't enquire what was going on between them, it wasn't my business.

He opened the front door. The cool night air rushed inside and made me shiver. He stood on the step and turned back around to me.

'Thanks for tonight, I really appreciate you listening to me like that – you're the only other person who gets how awful this is...' He paused and his eyes fell to the floor. 'I was wondering... what are we going to tell Robyn?'

'Do we need to tell her?' I asked.

'Shouldn't we be preparing her for what lies ahead?'

'She's four years old.' I shook my head at the cruelty of it all. 'She doesn't understand death, let alone her own.' In my darker moments, I wondered what was going on inside her head. It broke my heart to think she might be scared or worried but unable to verbalise it to us.

'So we should say nothing?' His tone wasn't accusatory, just curious.

'I don't think she needs a big explanation. I hate the idea of her being frightened by what's ahead, but let's just take each day as it comes.'

He nodded. 'We'll have to tell Harry though; we can't hide it from him any more.'

I nodded in agreement, feeling my heart tear at the pain that lay ahead for him. As an adult it was awful to endure, but watching my child try to come to terms with it too, knowing that I couldn't fix his pain, was going to unbearable. 'What are we meant to say? How are we going to explain it? How do you tell a nine-year-old that his sister is going to die?' I said, feeling desperate.

'Who's going to die?' we heard Harry's small voice ask from behind.

JP and I swung around immediately. Neither of us had heard Harry come back downstairs. He must have heard us talking on the doorstep. I looked at JP and JP looked at me. The air around us seemed to change as if we could smell fear. The moment we had both been dreading had arrived.

'What's going on, Mam and Dad?' he demanded, looking at me first, then at JP and back to me again. Then the realisation hit him. 'Is Robyn going to die?' His eyes were wide and fearful and his teeth bit into his bottom lip.

We both knew the time had come to tell him. 'Let's go inside and sit down,' I said.

The three of us went back into the house and into the living room.

JP's phone rang again, cutting through the moment. 'For God's sake!' he groaned impatiently as he fumbled to turn it off.

My heart was pounding, and blood pulsed through my ears. I had known this moment was coming, but I still didn't feel ready for it. The truth was I didn't think I'd ever be ready for it. No matter how much I had thought about it or researched it, I still didn't know the right way to say these words. Whatever I said next was going to be a defining moment in Harry's life forever. He would carry this moment around with him like a scar upon his heart for the rest of his life.

I waited until he was sitting down on the sofa next to JP, then I took a deep breath before beginning to say the words I had been putting off for so long.

'Harry, love, you know the way Robyn has bad cells growing inside her head and we were going into the hospital to zap them?'

'Yeah?'

'Well, the zapping machine can't keep up with the bad cells – they keep coming back,' I said.

'Is the machine broken?' he asked with all of the innocence of a nine-year-old.

'No, it's just the bad cells are too strong.' I paused.

'Robyn is very sick, Harry,' JP said, taking up my lead.

'Well, can't the doctors just give her different medicine?' he asked.

'Sometimes they can, but unfortunately the doctors have no medicine that can fix Robyn...'

'So, she's going to die?' Tears pooled in his blue eyes and I wanted to take back my words and take away his sadness and fix everything like I usually did, but this time I couldn't.

'I'm sorry,' I said, confirming his worst fears.

I watched his eyes flicker as he tried to process what we were telling him. I could see his brain working hard to understand, but he was too young. He was nine years old; the concept of death hadn't formed properly in his mind, so how on earth was he supposed to make sense of any of this?

'But where will she go when she dies?'

'Remember when Granny died, and she went to heaven and Grandad was going to mind her for us?' My mother had died just three years ago and although Robyn had no memories of her grandmother, Harry did. When she had passed away, we had explained to Harry that Granny was going to meet Grandad in heaven.

'Uh-huh,' he nodded.

'Well, it'll be the same for Robyn. She'll go to heaven with Grandad and Granny and they're both going to mind her there for us.' I felt my voice choke up with tears.

JP reached across to the armchair where I was sitting and rubbed my shoulder with his thumb. I knew he was finding this conversation just as hard as I was.

'But she'll always be with us right here,' I said, placing my palm over my heart.

'But what will we do without Robyn? Our family will be all wrong! Who will I play with?' His little eyes were locked on mine, begging me for reassurance.

It was the simplicity of his question that summed up everything for me. Life without her was unimaginable. And that was when I came undone, I had tried my best to hold it together in front of Harry, but tears flooded down my face and landed onto my grey marl T-shirt in dark stains.

JP started sobbing too, his shoulders heaved up and down as the grief wrung him out and then we were all crying. We were in each other's arms, holding on to one another tightly as the three of us cried together, broken-hearted.

Harry lifted his head from my chest after a while. 'Mam?' he asked in a small voice.

'Yes?'

'Is it my fault because I was giving out about you always being in the hospital? I didn't mean it. I'm really sorry.' His eyes were red from tears.

I reached out and gripped him on either side of his shoulders.

'Harry, love, it's not your fault that this is happening, do you hear me? This is nobody's fault, it's just one of those bad things in life that sometimes happen, do you understand me?' This was everything I didn't want; I didn't want him carrying guilt for his sister's death – something like that could destroy a person. He was too young to understand the fragility of life and I needed it to be clear that it was nothing to do with his behaviour. It was outside of all our control.

'I'm scared, Mam,' he whispered. His eyes were wide and round, and I hated that for the first time in his life I couldn't fix this for him. Every piece of advice I had read had said it was important to be honest with your feelings when breaking bad news to children, it was okay not to have all the answers.

I squeezed his hand hard. 'I'm scared too, Harry, and so is your dad.' JP nodded in agreement. 'This is going to be the hardest thing we've ever faced, but the three of us are going to help each other through this,' I continued.

'We need to make a pact that we'll be honest with one another,' JP said. 'If me or your mam are having a bad day, you'll help us, and if you're having a bad day, we'll help you. Deal?' He clenched his hand to make a fist bump.

Harry nodded. 'Deal,' he said as he bumped his small fist against JP's.

'From now on, we need to make every day special for her,' JP said, leaning in towards Harry. 'So your mam and I are going to need your help, little man.'

'Do you think we can get Santa to come early this year because it's not fair if Robyn misses Christmas?' His face grew animated as his mind began to run with his idea. 'I could write a letter to him and tell him all about Robyn and that she has bad things growing in her brain and even though the doctors ran out of medicine, she is so brave because she is always getting needles in the hospital. And I'll tell him that I know he can't come twice in one year because that's not fair on all the other boys and girls, but it's okay if he doesn't come to our family again at the real Christmastime this year because I just want to have our family together for one last time.'

'Do you know what, Harry?' I said as I wiped tears away with the back of my hand. 'I think that's a great idea.'

HARRY

I never saw Dad cry before, but today I did because Robyn is going to die. Even though we sometimes fight, and she can be kinda annoying when she takes my stuff, I don't want her to die because I'll miss her. When you die it's forever and that's a really long time. I only know one other person who died and that was Granny, but she was really old so even though it was kinda sad that was okay. Dad said she would be going to live in heaven, and I asked if we can go there to see her, but he said, we're not even able to visit Robyn for a day and I said 'can we go even for five seconds?' and he said 'no, not even for five seconds'.

It's going to be really weird if Robyn isn't in our family any more. It's going to be so boring. What will I do without Robyn? Who will I play with? Mam said 'she will always be a part of our family', but I told her if she lives in heaven then she can't be, can she? I remember from Granny that dead people are really cold, and I asked Dad if Robyn would be cold too and he said we could put a blanket on her to keep her warm. I told him that her Frozen *one is her favourite. I asked Dad if they have lights in heaven because Robyn is scared of the dark and she always has to sleep with her night light on and he said 'of course they do', but I don't know how he knows because he's never been there and* nobody that has gone there has ever come back again because you're not allowed to visit heaven, so I asked Dad how did he really know that and he just said 'I just do'. But that's not really a good answer. If teacher asked me a question in school and I said that answer she would give me a big red X in my copy. Then I asked him what they eat in heaven and he said he wasn't sure, 'maybe the same things that we eat here', and I said 'but without all the horrible things like broccoli and fish?'

'Yes, I think you're probably right, son,' Dad said.

And I said Robyn is soooo lucky she never has to eat fish pie ever again, but then he looked like he was going to cry and even though I have loads more questions about heaven I didn't ask any more.

36

We stood in the garden under a blistering blue sky streaked white with filmy plane vapours. Wispy clouds hung lazily above us as if dithering which way to go and the sun was warm on our skin. JP smiled at me and I smiled back at him.

A few days before, Geraldine had called me to let me know that the proceedings had been withdrawn by JP's legal team and she had seemed surprised when I admitted to her that I already knew. I explained about our last meeting with Dr Sharma and JP's realisation that Robyn hadn't long left to live. She wished us well on the rest of our journey and I thanked her for all her help. The media seemed to have lost interest in the story too, and I was glad to have that awful chapter behind us.

'One, two, three – are you ready?' Harry asked, just before he flicked the switch on the outdoor Christmas lights.

'Happy Chrissssstmaaaas!' we roared in unison.

Robyn smiled in my arms as she looked around at the fairy lights that JP had draped from tree to tree all around the garden and along the front of the house. The lights were muted under the bright sunlight, but I knew once night-time came it would be transformed into a magical scene.

After Harry had the idea to write to Santa, I decided that if Robyn couldn't be here for Christmas, although it was only June, I was going to bring Christmas forward to make sure we had one last one together and I wanted it to be the best one yet. Harry had been excitedly helping us to get ready to make it extra special for his sister. Even though Christmas had always been my favourite time of year, now I was terrified to face it. I was afraid of the emotions it might unleash in me. I was petrified that something wild and feral might break free from my heart and, once it did, I wouldn't be able to reel it back in again, but I desperately needed to hold it together, if I fell apart now, I would ruin our last Christmas with one another.

'The neighbours will think we're crazy,' JP laughed, looking around at the twinkling lights as the sound of a strimmer filtered through the air and the meaty smell of our neighbours' barbeques drifted over walls and fences.

'Let them! Come on, let's go back inside,' I said as I put my free arm around Harry's shoulder and we returned into the house to continue decorating.

The piney smell from the noble fir tree which we had picked up that morning had already begun to scent the whole house. Because it was the middle of summer, I thought we would have to resort to an artificial tree, but JP had managed to track down a Christmas-tree farmer in Wicklow who could give us a real one. Every year since the kids had been born, it had been a family tradition that we would all choose the tree together and then buy a hot chocolate afterwards, so, after much debating between JP and I about whether Robyn was up for the trip to collect it, we had made her as comfortable as we could, before we all piled into the car. JP had made a playlist of all the songs she used to dance to, like Pharrell Williams' 'Happy', but also the nursery rhymes that she had loved as a baby like 'The Wheels on the Bus' were on there too and we had it playing as we drove along. There was a time when that song was like a screwdriver through my brain, but now, I could listen to it all day long as I remembered Robyn as a toddler doing all the actions in the mother and toddler group we used to go to. Sometimes a memory would assail me from nowhere and be so painful and a cruel reminder of everything that I was losing. We all sang along as we drove across the impossibly narrow roads that clung to the mountainside. The landscape, dotted with marigold-coloured furze and mauve sprigs of heather, seemed to stretch out forever as we drove through the depths of the Wicklow countryside. We'd rounded a bend and had to swerve to avoid a herd of horned sheep grazing at the side of the road. As we had continued on with pounding hearts from the fright, the sheep had just stared at us with idle curiosity. Finally, we had begun to descend into a tree-clad valley and arrived at the farm.

'Too skinny,' Harry had said as the farmer led us over to a tree.

'Too wonky,' he'd said about the next one the man showed us.

'The top is crooked on that one.'

'Too tall,' Harry had continued.

'You're a hard taskmaster,' the farmer had laughed, shaking his head.

He had brought us to another one, with its branches evenly spread, and it had looked fairly okay. 'What do you think, Harry?' I'd asked. 'Does it meet your high standards?'

'Do you like it, Robyn?' he'd said, turning to his little sister who was wrapped up in her buggy.

She had smiled her lopsided smile back at him.

'This is the tree,' he'd announced to the man.

Tears had welled in my eyes and I felt my whole chest tighten.

JP slid his arm around my shoulders and pulled me in against him. He was finding this whole thing just as emotional as I was. The togetherness we were showing as a family was everything I had always wanted; it was just bittersweet that it was to be our last one as us.

Robyn was exhausted when we finally got home. JP had trussed the tree up onto the roof of the car and then, to continue the tradition, we'd stopped off in Bewley's on Grafton Street on the way home for a steaming hot chocolate, but I could see that the trip had taken its toll on her, so while JP climbed the ladder into the attic to find the decorations, I tucked her up in bed for a nap with Mr Bunny.

She slept a lot now and each day it seemed as though we were losing another little piece of her. Her speech was gone, and she couldn't walk any more. She could still smile though, and that smile meant the world to me. When she had been five weeks old, she had given me her first smile as I had been changing her nappy. After a sleepless night of breastfeeding, those gummy smiles would fill me with the warmest feeling and now as I saw her little facial muscles working so hard to do it, it felt like those new baby smiles all over again. I was trying to find joy in the everyday things, wherever I could, and that's how I felt when Robyn smiled.

When she was asleep, I covered her with the duvet and crept back downstairs.

'You've kept all their decorations,' JP said as he held up an angel made using a toilet roll insert that he had found in the box of decorations.

'My angel!' Harry cried, taking it from JP and hanging it on the tree alongside the new decorations that Harry and Robyn had made themselves the day before. I had traced their hand and footprints onto cardboard, Harry had cut them out and then we had helped Robyn to paint them with her right hand. When they had dried, I had laminated them, to preserve them, and attached string to hang them.

'That tree would put the one at the Mansion House to shame,' JP said as we stood back to admire it when we had finished. If the sun hadn't been beaming in through the windows from outside, you would swear it was actually Christmastime.

'Mam?' Harry asked.

'Yes, love?' I turned around from the tree to face him. I saw he was clutching a piece of paper in his hands.

'I wrote my letter to Santa.'

'Really? Can I see it?'

He shook his head. 'Only Santa can read it when he comes tonight.'

I smiled. 'Okay, love.'

'I'll hang up the stockings,' Harry said, taking them out of the box.

My heart stumbled as my eyes landed on the names that were embroidered across the top of each one: *John-Paul, Sarah, Harry, Robyn.* I found myself wondering what would we do with Robyn's stocking next Christmas? Would we hang it up as normal or would it be too painful a reminder of her absence every time we looked at it? Then I felt a smack of guilt, we couldn't forget about her. She would still be our daughter; even if she was no longer with us, we needed to make sure she was remembered.

'I'll put up Robyn's stocking for her next year, Mammy,' Harry said as if he sensed my upset.

I began taking my candleholders out of the box where I had stored them during my heartbroken haze last January. I couldn't help but think back to the crushing disappointment of the Christmas before. The last time I had set about lighting these was the night before everything had started to go wrong. I wished I had known then how perfect my life was right at that moment. I had been so blissfully unaware of the heartache that lay ahead for us. So much had changed since then.

JP spotted my candles and laughed. 'That collection multiplies every year.'

'What?' I said, pretending to be offended. 'It wouldn't be Christmas without them!'

I moved from candle to candle lighting them as Mariah Carey's 'All I Want for Christmas' came on the playlist that we were listening to on Spotify. That song was so bloody jingly and I remembered how Robyn and her friends had danced to it on stage at her playschool Christmas show the year before. Everywhere there were reminders that Robyn was departing soon.

We had dinner when Robyn woke, then we bathed the children and dressed them in new Christmas pyjamas that I had managed to find online. I loved when they were fresh from the bath; their skin so clean, their hair so silky. We put on the movie *Elf* and Robyn surprised us all by staying awake for most of it. JP and I were sipping mulled wine and we had the fire lit even though it was roasting, and I had to open the windows to let some of the heat out, but we had all agreed that if this was to be Christmas Eve, then a roaring fire was essential.

After the movie was over, Harry, with some help from Robyn, set out a gingerbread family for Santa with a glass of milk, then JP and I tucked them up together in my bed. We made Robyn comfortable on the pillows and I began reading ''Twas the Night Before Christmas'. Harry held her hand and I knew that she was happy.

As I recited the words like I did every year, it was hard not to let my mind get caught up in a tangle of 'last times'. I found that I had to keep pushing back tears. This was our last time reading this poem on Christmas Eve. Tomorrow it would be our last

Christmas opening presents as a family of four, our last Christmas dinner with all of us together. I kept tearing up whenever I was reminded of something else she would be missing out on – *we* would all be missing. We were so very close to the end of our time limit. A nurse from the hospice had been out to visit us and I knew the deadline was looming on the horizon and I was powerless to stop it. I desperately wished I could pause our lives, but time marched on regardless of our pleas. How would I deal with December when it was actually Christmas and the shops would be decorating their windows with swags and garlands and snow scenes or when heart-warming Christmas adverts with messages of love and togetherness, featuring happy families preparing for the big day, filled the TV screens? For the first time in my life, I now understood why people said Christmas could be a difficult time.

When the kids were asleep, JP and I came back downstairs and went into the kitchen to prepare the vegetables for dinner the following day. We were having a large crowd: JP's parents were coming over; Fiona and Seán were going to come too. Fiona had offered to cook, but I wanted it to be like every other Christmas, so she had relented on the condition that I allowed her to bring the trifle. Other friends and family were going to drop by over the course of the day, including Linda and Mel. Robyn's pal Lily was coming over with her mum and her playschool teachers were going to call too. I wanted everyone who mattered to be there for Robyn's last Christmas. Although nobody spoke about it, everybody realised that it was their chance to say goodbye to her. I knew tomorrow was going to be a tough day. My body felt like a cracked pane of glass that somehow still managed to hold together but was perilously close to shattering into millions of tiny pieces.

'Do you want another glass?' I said, gesturing to the mulled wine that was on the hob, when we had finished peeling a small mountain of potatoes.

'I'd better not, I've to drive home.'

I took a deep breath. 'Well, I was thinking... why don't you stay over? The kids would love to have you here when they're opening their presents... if you want to, I mean – unless there's somewhere you need to be...' I trailed off. JP had been spending the majority of his time with us since our last appointment with Dr Sharma and was only returning home once the children had gone to bed every evening. I had been wondering how it had been going down with Megan, but I never asked him. That wasn't my problem to deal with; I had enough worries on my plate right now.

I knew he was taken aback as he studied my face to make sure I was serious.

'In the spare room,' I added, feeling heat flood into my cheeks in case he had thought I was suggesting something else.

'There's nowhere else I'd rather be,' he said quickly. 'Thank you, Sarah... I really appreciate this.'

I filled both of our glasses with mulled wine and we went into the living room and flopped down wearily onto the sofa.

'I've wanted to say something to you for a while now,' JP spoke as the fire sparked in the grate.

'Go on,' I said with trepidation. Although we had recently reached a truce, I knew it was as fragile as antique china and I didn't have the energy to resurrect old war wounds. I hoped that wasn't the road that he was about to go down.

'You were right about the treatment in Arizona,' he began. 'Deep down I always knew it. I knew that clinic was a long shot, but I just needed hope, I needed something because I couldn't accept that there was nothing I could do – I'm her dad, I'm supposed to be able to protect her from all the bad things in the world.' He paused. 'You see, I always had this thing after Ellen died... we usually cycled home from school together, but that day I had hurling training after school so she was cycling on her own and I always wondered if maybe I could have saved her if I had been there with her... Maybe I would have seen the car or something... I don't know... that's why I had to try and do everything possible to save Robyn, but I was being selfish. I wasn't thinking of all that we'd be putting her through. I wasn't putting her needs above my own. I can see that now.'

'Oh, JP,' I said, as he confirmed what I had suspected all along that the impact of his sister's death had clouded his judgement about what was best for Robyn. 'Why didn't you ever say anything before?'

'I didn't even realise it myself until very recently.' He turned around to face me. 'I'm sorry for putting you through all of that and I'm sorry I didn't listen to you earlier. A huge part of me felt as though I was letting Robyn down by not fighting for her, but I can see now that letting her go peacefully is the more loving thing to do.'

'It doesn't make you selfish wanting more time with her. I want that too, more than anything in the world.'

'Yeah, but you instinctively knew that it wasn't the right thing to do – I didn't. I'm sorry for questioning your love for her. You're a great mother, Sarah. You've been brilliant throughout this whole nightmare – you've got me through the days when I didn't think I could go on...' He paused. 'You're the glue that holds our family together.'

'Thanks,' I muttered, taken aback by the surprise compliment. We had been fighting so much lately that it felt like a long time since JP had said anything nice to me.

'The kids adore you; you always get it right. You always know the right thing to say or do,' he continued.

'They love you too, you know.'

'Yeah, but it's different... you put them before yourself all the time. You'd walk through fire for them and they know that.'

'What's brought all this on?'

'I suppose it's a long-winded way of saying sorry. Leaving you like that...' He trailed off. 'Well, I'm not proud of myself.'

'Well, it wasn't one of your finer moments,' I agreed.

'You know, when we were watching the movie earlier with Harry snuggled in beside me and Robyn sitting on my knee... it was perfect. I didn't realise how much I missed all of that. I keep asking myself how did I walk out on it all? How had I ever thought there was something better out there?' His cheeks pinkened as he spoke.

I was stunned. 'Eh, in case you've forgotten, it was your choice to leave, JP – I was happy with us.' I didn't mean to sound harsh, but the truth needed to be heard.

He shook his head. 'I know, it's all my own fault – that's the worst part of it. I only have myself to blame. If only I could see then what I can see now, I never would have gone anywhere. I wish so much I could rewind the clock. When I look back, it's like I don't even recognise that person any more. How had I been that selfish?' He paused. 'I guess the grass isn't always greener...'

'Is everything okay with Megan? Is she being a support to you?' I asked.

'We broke up actually.'

My mouth dropped open. 'I'm sorry to hear that.'

He tilted his head at me sceptically. 'No, you're not,' he laughed.

I couldn't help but laugh too. 'No, really, I am,' I said. And I genuinely meant it, I knew he must be hurting, and lord knew both of us had enough pain to last a lifetime right now.

'After I went home the night that we broke it to Harry that

Robyn was dying, I told Megan it was over. I couldn't do it any more. We hadn't been getting along for a while and then when Robyn got sick... it's made me see everything in a new way. This thing has been thrown upon us and it's like it casts a magnifying glass over everything in your whole life and nothing is the same ever again. It's like suddenly you have clarity about what's really important to you and you want to grab all those things and hold on to them tightly, and on the flip side, you have to let go of anything that doesn't quite stand up any more.'

I nodded in agreement; I knew exactly what he meant because I felt the same way.

'What started out as fun and excitement turned out to be not what I wanted at all. I didn't love her – I thought I did, especially at the start, but now I can see that it was just infatuation. I thought I wanted sex, but really it was just intimacy and closeness that I needed, and I soon realised that Megan couldn't give me that. She was like a shiny penny that had turned my head, but then you flip it over and you see it for what it really is, tarnished and dull. And I can't really blame Megan, she was just being a normal twenty-six-year-old, but God, I missed our family and all the simple things, like tucking the kids up in bed. Just being able to sit and watch TV on a Saturday night, without having to glam it up and stand packed into a sweaty nightclub or the way we used to have lazy Sunday morning breakfasts together, reading the papers, with the kids playing around us, instead of being dragged around shopping centres. I just grew tired of it all...' His voice choked, and I saw he was close to tears.

'Where are you staying?' I asked.

'I'm still in the flat and she's moved in with her friend. I know I've fucked up,' he continued, 'and I certainly don't deserve any sympathy, but I hate it, I'm alone and I hate it. I miss what we had. I can now see what's important in life... it has put everything into perspective. I know what I really need and want.' He paused and his eyes locked with mine. 'I don't think I can get through this without you – you're the only one who understands what it's like...'

His words rang true with me. People tried to understand – people like Fiona tried to listen, but I always felt I needed to protect them from the true depths of my despair, I couldn't let them see how broken I really was because I knew it would hurt them to see me in such pain. When all was said and done, JP was the only other person who knew *exactly* what it was like. Just how awful and crushing this nightmare was. I could be completely honest with him because I knew he was thinking about the same horrible things that I was thinking about. I didn't need to put on a brave face for him and that in itself was a relief.

'I miss you,' he blurted. 'I miss what we had... I need you, Sarah – I can't do this without you.'

HARRY

Dear Santa,

I hope you and Mrs Claus and all the reindeers are well. This is Harry, aged nine and a half, from Dublin in Ireland. Remember you brought me a black skateboard and a remote-controlled car for Christmas last year?

I know this is weird because you probably never get letters in June when the weather is really hot, but I have some really important things to ask you. My little sister called Robyn (remember you brought her a Baby Annabell doll last year?), well Robyn is very sick, she has bad things growing in her brain and the doctors have no medicine that can make her better. Mam and Dad told me that she's going to die. Santa, I have to ask you for three things and I know that's a lot of things to ask for, but they're not toys and they're not really things for me.

I need to ask you for a big, humongous favour. Please can you come really early this year so we can have a special Christmas with Robyn? I know that's not fair on all the other boys and girls in the world, but it would make Robyn happy. Think of it, Santa – if you could come now, then you don't have to come again at the real Christmas so you would have one less house to do and everyone knows how busy you are on Christmas Eve .

The next thing I need to ask for and this is the most important bit please can you ask the elves if they have some magic medicine to make Robyn get better so she doesn't have to die?

The last thing I want to ask for is something for my Mam. She's really sad all the time since my dad went away to live in a different house so I think if you could bring my dad home to live in our house, she will be happy again.

Please, Santa, I know I've asked for a lot of stuff, but if you can help me, I will always eat my broccoli and I will never complain about stinky fish pie again. I promise I will try to be the best boy in the ENTIRE UNIVERSE.

Lots of love,

Harry aged nine and a half from Dublin, Ireland xxxx

37

After JP's confession the previous night, we had stayed up late talking and laughing and even crying together too. I had caught a glimpse of the way we used to be, back at a time when we used to really talk to each other, probably way before we had had the kids, if I was completely honest. I had forgotten what we were once like before the years had slipped past and time had muted our feelings for one another.

When I had climbed into bed beside Harry and Robyn that night, I had lain awake wondering when had we stopped kissing one another goodbye as he had left for work in the mornings. Or when was the last time we had said 'I love you' at night before we went to sleep? When had we stopped caring for one another? I knew our sex life had taken on a perfunctory role in our relationship over the years, especially after the IVF. Then, when you throw in the exhaustion that follows young kids, I guess it had sort of died away like a flower you forgot to water. How many times had I used the excuse that I had a headache when JP had wanted to make love? When exactly had we stopped looking at one another as a person we loved and begun taking one another for granted? Why had we just assumed that the other would always be there?

The next morning while the house was still sleeping, I crept downstairs and left a note in the kitchen for JP explaining that I needed to go out for a while. As I reversed out of the driveway, the clock in my car told me it was 6.03 a.m. The sun was rising in an indigo sky and I knew it was set to be another scorcher. I could see the towering spire of St Sylvester's Church like a beacon in the distance. I kept driving until eventually I pulled up outside. Its old limestone façade and formidable gothic windows were lit up in the morning sunlight. This was the church where JP and I had got married, where Harry and Robyn had been baptised. It was here that Harry had made his first communion and where Robyn would have made hers in a few years' time. I knew JP would probably scoff at the idea of me going to a church, his views on religion and spirituality were different to mine, but today was going to be our last Christmas Day together and I needed strength to get through it. St Sylvester's had been the first place I had thought of and so I drove there seeking solace.

It was only as I walked across the churchyard that I realised the church might not even be open at that hour of the morning. I pushed the door and was relieved when it moved with my hand. I went inside and dipped my finger into the font of cool holy water and blessed myself. I continued into the nave of the church, where familiar religious statues stood atop pedestals and pictures depicting the stations of the cross hung along the walls. I walked over to the candles and, after putting money through the slot, I lit one, watching the flame as it struggled to come to life before it finally flourished and glowed. Then I sat on a pew near the back, where sunlight flooded in through the stained-glass windows, scattering beams in bright colours around on the bench beside me.

In the stillness, I could hear the echoes of happier times: strains of laughter when I couldn't get JP's wedding band onto his finger; Robyn's shriek as the cold baptismal water startled her awake; the sweet sound of children's voices as they sang at Harry's communion.

I bent my head and prayed for the courage and strength to get through this day and for all the other days to come. I prayed for all of us, for Robyn, for Harry and for JP. I prayed until warm tears streamed down my face.

* * *

My note was still sitting on the worktop when I got home. The house was quiet, and everyone was asleep, so I went into the kitchen and made myself a black coffee. I was feeling calmer after my visit to St Sylvester's, my heart more peaceful. I would get through this day, no matter what.

When JP got up a while later, he came into the kitchen bleary-eyed and I knew he had slept as badly as I had.

'How did you sleep?' he asked, joining me at the table.

I shrugged my shoulders.

'Stupid question, isn't it?'

He seemed sheepish and I guessed he was feeling embar-rassed after our heart-to-heart the night before. Despite every-thing that had gone on between us and the mistakes he had made, I think I finally understood him. I knew that he wasn't a bad person – he had just needed a connection with someone, and he had found that in Megan. It was as though the slate had been wiped clean and we were ready to start a new chapter – a chapter that we both knew was going to be our most difficult yet.

'I found this under the tree,' he continued.

'What is it?'

He handed me a page with blue feint lines ripped from a copybook. It was the letter Harry had written to Santa. As I read through Harry's scrawled handwriting, my breath hitched in my chest. I realised with a slap that he was counting on Santa to fix all of this sadness in his life. In Harry's eyes they were simple requests, he didn't understand things like terminal illness and mortality. His innocence on the paper was crushing to read; he was going to be so disappointed when he realised that Santa had no magic cure for Robyn.

'Oh God, JP,' I said, shaking my head.

When Harry got up, he was shocked to see his dad sitting at the kitchen table.

'Dad!' he sang.

'Come up here, son,' JP said, opening his arms.

He ran and climbed up onto his knee. I immediately thought of the letter JP had just shown me. I hoped Harry didn't think that JP being here this morning was part of Santa's gift to him.

'Dad came to see you open your presents,' I said in case there was any confusion about JP coming back home.

'Did Santa come?' Harry asked.

'Well, I just peeped into the living room – now, I didn't go in – but it did look like there were presents in there! Will we go have a peek?'

Harry shook his head. 'Let's wait for Robyn.'

We waited until Robyn woke and then we carried her downstairs and crept into the living room to see what Santa had brought.

'He drank all the milk – and look – the reindeers ate the carrot too!' Harry cried, running over to the plate we had left out for Santa. He looked around the room in amazement. The floor was covered in toys. There was no carpet visible.

I could see the gleam of excitement in Robyn's cerulean eyes too as she took in the scene before her and my heart soared. I had been worried she might be too sick to enjoy the magic of Santa. I carried her over, and we sat down on the floor while JP brought a present with her name on it over to her. We both helped her to tear it open and she smiled when she saw it was a unicorn that lit up like a rainbow when you pressed a button. As I helped her to use it, I noticed JP was videoing us on his phone. I was so glad he had remembered to do that. I gave the camera a smile and he smiled back at me. I wanted to capture every little detail and memory because I knew we would need them in the awful days that were to come.

'Mam!' Harry cried after a few minutes. 'Santa brought you one too!'

'Really?' I said in surprise as Harry handed me a gift. I hadn't put anything out for myself. 'Are you sure?'

'It says your name, look.' He pointed to the handwritten gift tag that said *Sarah* in cursive script. I began to unwrap the silver bow that secured the red paper. There was a box inside and, as I removed the lid, it revealed a robin made from glass. I lifted the ornament out to take a closer look, taking care of its delicate structure, and I realised it was a bauble. I saw it had painted black eyes and an auburn breast, but otherwise the light filled the clear glass. Words deserted me. 'It's beautiful,' I said eventually. 'Thank you, Santa.' Tears welled up in my eyes and I saw JP was looking down at the floor. 'Thank you so, so much!'

When all the presents had been unwrapped, I noticed Harry seemed to be a little subdued and I knew it was disappointment. He had been counting on Santa to deliver something that would save Robyn. My heart ached for my little boy.

It was after midday when our families began to arrive. Everybody had got into the spirit and had worn Christmas jumpers even though they must have been sweating in the thick wool. I couldn't help but smile when JP's father, Richard, arrived wearing felt antlers and my usually uptight mother-in-law, Joan, wore an elf hat. Although she clearly felt self-conscious with it on, it touched me that everyone had made an effort and wanted this day to be just as special as I did. Fiona and Seán were helping all the children to decorate gingerbread men at the dining-room table. They were sticking on far too many jellies and Smarties, but they were having a ball. Robyn was showered with gifts from relatives and friends. Her friend Lily brought her an Elsa costume. 'You can be Elsa now, Robyn,' Lily said, handing her the dress, and Robyn's eyes lit up with excitement as we helped to put it on her. I was so touched when her playschool teachers handed me a scrapbook of all her artwork from earlier in the year before she had got sick. I knew I would treasure it forever.

I went into the kitchen to baste the turkey and I had just opened the oven door when I heard footsteps behind me. I turned around to see my mother-in-law had followed me and she was looking at me nervously.

'Is everything okay, Joan?'

She cleared her throat. 'I owe you an apology, Sarah,' she began.

'Really?' I asked, closing the oven to give her my attention.

'Well, for what I said to you about not letting John-Paul take her to the States. I'm sorry, Sarah, I just couldn't bear to lose her – I still can't...' she quivered.

'I know, Joan,' I consoled. 'I don't think I'll ever accept what is happening.'

'I also need to apologise for being – so – so... harsh on you when John-Paul left. I shouldn't have been like that. I'm sorry, Sarah.'

'That's okay.' I meant it too; if there was one lesson that Robyn's illness had taught me it was that life was too short for grudges and grievances.

She checked behind her to make sure nobody could overhear us before continuing. 'You see, John-Paul's dad used to carry on the same way. Now, he never left me – you wouldn't get away with that in those days – but all the same I was expected to just put up with it, turn a blind eye and get on with things. It stung though, and of course when everyone else knew about it, it was humiliating. Those early years while the kids were small were tough, but there were plenty of women in my position, you certainly never left the family home, or you would have been a social pariah. Times have changed, I can see that now, and you were right not to tolerate it. John-Paul did an awful thing, but I admire how you handled it, Sarah. You've been very dignified throughout it all. I am proud to call you my daughter-in-law.'

'Thanks,' I mumbled, feeling embarrassed by the unexpected compliment but also unsure of what to say to this woman who had just exposed a huge vulnerability to me. I looked beyond the glass panel in the door leading to the living room where JP's father was cradling Robyn gently on his knee. I had never known that Richard had lived a double life. He had always struck me as such a family man.

'As you know, he's a great husband now, he doesn't stray, or at least not that I know of... I guess what I'm trying to say is...' She broke off. 'Don't rule things out... people can change, remember that.'

I nodded. 'I don't know if JP and I will ever reconcile in that way, Joan, but for now we are together for Robyn and that's enough for me.'

She reached out and clasped my hands between her own and gave them a squeeze. 'I just wanted to say, thank you, Sarah, for allowing us to be here today and for being so good to John-Paul and for letting him still be part of the family at this time. It's the greatest gift you could give him.'

* * *

A long table ran from the kitchen at the back of the house right through the double doors and into the living room at the front of the house. We had over twenty people sitting down for dinner and JP and I had set the food out like a buffet on the kitchen worktops. Everybody helped themselves and then we all sat down to eat together under the candlelight. We talked and laughed. We pulled crackers, wore silly paper hats, read even sillier jokes and it was lovely. Robyn sat on JP's knee at the head of the table and managed to eat a tiny bit of puréed dinner and seemed to enjoy the taste. I was trying to take it all in, to switch off the part of my brain that was aching at all we were losing and just savour every detail, but it was hard when a booming gong seemed to be following me around, shadowing over me, sounding 'this is the last time you will do this' with every step I took.

I watched Robyn grow tired as the meal wore on and I knew she needed to sleep.

'I think I should take her up to bed,' I said after dinner.

One by one, the family gathered around and placed gentle kisses on her hair. Their eyes were misty, and I couldn't look at them. We all knew they were saying goodbye.

JP helped me up the stairs and then I put her under the covers in my bed. I felt bone-tired – every part of me, every muscle, even my skin ached. I was wearisome from the emotional toll of the day and I guess my lack of sleep from the night before. Even though I could still hear the chatter from all our guests down below, I climbed into bed beside her and wrapped her warmth in mine. I traced my fingers along the contours of her face, along the conch shape of her ear while she slept. Every time I looked at her, my stomach churned with fear.

When I woke next, I was unsure of the time. It was dark outside, and I could hear the muffled sounds of TV from downstairs. Robyn was still sleeping soundly so I got out of bed and crept down to find JP sitting alone in the living room. There was no sign of a party and the house had been restored back to normal.

'I'm sorry, I fell asleep...'

'You're exhausted, everyone understands.'

'When did they go home?' I asked.

'They left about an hour ago.'

'Did Harry go to bed okay?'

'He fell asleep on the couch, so I took him up to his room a while ago.'

I sat down onto the sofa. I still felt tired. No matter how much I slept, I felt exhausted. I recognised one of the Bourne movies on the TV. My eyes looked at the screen, but I couldn't concentrate on anything right now.

'Thank you for making today so special, I think we'll all hold on to these memories forever,' JP said.

'You did your bit too; I can't take all the credit. It was having everyone together that made it really special.' Despite everything, all the painful goodbyes and undercurrent of sadness, it had been joyous in a way I could never have imagined. All the people who meant the most to me had been there; we were together and that's what Christmas was all about.

'I know Santa forgot you last year, so I just wanted to give you this.' JP got up from his armchair and took a small box down from the top of the mantlepiece.

'But what about the robin...'

'That was from Santa, this is from me.'

'But I never got you anything,' I said quickly. 'With everything going on I forgot – I'm sorry...'

JP laughed. 'That's payback for last year.'

I couldn't help but laugh too. 'What is it?' I said, taking it from him.

'Open it.'

I pulled back the lid of the box to find a gold locket sitting on the black velvet cushion. I lifted it out and opened the clasp to see Robyn's toothy grin beam back at me from the photograph inside.

'It's beautiful,' I whispered as he helped me to secure it around my neck.

'When she's no longer around, she'll always be with you.'

'I can't believe that this is the last one...' I said, feeling desolate beyond words. I had put so much energy into preparing for this day to make our last Christmas together perfect and I was left feeling so low now. I began to sob suddenly. It took me by surprise. My whole body was trembling. 'I can't do this,' I whispered, shaking my head. The mountain ahead of me seemed impossible.

JP sat down onto the sofa beside me. Then he put his arms around me and held me close, so close that I could smell his musky aftershave, the scent intense and manly. I had chosen it with the kids for Father's Day last year. I was glad to have the safety net of his strong arms around me, somebody to catch me and soften the fall.

'Yes, you can,' he said. 'You're the strongest woman I know. We'll do it together, when you feel like you can't go on, I'll get you through it, and on the days when I'm falling apart, you'll carry me through.'

Suddenly his face was in front of mine and our eyes locked with one another and I could sense a longing behind them. I felt it too. He leaned across so his breath was hot on my face. We had been through so much together. Years of understanding passed between us as our lips met. And I needed that. I needed the easiness of someone I knew – someone who knew me better than I knew myself. Right then, I needed closeness. I craved intimacy with someone, it had been a long six months and I wanted to surrender into someone's arms. I wanted someone to hold me, to catch me from my fall because I was sinking. Having a terminally ill child and all the pain and tormented thoughts that it brought was a lonely place to be on your own. I knew my barriers were softened by exhaustion, but there was comfort in the familiar and before my head could catch up with my heart and make me think twice, I melted into his embrace as our mouths searched for one another. It was too familiar not to instinctively keep kissing. It was like sitting on a bike and automatically pedalling. His kiss was slow and tender, and it was a balm being applied to my broken heart. Past hurts were left in the past and we were just JP and Sarah once more, with no history or backstory.

I knew I should stop this. I should stop this right now because I didn't need any more drama in my life, but I couldn't. I wanted to touch and be touched, I needed someone to pull me out of this pain, before I sank underneath it all.

HARRY

Santa didn't bring me what I asked for in my letter. Mam asked me why I looked sad when I opened my presents. She thought that I didn't like my new Liverpool jersey with 'Harry' printed on the back, but I didn't want to tell her, so I pretended to smile and said I was happy and I told her that this was the best Christmas ever. I know it was very nice that Santa came early just for us and that he brought me the new Liverpool jersey (Santa, if you're reading this, THANK YOU VERY MUCH) and Dad even had a sleepover last night, so I do think that he read my letter, but he forgot one thing because he didn't bring the medicine for Robyn. That's the present I really wanted the most. Santa was the only person who could fix her. Dad said I'm very lucky because not everybody gets two visits from Santa in the same year, but I know it's only because Santa feels sorry for us because Robyn is going to die. Even though I have the new jersey I'd give it back to Santa if he could make her better the way she was before.

Loads of people came to our house for our Christmas dinner today. I didn't eat my vegetables, but no one minded. Mam just said to eat what I wanted so I only ate a small bit of dinner and then a big bit of ice cream for dessert. I think Robyn is going to die soon because they were all crying when they were going home.

I'm trying really hard to be brave, but sometimes when I'm in bed on my own and Mam thinks I'm asleep, I cry then because I'm really sad. I know everyone else is sad too that's why I don't want them to see me crying because I don't want to make them sadder, but if the doctors and Santa can't save Robyn then I don't know who will. I don't want her to go to heaven because I can't see her there and I'm really going to miss her lots and lots.

38

The next morning, I lay awake in bed as the morning sunlight cast shadows across the ceiling. I felt mortified. I couldn't believe I had allowed it to happen. What the hell were we doing being intimate while our daughter was dying in the bedroom upstairs? In that moment, we had both needed to let our guard down and be vulnerable. We had both needed to hold and be held, and it had felt so good to melt into his familiar embrace, but in the cold light of day I realised I should never have done it. Afterwards, as shame had flooded through me, I had told JP he could sleep in the spare room while I had climbed into bed beside Robyn. How was I supposed to look him in the eye when we saw each other this morning? Everything would be strained and awkward now just as we were starting to get back on an even keel again. I groaned at my own stupidity.

I got out of bed, left Robyn to sleep on and I went downstairs to make myself a coffee in the solitude of the kitchen, but after a while I heard JP's footsteps descending the stairs and my heart started to ratchet.

'How was she last night?' he asked when he came through the kitchen door.

'She was good, she's still asleep,' I replied, unable to look directly at him as embarrassment wormed its way through my body.

Silence cloaked the air between us. I got up and made him a coffee and I couldn't help but recall how my whole body had been left tingling as his stubble had brushed against my cheek. I felt my face blush as I remembered it. *Stop it, Sarah*, I tried telling myself, praying that he didn't notice.

When the Nespresso had finished spurting out coffee, I placed the mug down in front of him. Despite the awkwardness I felt, I knew I needed to say something to clear the air and remove any lingering tension. We needed to be 100 per cent together, without even a trace of awkwardness, for Robyn's sake.

'About last night...' I blurted. 'We shouldn't have done that...'

He exhaled. 'Look, I know... I think it was just the emotional toll of the day... we're both feeling a little all over the place right now, so let's just forget it ever happened.'

I nodded, grateful that he was willing to move on from it.

We both fell quiet as the weather reporter on the radio in the background was saying that the recent heatwave was set to continue.

'Do you want to head to the beach for a walk when she wakes up?' I suggested. 'It's a great day out there.'

'Good idea.'

* * *

The day was balmy and bright as JP lifted Robyn from the car into her buggy. Although the weather was warm, the strong onshore wind meant it was much cooler by the coast. The wind was blustery and blew through the dunes in silvery waves, so we wrapped a blanket around Robyn to protect her from the elements.

Portmarnock beach was quiet that day, but come the weekend it would be packed with families sitting on rugs and eating picnics from baskets. Gulls arced and soared and cawed hoarsely through the brilliant blue sky above us. I breathed in the briny air and felt it fortify me with goodness. Fresh sea air was like a medicine. I felt alive and invigorated under the sunlight.

JP pushed the buggy with difficulty as the wheels sank in soft sand, but, eventually, we managed to get to the part left smooth and flat by the outgoing tide.

Harry ran down towards the water, where foamy waves rushed up along the sand making an angry hiss before retreating cowardly again. The school year had finished up and he was now on his summer holidays. We watched as he found a piece of driftwood and began writing our names along the strand as his T-shirt flapped in the breeze. He dragged the stick through the sand which was crumbly like demerara sugar, to write *Mammy, Daddy, Harry* and *Robyn*. Then he ran along the outside of our names to ring a heart around them all.

I looked down and saw Robyn was smiling at him from the buggy. She looked radiant, as if the sunlight was shining right through her. This was the image of her that I wanted to come to mind in the darker days that lay ahead. If I sliced my life with a cheese grater, the wire cutting through it in perfect even slices – then this slice was utterly perfect. *Don't think,* I told myself. This day is too precious to waste it being sad. It was me and my husband, our son and daughter all together in the sunshine. My unit, my world. In this snapshot, I could forget the hurt and pain. This slice of my life was perfect.

'Do you remember that summer when we all went to

Lahinch?' JP asked as we watched Harry. We had headed down with JP's parents. We had rented a holiday home and the kids had spent a glorious week running wild and free on the beach.

I nodded. 'Robyn spent the whole time running around chasing the seagulls. Remember she tried her best to catch one while all the other children on the beach were terrified of them?' I said, smiling at the memory.

'She was so full of life – out of all the kids on the beach that day, she definitely had the most energy. I was so proud of that, y'know, when people would tell me that she was a real little livewire, I loved her spirit and secretly would think "that's my girl". I always imagined that she would grow up into the kind of woman that never took shit from anyone. She could be the President of Ireland if she wanted to.'

I nodded. 'She could,' I agreed.

'I can't believe these are the last days of *us*,' he said, shaking his head sadly, his eyes turning cloudy as he looked out over the horizon. The rocky terrain of Lambay Island was on our left, and Ireland's Eye and Howth Head on our right. Some people said if you climbed Howth Head on a clear day, you could see the white peak of Snowdon in Wales.

JP lifted a stone and skimmed it into the water. My eyes followed it for a moment until it sank without a trace. The sun disappeared behind a cloud and I shivered in the nippy wind. I was always cold lately and the cardigan I had brought with me, which had seemed a sensible option when leaving the house earlier, now offered little in the way of warmth.

'Here,' JP said, noticing. 'Take my sweatshirt, you're freezing.'

'But you'll be cold...'

'I won't feel it, I promise.' He draped it over my shoulders.

Our eyes met and for the first time in a long time, I felt that he could see me. I realised how invisible I had been feeling for the last few years as a stay-at-home mum. I couldn't remember the last time that he had looked at me properly, instead of looking sideways, avoiding my eyes. I thought it was something that came with long-term marriage, but now I realised it had been because he couldn't look me in the eye. He now heard me too. Whereas previously I could see a glaze come over his eyes as I recounted something that had happened in my day – now he really listened to what I was saying.

Recently, I had come to the realisation that during the course of our marriage, I had lost a part of myself, but over the last few months, I had started to uncover the old me again, not the person I had become after all those years spent with JP. Once more, I was the woman who knew her own mind and could make her own decisions without questioning herself constantly. It wasn't JP's fault – I guess I had allowed it to happen during the years of IVF and then having young children. Somehow, I had crept into a shell and taken a back seat in my life where everyone else was more important than me. And I had been happy with that, nothing had made me happier than our family unit, but when that is so cruelly swept away from you, it leaves you with no choice but to start all over again. I had gone back to my foundations and was trying to rebuild myself up brick by brick, but this time my walls were much stronger.

'JP, I've been thinking...' I began. There had been something on my mind that I had wanted to ask him. 'Now if this isn't a runner for you, that's fine. I just thought it would be good for Robyn – and Harry too...'

'What is it?'

I took a deep breath. 'Well... you saw how happy they were when you were there at breakfast this morning and, well, I was thinking... maybe you could move back in for a while... so we're all together as a family for as long as we have left...'

He looked shocked.

'Really?' he asked. His eyes met mine and I found myself looking away as I had a sudden flashback of those same eyes searching my face the night before.

I nodded. The wind whipped my hair around my face, and I had to pull it out of my mouth to talk. 'I don't want you to miss out on any precious time we have left with her.' Robyn deserved to have both her parents around her for the short time she had left in this world, and I knew I could do with his support too. He was the only other person who got how painful this all was. With everyone else, I felt I had to keep it together and keep my good side out because they didn't know what to do or say whenever I got upset. It was exhausting. But with JP, I didn't have to do that. He was the only person I felt I could fall apart in front of, I didn't have to put on an act or a brave face.

'Are you sure? I mean, I don't want to put any more burden on you than I already have…'

'I'm sure. Anything that puts a smile on my baby girl's face is good. No matter what has happened between us, this is about Robyn and Harry too. I want to make this time as special as I can for them, and I think this is a good way.' Despite everything that had happened between us, he was a good dad. I couldn't take that away from him. He had adored his children from the moment they were placed into his arms with their round pink faces peeping out from their towelling blankets.

A smile broke out across his whole face and his eyes glistened with tears. 'Thank you, Sarah – thank you so much – you don't know how much this means.'

39

Days crept past and all around us were little signs that the egg timer counting down Robyn's life was running out of sand. A palliative care team from the hospice now visited daily to stay on top of her pain medication and to make sure she was comfortable. The team had also organised for a night nurse called Julia to come to help us. Although unspoken, we knew it meant that the end was near.

Julia was like an angel. You never heard her when she came into the room, she moved quietly and unobtrusively. She knew our family time was precious and she melted into the background as much as she possibly could. She kept Robyn's pain levels in check and, if there was any breakthrough pain, she immediately remedied it. Robyn seemed to be sleeping peacefully most of the time. I still wanted to have Robyn sleep beside me in my bed and, when she wasn't nursing Robyn, Julia sat quietly in an armchair in the corner of the bedroom. As much as she was a nurse to Robyn, she was a support to JP, Harry and me. Her role was more than a nurse; there would be a warm coffee waiting beside you when you felt your eyes burn with tiredness. She took family photos of us all surrounding Robyn in bed, she even played a game of draughts with Harry when he couldn't sleep one night. Other times she just talked to us, reassured us about what was to come. Often, JP would join us during the night, I knew he wasn't sleeping great – I was the same and whenever my eyes did finally succumb to tiredness, my sleep was always feather-light, the slightest noise or movement in the room would cause me to startle wide awake again. I could never switch off completely.

One afternoon, we took Robyn for a short walk around Malahide Castle and when we came home and put her to bed, she fell asleep for the rest of the evening. I rubbed the soft skin on her arms as she slept and as the hours crept past and she still wasn't waking up, I started to worry. I was watching her like a hawk, I was terrified she was just going to slip away from me. When Julia arrived through the door that night, my shoulders sagged with relief. I was so glad to have her nearby, her presence was reassuring when everything was so terrifying.

'She's very weak,' Julia announced to JP and me, after she had listened to her breathing and checked her pulse. But she didn't have to tell us, I could see it with my own eyes. We were watching for the signs. I knew her life now balanced precariously on a knife-edge; she was so near to tipping over. I wasn't ready to lose her yet. We were close though and that frightened the life out of me.

I could tell that Julia was concerned when she still hadn't woken several hours later, so we were all relieved when, just as the sun rose on a new day, she woke up once more.

'I thought we were going to lose her,' I whispered as I lifted a teaspoon of apple purée towards her lips.

'She's hanging in there,' Julia said. 'She's a tough little cookie.'

I said a silent prayer of thanks for giving me another day with her.

Harry got up soon after, climbed up on the bed and hugged his sister. His hair was tousled with sleep and I was glad that at least one of us had slept well.

'I'm hungry,' he announced after a while.

'Come on, son, I'll take you down and make breakfast,' JP said as the two of them left the room.

'Something smells good,' Julia said to me a few minutes later as the smell of breakfast wafted up the stairs to us. 'It'll be time for me to go soon, so I want you to go downstairs and get some food into you,' she ordered. 'You need to keep your strength up.'

I did as I was told and, even though I had no appetite, I left the room and headed downstairs.

JP and Harry were sitting at the kitchen table eating.

'I've left you some bacon and eggs in the oven,' JP said. 'I hope they're not too rubbery now. I'll go on up to sit with Robyn, while you eat.'

We were taking turns to stay with her even though Julia was there with her and she spent most of time asleep anyway. Sometimes if I got up to use the bathroom, I would come back to find Harry had climbed in beside her and was rubbing her back gently. One of us was always with her and that gave me peace of mind.

I was so glad to have JP's presence in the house again. He could help me lift Robyn or bathe her or he could play with Harry, so he didn't feel overlooked. We were united in our care for our children and I knew I couldn't have done it on my own. I couldn't believe how easily we had slotted back into our old lives together; it was almost as if JP's affair and the time spent apart had never happened. We had been shaped by the scars we bore together, and somehow, we had emerged stronger. We were now kinder and more considerate of each other, like housemates who feel the need to put out their best selves. Instead of making a cuppa for myself like I might have done in the past, we now would offer to make the other person a mug too. I cringed thinking back to it. The little acts of unkindness that had built up as normal over the years. When had our marriage changed? Maybe if we had been more caring towards one another all along, the affair would never have happened. It seemed obvious now in hindsight, but we should have been giving one another our best selves all the time.

That morning after we said goodbye to Julia, who was going home to get some much-needed sleep before returning to us later that night, JP helped to carry Robyn downstairs. He brought her into the kitchen and sat down onto a chair with her. It felt nice, like the way it all was before, just the four of us having a lazy morning together. Suddenly, Robyn's right index finger twitched, the last bit of movement she had left. She was trying to point at something beyond the patio glass.

'What is it? What do you want?' I asked, getting up.

Her finger jabbed the air again.

'Do you want a drink?' I went to open a cupboard door.

I could see frustration in her eyes.

'Maybe she is hungry?' JP tried.

She started to become agitated and I hated that I couldn't understand her. This was the cruellest part of it all.

'She's pointing at something in the garden, Mam,' Harry said.

She kept jabbing her finger and suddenly Harry spotted what it was that she was trying to show us.

'Look, there's a robin!'

My eyes followed theirs and I saw there was a little robin perched on the fence at the end of the garden.

'Oh, sweetheart, it's your bird!' I cried.

The small bird must have known he had an audience because he fluttered down onto the patio and looked up at us with calm bravery. Harry quickly jumped up, opened the bread bin and took out a slice. He opened the patio doors as warm sunlight flooded into the kitchen and tossed it onto the ground in tiny pieces for the bird. We saw Robyn's face relax as she watched him peck around on the paving before sending his wings in a whir as he flew off again.

'Did you know,' I began, 'that on the day you were born a beautiful robin flew onto my window ledge in the hospital and he looked at me with his dark, clever eyes and I knew he was telling me to call you after him and that's how you got your name.'

And even though she could no longer speak, I could see her eyes dance with a smile.

40

A shadowy black outline filled the spot where her face should be, I tried to stretch out my hands to pull it away, but the shape wouldn't move. I opened my eyes, sat up in the bed and gulped back air. I stretched my hand across to her chest and relief flooded through me when I found she was still breathing.

'Are you okay, Sarah?' I heard Julia's voice ask.

'I can't see her face!' Beads of sweat had broken out across my body and the sheets were damp beneath me.

I was waking up in the middle of the night with awful nightmares. I would wake in a cold sweat, terrified that I couldn't remember her. I would sit up in the bed and try to call to mind her face, but sometimes it was blank. Sometimes I had nightmares imagining her terror that she couldn't voice. Did she wonder why her body was failing her and she couldn't tell us? Did she know she was dying? I would lie in bed beside her, stroking her face, willing myself to remember every detail. We had taken countless photos and videos of her and prints of her small hands and feet too, but I was so afraid my mind wouldn't be able to recall her. That was my greatest fear; that I would try to evoke the planes and contours of her face and they wouldn't come to me.

Julia switched on the lamp, casting a warm glow around the room. I looked at my daughter sleeping peacefully beside me.

'There she is, Sarah, she's just asleep,' she said, coming over to the bedside.

My heart was hammering inside my chest and I could hear the blood pounding through my ears.

Julia checked her pulse and listened to her breathing with the stethoscope. 'She's very weak,' she professed.

I exhaled heavily.

When she had last woken, I had tried to feed her droplets of water and a spoonful of apple purée, but she had refused them both and Julia had explained to us softly how Robyn's body was shutting down and this was a new sign that the end was almost upon us. 'Her body is preparing itself to go on its final journey,' she had said.

I was getting used to Julia's spiritual ways and although I knew JP found her airy thoughts and metaphors difficult to comprehend at times, I found them strangely comforting.

'Go down and get yourself a coffee,' Julia advised.

I didn't move.

'Go on,' she ordered. 'Don't worry, I'll call you if anything changes.'

Reluctantly, I headed downstairs and I met JP in the kitchen. 'Hi there,' I whispered.

'Can't sleep either?' he said.

I shook my head and looked out beyond the window where darkness cloaked the sun that was attempting to rise outside. The wind howled beyond the glass. I had heard on the radio that a tropical storm was due in off the Atlantic and was tracking across Ireland.

'I keep getting these nightmares,' I said to him. 'I'm worried that I won't be able to remember her...'

JP got up from the table and put his arms around me. 'We'll never forget her, Sarah, she is part of us – she is in me, and in you, and in Harry. She is in your eyes; she is in Harry's laughter and although I hate to admit it... she is in my stubborn streak.'

I smiled even though tears streamed down my face.

'As long as we're all here and we're able to breathe, we'll never forget her,' he continued. 'We won't let it happen.'

'Julia said it's close now.' I stood shivering in the cool morning air. I wrapped my cardigan tightly around me and poked my thumbs out through the ripped holes in the sleeves.

He nodded and put his arms around me. 'I know.'

A photo reel of memories was continuously playing in my head: the sheer shock of that positive pregnancy test that told me, after all our years of infertility, we had managed to conceive a baby naturally; when Harry came into the hospital to meet Robyn after she was born for the first time, and we became a family of four; Robyn clutching her Peppa Pig lunch bag on her first day of playschool; her smile at our Christmas dinner just a few days earlier.

I looked out on the bleak day outside as the plants fought against the gale. Suddenly, the robin from the previous day appeared again on the patio, just inches from the glass. He remained still and composed as he looked in at me, his dark, clever eyes meeting mine. JP looked at me, his eyes wide with disbelief. I got up and found a stale heel of bread and pulled the crust off for the bird. I slid back the patio door and threw the pieces onto the ground for him. He fluttered back to a safe distance still watching me until I went back inside, and he began pecking at the bread.

* * *

The storm arrived first with a smattering of raindrops drizzling down the glass, but it quickly picked up into a howling wind, battering the house and rattling against the windowpanes, causing rain to hit the house in diagonal slants and dance off the pavement below. Although outside it was wild and raging, inside the bedroom was calm and tranquil.

Robyn had slept for the whole day with Mr Bunny beside her and, as day changed to night, the four of us lay in my bed covered up with a duvet like we had done on so many lazy Sunday mornings gone by. Harry had been out of sorts that day, he hadn't left Robyn's side, even when JP had tried to coax him downstairs to play the PlayStation for a little while. It was as if he could sense that she would depart soon. He eventually fell asleep in bed beside Robyn, and JP and I had climbed into the bed too and sandwiched the children on either side.

When Julia arrived that night, she lit tea lights and scattered them around and the soft candlelight sent flickering shadows across the room. Gentle lullabies were playing to make it as peaceful as possible. JP and I stroked Robyn's face, her translucent skin showing a network of blue veins beneath. Nobody wants to imagine a setting where they have to say goodbye to their child, but I was thankful that we weren't in a sterile hospital room, we were at home, in our bed, the four of us together where Robyn belonged. It was the most special way.

Her breathing became faint as the night wore on, so faint that several times I put my head against her chest to make sure she was still with us. How strange it was that the only thing separating her from this world and the next was something as simple as a breath. An instinctive reflex straight after our birth as our lungs learnt quickly to inflate; something humans did subconsciously thousands of times a day. But when those breaths were going to stop, that final breath became everything. A breath was all that stood between life and death.

Julia encouraged us to talk to her, she said our hearing was the last sense to depart us, so we spoke to her and told her stories. We told her that we loved her and that it was okay for her to go. We told her that her grandad and granny were waiting for her.

She was cradled in my arms, her head against my heart, when she took a shuddering last breath, longer and louder than any that had come before it and I held my own breath waiting for another one, but when it didn't come, we knew she had left our world.

People say they can feel a loved one's spirit in the air after they die and, after Robyn passed on, the storm which had been raging outside suddenly calmed. Although the rain stopped pelting against the glass and the wind ceased, the air around us was electrically charged. I could feel her close by – it was physical – the same way that you can feel your heart grow when somebody you love hugs you. I knew she was with us.

Julia pulled back the curtains and opened the bedroom window.

'It's an old Irish tradition. Her soul is starting its transition and we have to help send it on its way,' she explained as the air in the room grew cooler. Sweet birdsong filtered into the room, heralding the dawn of a new day, a day that was the start of a new world for all of us.

JP and I hugged and cried for a while and then we woke Harry and told him that she was gone. He was very upset as he hugged and caressed his sister. The only comfort was that her suffering and pain were finally over but ours was only beginning. I had carried her inside me; for nine months, we had shared a body, our hearts had beat together – she was a part of me – I had lost a part of myself.

Once again, I was so grateful to have Julia in our lives – she was guiding us through this alien landscape, and I would never be able to thank her enough. As well as her official duties like recording the time of death and completing the paperwork, she had let us be a family for the short time we had left. She didn't intrude into the last hours of togetherness that we needed right then and so we stayed in bed as a family of four until morning broke and we prepared ourselves to tell our families and friends.

'Will we bathe her?' Julia suggested as the rising sun filled the room with a salmon-coloured glow.

I thought of the day she was born when JP had given her her first bath. 'You do it,' I said, turning to JP. It was a fitting bookend to her short life that he should give her her last bath too.

'Okay,' he nodded.

In the bathroom, I sat on the downturned toilet lid, with Harry on my lap. I was stroking his hair while we watched Julia guide JP as they began to wash Robyn carefully with a soft cloth, treating her as delicately as a newborn as they sponged water around her small body.

HARRY

It really happened. Robyn died. I know Mam and Dad said it was going to happen, but sometimes grown-ups get things wrong. When they were putting the lid on the coffin Mam asked me if I wanted to say goodbye, but I was afraid to touch her because it didn't look like Robyn in there.

We went to the church for the funeral and there were so many people there. I had to read a prayer and Dad came up to the altar with me because he knew I was scared with all the people looking at me and when I was finished, he whispered that I did a good job, and that Robyn was proud of me. I asked him how he knew that she was proud of me because she can't tell us that now and he said 'I just know'. When the priest was finished talking, all these people that I didn't know kept coming up shaking Mam and Dad's hands and hugging me and they were all crying and squeezing me too tight and I just wanted everyone to go away and stop hugging me and leave us alone. Then we had to go to the graveyard, and they put Robyn's coffin into the ground, and they were putting all the muck on top of her and that was really scary because what if she woke up and was trapped under it all? So I shouted 'Stop!' at the men and they put down their shovels and then everyone was staring at me and they all looked really sad and I got embarrassed. Dad said it was okay because she is in heaven now and I said 'she's not, she's still in the coffin' and Mam squeezed my hand really tightly and Dad was trying to hide that he was crying but I could see the tears running down his face and then the men picked up their shovels and started putting the muck on her again.

Mam said that she's all around us and she can hear us, so sometimes I talk to her when nobody can hear me, and I tell her all the stuff that is happening and that I'm taking really good care of Mr Bunny. Mam and Dad asked me to mind him for her. I'd be really embarrassed if my friends knew I was sleeping with a teddy, but I like it because it still smells of her and if I shut my eyes really tight it's just like the way it used to be. I can pretend she is still beside me and we are just snuggled up together under the duvet again.

41

JP crept into the bedroom where I lay underneath the covers, staring at the walls. Everything was flattened. I was flattened and all the colour had been sucked out of the world.

'Here, thought you might like a cuppa,' he said.

As I sat up in the bed, pins and needles prickled through my legs and my neck was aching from the awkward angle I had been lying at. He handed me the mug and I took it between my hands. I didn't want to eat anything; I didn't want to drink anything either, but the warmth against my cold fingers was welcome.

'You're freezing,' he said, taking the throw from the end of the bed and putting it over me. 'I'll get you a hot-water bottle.'

JP was taking care of everything, including me. He had spoken with the priest to arrange the funeral. He had chosen readings and songs for the choir to sing. He had gone to the undertakers and chosen a tiny white wicker coffin. Things I knew I would never be able to do, somehow, he had found the strength to.

Visitors came and went; so many people were coming to pay their respects and he let them in, served them tea and chatted with them. When they asked where I was, I could hear him from downstairs explaining that I wasn't up to seeing people. I listened to their platitudes filter up through the ceiling about how Robyn was 'in a better place'. Where was that place? I wanted to die too and go to it. Or another one was that 'she was too good for this world'. *Like what does that even mean?* And I hated those words. There was no better place than here with her family, the people who loved and cherished her.

JP was taking care of Harry too. Poor Harry, he would come and lie down on the bed beside me, suddenly looking so small and lost. His head would rest on my chest, his body curled in against mine like a seahorse. We wouldn't say anything to one another; it was as if neither of us could put words on our pain, but we would just cry together until JP would coax him back downstairs with some promise of a movie or a game of football. And some part of me somewhere, the part that was Harry's mother, realised that life had to go on and I was so grateful that JP was able to do that – to keep parenting when I was too broken.

I thought I had been prepared for Robyn's death – as much as you could be, I had accepted that she was going to die several weeks ago, but now I realised, I could never have been prepared for it. How can you prepare for something so awful? The human brain simply can't comprehend that level of terror until it happens and then it hits you like a tidal wave and wipes you out.

Grief is a funny thing. Nobody tells you about the awful crying that physically hurts; it comes from deep within your stomach and hurts your whole body – 'keening' was the old Irish word for it and I could see why it was called that – sometimes it came out of my mouth and I sounded like a wailing banshee. All the love you still have to give now has nowhere to go and so it pools at the corners of your eyes and sits like a brick upon your chest until you can't breathe. Nobody tells you how every cell, every synapse aches, right down into your very core. And nobody had warned me about the tiredness. The weeks of sleepless nights and living on adrenaline suddenly hit me like a tsunami and I was exhausted. I was so tired, my bones hurt, but still I couldn't sleep. I couldn't face waking up again to realise she was gone. My darling Robyn was no longer here. At least the exhaustion subdued me into a numb state where I felt as though I was watching everyone from afar. Fiona would come up and sit by my bedside and I could see her, I could hear what she was saying to me, but it was as though I was not really there with her. I was in my head, where Robyn was.

Once, when Robyn had been around two years old, we had been walking through long meadow grass and when I turned around, I couldn't see her. My heart had stopped – that stomach-churning panic that only parents know, the sheer terror of losing your child – and then after what felt like minutes but could only have been seconds, I saw some blonde curls emerge from above the green grass and my heart started beating again. That day I wondered how I would survive if anything should ever happen to my children. I thought I would have to die with them because how could you not? Being a parent was like handing over your heart to someone and hoping they would mind it. Except now my terror had been realised, I had lost a child, but somehow the human body kept going and the days were going past and I don't know how they did, but time marched on. People still went to work, the post still arrived through the letterbox, bananas turned spotted brown in the fruit bowl, and everything kept going on and nothing stopped to grieve for my Robyn. Nothing stops. Everything keeps going on.

I miss my baby.
I miss her laugh; her head thrown back in a giggle to show,

Every gap in her teeth,
That I have imprinted on my mind.
I want to feel those pudgy arms around my neck;
Her breath as sweet as jasmine on my cheek.
I yearn for her warmth as she climbs into bed beside me in the
morning.
The way she just knew if I needed a hug or a flower picked
from the garden.
That special essence that made her her.
I miss my baby.

EPILOGUE

Beams of slanted sunlight filtered in through the kitchen window and dust motes hovered in the rays. The toaster popped, causing me to jump out of my daydream. JP got up from the table, his dressing gown wrapped around him to stave off the chilly morning air. He lifted the bread out and put it onto a plate. He spread butter thickly across it before handing it to Harry and tousling his hair.

'Thanks, Dad,' Harry said, his teeth crunching into the bread.

JP made two mugs of coffee and handed one to me.

'Thanks,' I said, taking it from him. I felt his hand rest on my shoulder as he leant forward and kissed my cheek before sitting back down at the table again.

I clasped the mug between my hands and looked out through the patio doors at the frost-tipped grass. February frosts still arrived, but there was a glorious china-blue sky above and a hint that spring was on its way. It had been a long winter.

An email pinged on my phone. When I saw it was from a journalist I had been trying to set up a meeting with, I held my breath. I could have punched the air when I read that she wished to set up an interview with me for the following week. My charity work in the Robyn McIntyre Foundation was keeping me busy these days. JP and I had set up the charity using the funds raised from his JustGiving page and it had given me a focus in the dark days after Robyn's death. Our primary aim was to use Robyn's story to create awareness of this cruel illness, as well as highlighting just how underfunded research into DIPG was. I wanted the whole world to know about this horrible disease. We were lobbying the government and pharmaceutical companies to increase their budgets for DIPG research. It wouldn't bring Robyn back, but I was proud that my girl had left behind a legacy and I hoped that, in time, if a cure could be found, Robyn's death wouldn't be in vain and other families would be spared our pain.

'Remember that journalist that I was telling you about?' I told JP excitedly. 'Well, she just emailed to say she wants to meet me next week!'

'That's fantastic, I know how much you wanted to get a meeting with her.' JP smiled at me. 'Well done, you.' He reached out for my hand across the table and gave it a squeeze.

JP never went back to the flat after Robyn died. Instead, he had stayed in the house with Harry and I, and the three of us had helped piece one another back together again. We had been through hell and back together, but our foundations were stronger now than ever before and we were slowly rebuilding our marriage.

'It's a nice day out there, how about we go for a cycle around the castle today?' JP suggested, looking at me.

'Can we get hot chocolate afterwards?' Harry asked through a mouthful of toast.

'Good idea,' I said, bringing my mug towards my lips.

'But we have to be home in time for my football match,' Harry warned.

'Absolutely,' JP agreed. 'The captain can't be late.'

JP and I exchanged a smile. Harry had recently been made captain of his football team and he was taking his duties very seriously.

Beyond the glass, I noticed a robin fly down and perch on the windowsill. The bird fluttered up into the air again, proudly showing off its russet-coloured breast. Its wings moved in a whir before it settled back down onto the ledge again. There was an urgency to its movements, as if wanting to catch my attention. Through the glass, its dark, clever-eyed gaze met mine and I smiled at my darling girl. She was always with us.

AUTHOR'S NOTE

Thank you for reading *The Last Days of Us*. I hope that Sarah, JP, Harry and Robyn's story touched you. DIPG is a devastating illness usually affecting children between four and eleven years of age. Every year approximately 100–300 children in the United States and a similar number in Europe will receive this crushing diagnosis. In writing *The Last Days of Us* I have tried to portray this cruel disease as accurately as possible, and I hope you will forgive any errors that may be contained within. I should also mention that the US clinic referred to in the story is entirely fictional. I dearly hope that we will finally see a breakthrough in the fight against DIPG soon.

If you wish to learn more about DIPG or donate towards research, you can find out more on:

www.dipg.ie
www.abbiesarmy.co.uk
www.dipg.org

ACKNOWLEDGMENTS

To Catherine Cho and Hayley Steed from the Madeleine Milburn Agency, thank you both for guiding me through the extraordinary year that was 2020, while we bounced from lockdown to lockdown and all the uncertainties that it threw up. Thank you for keeping me calm and for your belief in this book and in me.

To my brilliant editor Caroline Ridding and all at Boldwood, what a joy it has been to join the Boldwood team. Thank you for your faith in this book. I knew as soon as we Zoomed that day I had found the best editor and home for my book. Your energy and enthusiasm are a breath of fresh air and I am really excited for what is to come. Also to Jade Craddock for her insightful and thorough copy-edit and to Ross Dickinson for his excellent proofread.

Thank you to my family, both Finnertys and Van Lonkhuyzens; Mam and Dad, Mary and Neil and my siblings Niall, Tom and Dee for all their love and support. Niall and Nita, having you all move back to Ireland has been one of the best things to happen in 2020.

To all my dear friends too, for always cheering me on. I hate mentioning names in case I forget somebody, but you know who you are. I'm so lucky to have friends like you.

A special mention has to go to my super-talented friend and fellow author Janelle Harris, who has listened to me going on about this story for far longer than she should have had to. I cannot thank you enough for all your help and encouraging words and I'm so glad to have somebody who 'gets' this writing life.

A big thanks also to my friend Katie O'Connor for taking the time out of her very hectic life to share her legal knowledge with me. It is much appreciated and any errors within are wholly my own.

To all the booksellers, bloggers and libraries for their support. To the readers who contact me with lovely messages and kind words. You'll never know how much those messages mean. There is not a day that goes by where I don't thank my lucky stars for the privilege of being able to do this; of all the books you could choose, thank you for picking up my book.

To my husband Simon, Lila, Tom, Bea and Charlie. There is no one else I'd rather be locked down with. You are the best support crew. I love you all beyond words.

Lastly, to all the robins who showed up when I was writing this book and told me I was on the right path.

MORE FROM CAROLINE FINNERTY

We hope you enjoyed reading *The Last Days of Us*. If you did, please leave a review.

If you'd like to gift a copy, this book is also available as an ebook, digital audio download and audiobook CD.

Sign up to Caroline Finnerty's mailing list for news, competitions and updates on future books.

http://bit.ly/CarolineFinnertyNewsletter

ABOUT THE AUTHOR

Caroline Finnerty is an Irish author of heart-wrenching family dramas and has published four novels and compiled a non-fiction charity anthology. She has been shortlisted for several short-story awards and lives in County Kildare with her husband and four young children.

Visit Caroline's Website: www.carolinefinnerty.ie

twitter.com/cfinnertywriter

facebook.com/carolinefinnertywriter

instagram.com/carolinefinnerty

goodreads.com/carolinefinnerty

bookbub.com/profile/caroline-finnerty

ABOUT BOLDWOOD BOOKS

Boldwood Books is a fiction publishing company seeking out the best stories from around the world.

Find out more at www.boldwoodbooks.com

Sign up to the Book and Tonic newsletter for news, offers and competitions from Boldwood Books!

http://www.bit.ly/bookandtonic

We'd love to hear from you, follow us on social media:

facebook.com/BookandTonic

twitter.com/BoldwoodBooks

instagram.com/BookandTonic

Printed in Great Britain
by Amazon

65135010R00180